W9-CMB-036

POISON, YOUR GRACE

A SIMON & ELIZABETH MYSTERY

POISON, YOUR GRACE

PEG HERRING

FIVE STAR
A part of Gale, Cengage Learning

GALE
CENGAGE Learning™

Detroit • New York • San Francisco • New Haven, Conn • Waterville, Maine • London

RODMAN PUBLIC LIBRARY

GALE
CENGAGE Learning™

Copyright © 2011 by Peg Herring.
Five Star Publishing, a part of Gale, Cengage Learning.

ALL RIGHTS RESERVED
This novel is a work of fiction. Names, characters, places and incidents are either the product of the author's imagination, or, if real, used fictiously.

No part of this work covered by the copyright herein may be reproduced, transmitted, stored, or used in any form or by any means graphic, electronic, or mechanical, including but not limited to photocopying, recording, scanning, digitizing, taping, Web distribution, information networks, or information storage and retrieval systems, except as permitted under Section 107 or 108 of the 1976 United States Copyright Act, without the prior written permission of the publisher.

The publisher bears no responsibility for the quality of information provided through author or third-party Web sites and does not have any control over, nor assume any responsibility for, information contained in these sites. Providing these sites should not be construed as an endorsement or approval by the publisher of these organizations or of the positions they may take on various issues.

Set in 11 pt. Plantin.

LIBRARY OF CONGRESS CATALOGING-IN-PUBLICATION DATA

Herring, Peg.
   Poison, your grace : a Simon & Elizabeth mystery / Peg Herring. — 1st ed.
     p. cm.
   ISBN-13: 978-1-4328-2536-2 (hardcover)
   ISBN-10: 1-4328-2536-4 (hardcover)
   1. Elizabeth I, Queen of England, 1533–1603—Fiction. 2. Murder—Investigation—Fiction. I. Title.
PS3558.E75478P65 2011
813'.54—dc23   2011031298

First Edition. First Printing: November 2011.
Published in 2011 in conjunction with Tekno Books and Ed Gorman.

38212005049066

Main Adult Mystery

Herring, P

Herring, Peg

Poison, your grace

Printed in the United States of America
1 2 3 4 5 6 7 15 14 13 12 11

POISON, YOUR GRACE

CHAPTER ONE

Spring 1552

"I require tooth powder," the lady announced without deigning to meet Simon's eyes. She looked instead at the amazing variety of oils, lozenges, liquids, and more that lay about the apothecary shop. Used to being ignored by their noble customers, Simon reached for the jar of powdered rabbit's head sold as dentifrice and twisted a bit of paper to make a container for the purchase.

"Is the preparation effective?" There was petulance, superiority, and a pitiful sort of hope in the tone.

"Some find honey a more pleasant experience, but a slightly abrasive substance sprinkled on the tooth cloth cleans better." Ignoring the musty smell emanating from the jar, he spooned the gritty substance into the cone of paper. Small, bright eyes watched as he measured. Like all honest tradesmen, Simon worked in full view of customers to demonstrate both quality and quantity. Cheating the public might bring fines, time at the pillory, even branding. The woman's manner made it clear that she would demand full value for her money.

He folded the top of the cone closed. The lady's face changed slightly when she noticed the withered arm he used minimally, efficiently accomplishing most of the task with his right hand. When he met her gaze, she lowered her eyes to the packed-dirt floor and coughed weakly.

As the haughty woman watched him, Simon subtly observed her as well. Noting her ostentatious if slightly outdated finery, many an apprentice would have inflated the price a bit to line his own pocket, seeing that she could afford it. Some apothecaries would have done the same, considering it their due for debts the rich ran up and never paid. Neither Simon nor his master, Thomas Carthburt, was that sort. The price asked was what everyone paid, despite the lady's apparent means and superior manner.

From the back of the shop, several hammer blows interrupted his thoughts. Carthburt worked at a small table, making physic for pain. He lived with a great deal of it himself, with arthritis so advanced that his back twisted and his hands curled into strange shapes, knuckles protruding grotesquely. Still he worked doggedly, mixing tiny leaves of newly sprung lettuce with the gall of a castrated boar, adding briony for its emetic properties, then opium and henbane, well-known pain relievers, and a precise amount of hemlock juice. Although effective, such physic brought death in too great a dose, so Carthburt always did the measuring himself. He ignored the customer, trusting his assistant to handle the transaction.

When Simon finished, the woman asked in an accusing tone, "Is it pure? I will not have it mixed with sand or talc. My teeth are sensitive." He had guessed that from the way she spoke without opening her mouth more than necessary. Her teeth were in fact rotting away, and no amount of cleaning would help now. Despite expensive clothes, she looked haggard, her frame shrunken. Rotten teeth made it painful to eat, which brought on malnutrition and illness. The gentlewoman was starving, though surrounded by plenty. No wonder she was peevish.

"The preparation is pure, madam. My master's reputation is well known."

"I have heard it. Still, if I am not satisfied, I shall return for my money."

"Of course. Perhaps something for toothache would be helpful as well?"

The proud expression dropped for an instant, replaced by hope. "Have you something that truly works?"

"Let us ask Master Carthburt."

Ten minutes later, the lady seemed slightly more optimistic. Carthburt had given her some of his mixture and suggested foods that would provide adequate nutrition without placing too much strain on her decayed teeth. "Your humors are unbalanced," he said with the sternness that only an old man may use with his betters. "Eat foods opposite to those you are presently taking. With a balanced diet, the humors will balance as well."

Simon saw the woman to the door, handing her parcel to the servant who waited outside. The London street was a blur of movement as carts, riders on horseback, and pedestrians jostled along its crooked path. Some looked down, watching lest they step in something offensive. Others scanned the crowd for acquaintances or potential customers. Shouts rang out periodically, proclaiming goods or services for sale. As a cart passed, he caught the scent of several spices, cinnamon and nutmeg for sure, several others as well. If a person stood on the market street long enough, he might buy anything available in the nation, from lace to lances, from hay to harlots.

As his glance took in a passing litter, Simon froze. The face visible through the small window was familiar, and he smiled with joy. Elizabeth Tudor! Though it was years since they last met, she looked the same: pale skin, reddish hair pulled back from a heart-shaped face, direct eyes lit with curiosity under brows so pale as to be almost invisible, slim nose rising slightly in the center, and thin lips set firmly over a rather pointed chin.

Her gaze met Simon's briefly, and there was a blaze of recognition. Then her expression fell into blandness and she turned away, ignoring the fact that he stood grinning at her like a lapdog. As the litter passed on, Simon stood on the stone threshold, feeling stupid. The hand half-raised in greeting fell, and he looked around to see if anyone had noticed. No.

A flush crawled up his neck, and he waited for it to cool before going back inside. There was no reason for the princess to acknowledge him, he told himself. He was someone she'd known briefly several years ago. She owed him nothing.

As he returned to his workbench, his master commented on the customer who'd just left. "They come to us too late, when there is little hope of restoring their health."

Simon kept his tone even, though the sting of the princess' snub still rankled. "My father says it is the way of folk to ignore their bodies' needs until they fail. Then they look to others to save them, either men of medicine like him or those who practice magic."

"Or those like us, who do a bit of both!" Carthburt had become Simon Maldon's master in part because he and Jacob Maldon saw eye-to-eye on most things. Although neither was foolish enough to take on every misguided belief of the times, each sought to heal with logic rather than superstition. Jacob often reminded his patients that no doctor could restore squandered health, no matter their station or resources. Likewise, Carthburt sold no powdered dog feces in his shop and carefully acquainted customers with the possible ill effects of his medicines. "What can heal can also kill!" he always warned. Still, many ignored him in their impatience for relief and as a result suffered stomach upset, sluggishness, or even permanent damage from too much physic.

Simon returned to his work but found it difficult to concentrate. Elizabeth's rejection stayed with him even as he explained it to himself a dozen different ways. She had recognized him; he knew it. Could she not even nod a greeting to an old—what was he to her? Friend? He had once thought so, but could friend-ship exist between a princess and an apprentice? Still, she might have acknowledged him.

"Father?" Simon turned to see Carthburt's daughter in the curtained doorway that led to the back of the shop, her fingers drumming nervously on the frame. The old man's face melted to softness, as it always did when his daughter appeared. Rachel was lovely, with her father's blue eyes and a softly rounded face. Fair-skinned and daintily made, she stood only as high as Simon's shoulder, though they were about the same age.

Carthburt's whole body signaled devotion. "Yes, my pet?"

Rachel almost never came into the shop, seldom came to the door. She was terrified of everyone, even Simon, who had learned to keep his distance if required to venture into Carth-burt's living quarters. Because of this, he did not live with his master as most apprentices did but returned at night to his parents' home.

"I cannot unlatch the grain bin." One of Rachel's interests, and she had very few, was pigeons. In a dovecote at the back of the house she spent hours with the birds, letting them rest on her shoulders and eat from her hands. Simon found it droll that she didn't seem to notice a few less when there was pigeon pie for dinner.

"I will go." He moved quickly to save Master Carthburt the task of lifting the heavy bin lid, probably wedged at one corner from a careless drop into place. Rachel's eyes grew large at the prospect of Simon invading her territory, and he moved slowly to reassure her. Staring at a spot on the floor behind him, she stood like a young child, one finger pressed between her lips, the other hand buried in the folds of her skirt, squeezing the fabric into a mass of wrinkles. Her foot tapped in rhythm with the clenching and unclenching of the fist that mussed her dress. "Stand there, beside your father, until I return. You must feed your birds, or they will wonder why you do not."

"Yes." The girl could comprehend that much, and she walked to her father, who put an arm round her slim waist for reassurance. Simon moved briskly into the medium-sized room at the rear of the shop. Two corners could be closed off with hangings. One, obviously Carthburt's, was exposed, the draperies pulled back around a pallet bed with several books piled beside it. A wooden peg on the wall held his other, better, set of garments and a hat with a rather dilapidated plume. The opposite corner was hidden, the hanging closed to protect Rachel's things from the view of the outside world. Other than that, the room held a brazier for warmth, some stools, and a large chair with pillows piled on the seat, comfort for the old man's evenings.

At the back of the room, a fragrant pot of some kind of stew sat off to one side of the fireplace. A neighbor came in several mornings each week and saw to such things as meals and laundry. Carthburt handled most of the rest of their domestic affairs. Over time, Simon had taken on more and more of the duties around the shop. Although the master insisted on doing what he considered his share of the work, his assistant tried to anticipate his needs, to do the more physically demanding tasks when possible.

Dozens of pigeons flocked near the back door, cooing and crowding around his feet. Chuckling at their boldness, he waded through them to the grain bin, which was indeed jammed. A quick check of the area uncovered a metal file in a box of tools, and he used this to pry the edge of the lid free. Finding a small chunk of wood, he pushed it into the corner near the hinge so that the lid would not stick again.

Returning to the shop, he found Rachel clinging to her father, tense until Simon moved to the opposite side of the room. Carthburt gestured apologetically as she fled the room. "She forgets to speak her thanks in eagerness to care for her pigeons."

"I am glad to be of help."

"It is not only you, lad. Rachel is afraid of . . . many things."

"It is often so with such folk," he agreed, interested because the apothecary seldom spoke directly of his daughter's oddness. "Father says their timid ways protect them from harm, which may be as God intends." The old man frowned, and Simon immediately regretted the generalization. Obviously, Carthburt did not appreciate the generalized reference to "such folk." Dropping the subject, he returned to his pestle.

For some time the two worked in their usual, comfortable silence, the only sounds exterior and therefore removed from them. Both looked up as a man entered the shop, his tall form darkening the doorway for a moment before he stepped inside. His livery bore a single red rose. "Are you the apothecary called Carthburt?"

"I am."

"Greetings from His Majesty, Edward the Sixth. I am to escort you to the palace on a matter most urgent."

Carthburt did not hesitate. Such a summons called for immediate action. "Close the shop, Simon, and accompany me." As his joints stiffened, the old man's sense of balance often failed, and he needed Simon's support to walk any distance. "We will see what His Majesty requires."

From his tone, Simon discerned that his master considered this the chance of a lifetime for his apprentice: a visit to White-hall, possibly a glimpse of the king. He had never had reason to reveal that although he had never met this king, he had met the one before him, Henry VIII.

The apothecary moved to the back of the shop and murmured a few words to Rachel, who made no response. Picking up a leather satchel kept stocked with medicines of likely use outside the shop, Simon followed him and the messenger into the street, moving to his master's left in order to allow Carthburt to lean

13

on his strong right arm. The palace was not far, which was fortunate. The messenger patiently matched his pace to what was comfortable for the old man, but he was either unable or unwilling to explain the reason for their abrupt summons.

Whitehall, the largest palace in Europe, sat astride the road between Charing Cross and Westminster, occupying an amazing twenty-three acres of land. The first thing approaching visitors saw was two huge gates that allowed passage from one side of the palace to the other without descending to the street itself. The three passed under the Holbein Gate, two stories built over an arched passage with twin towers rising to four-story height on either side. The outside of the gate was a mass of badges, armaments, and terra cotta roundels formed into busts of various Roman emperors. Windows along the passageways above allowed inhabitants to look down upon the throng below. Simon could not help but reflect on the differences between those above and those on the ground. Inside the palace was pomp and pageantry. Outside was a reality most inhabitants of Whitehall barely comprehended.

Once under the archway, they saw on the west the recreational facilities, where some noisy game brought shouts of encouragement from some and cries of disapproval from others. The majority of palace buildings: government offices, ceremonial areas, and apartments of those who dwelt with the king, were on the east side, sprawling down to the river where brightly painted boats made passage up and down the Thames easier than navigating London's inadequate streets. It was to this side that the attendant turned.

At the entry, they met two yeomen of the King's Guard in their colorful uniforms. Simon looked hopefully into each face but recognized neither. After passing through seven outer rooms, they approached the door to the audience room, where an officious clerk said brusquely, "The apothecary Carthburt is requested, none else." He obviously enjoyed wielding the tiny bit of power he was allowed.

"I shall wait here," Simon said. "If something is needed from the shop, send word and I will go with all speed."

They had naturally concluded that medical need summoned them, although the king had physicians enough. Edward had always been sickly, and it was rumored his condition grew worse each day. Only fifteen years old, he was consumptive and weak. The emergency that called them here was likely to concern keeping the boy king alive another day, another week, another month.

Simon stood patiently in the anteroom for half an hour, amusing himself by wondering what those nearby sought from the king: a favor, news of their fate or the fate of a loved one, redress of a grievance. In one corner, a man in plain brown clothing waited with patient despair, his face betraying loss of hope. Around the room several others paced, better dressed and expensively perfumed, practicing silently the words they would use to convince someone to listen to them. Others were still and grimly silent. Each time the door opened, all eyes went to it. Faces lit with anticipation, smiles of servile amity appeared.

After some time, Carthburt returned, looking grave. "Come," he ordered. Following their guide as he wound his way through the palace, Simon soon wondered how one ever learned his way around. They moved slowly due to Carthburt's hobbling steps, so Simon saw bits of palace life framed like illustrations in a book. He glimpsed a chapel through an open door, a woman inside appearing to be at prayer until he saw the scrub brush in her hands. In another room an accounts clerk wrote at a desk, head resting on one hand as he labored. Two men talked in low tones as they passed, gossiping by the quick way they pulled their lips shut when they noticed his curious gaze. A maid carried a bundle of laundry, leaning her body forward against its weight.

Their guide was no gossip, probably an excellent trait in one who so closely served the king. Instead of commenting on the people they saw, he acquainted them with the grandeur of the building once called York Palace.

"Whitehall was taken over by Henry VIII when Cardinal Wolsey fell," he said pedantically. "It has since become the king's main residence. Outside you saw the bowling green, tennis courts, the tiltyard for jousting, and the pit for cock fighting. Over his lifetime the old king expanded and rebuilt several areas, and now there are hundreds of rooms, from the grand Great Hall to small chambers for living and working." Their guide did not mention cost, but Simon knew that estimates of Henry's renovations ranged as high as thirty thousand pounds, more than the sum required to build most royal residences.

At last they entered a corridor along which closed double doors afforded the inhabitants some measure of privacy. Entering one on the right, they found a small sitting room with two doors on opposite sides of it. Simon sniffed at the smell of fresh paint. "There was a fire," the attendant murmured, turning his head so as not to have to raise his voice. "Workmen are to finish the repairs this week." Trim boards, freshly cut from the woody smell, lay stacked against a wall. Draperies for the horn windows lay spread over a stool, the tools for hanging them on the floor nearby.

The attendant opened the door on the right and moved ahead to pull aside the curtains around a bed on a raised platform. Simon's perusal of the renovations halted suddenly. On the bed lay a form so still that he knew their presence was not healing in this case. The man was dead. Carthburt, breathless from exertion and perhaps tension as well, murmured, "I'm to tell the cause of this if I can. There is much ado over it, since he dined with the king yesternight."

"Poison?"

"Likely. He was well enough at noon but complained of stomach upset at bedtime."

"A terrible deed. God will not let it go unpunished." They turned to see a man just rising to his feet, apparently having been in prayer when they arrived. In contrast to most in the palace, everything about him was plain. His clothes were gray and unadorned, his hair mid-length and simply combed. He held himself tightly erect, as if holding emotion at bay, but Simon got the impression that for him that state was common practice.

The attendant addressed the man primly. "I apologize for disturbing your grief, Master Seawell. The king commands that these gentlemen examine your father's, um, body."

Seawell regarded Carthburt and Simon closely for several seconds, giving them the chance to do the same. About twenty-five, he was neither death-pale nor old, but his resemblance to the corpse was obvious. The same strong nose and chin, the same grooves between the brows that gave the impression of a frown but were more likely due to vision defect.

"Do as you must. My father at this moment stands before his Creator's judgment, for better or for worse." A brief squint narrowed Carthburt's eyes, perhaps a sign of disapproval. He moved to the bed and began his examination.

The fact that the man had died in agony was plain from various ill smells and stains upon the bed clothing. The face retained traces of the pain he was now free of forever. Death had surprised him, filled him with anguish, and taken him, all in a relatively brief time. Carthburt leaned close, sniffing the body, touching the face, the hands, and the stomach, then testing the rigor of the limbs. Once satisfied, the old apothecary nodded to the attendant, who bowed slightly to Seawell and led them away.

17

Men posted outside the room entered as they left, carrying a litter between them.

CHAPTER TWO

When they had retraced their path, Simon was again left alone while Carthburt returned to the audience room. Through the doorway, he caught a glimpse of a figure he recognized from public events, John Dudley. A man of great physical attractiveness, courage, and military skill, Dudley, now Duke of Northumberland, had recently become the Privy Council's Lord President and as such commanded England from behind the throne. His task was gargantuan. After years of mismanagement, the country's economy was in tatters, the navy in ruins, unemployment rampant, and religious questions unsolved. If Edward lived and if Dudley turned out to be fair and strong, things might improve. Neither was likely, for Edward grew weaker every day, and the duke was said to have an avaricious nature.

Pacing the anteroom, his steps hollow on the cold stone floor, Simon wondered who the dead man had been. Someone important, that was certain. Fine apartments within Whitehall were not for everyone, and few dined privately with His Highness. The door opened, and a striking, dark-haired man put his head out, surveying the room. "Apothecary's boy is wanted."

Simon stepped forward and made a courteous bow. The man retreated into the room, assuming that he would follow. His new guide was dressed richly, his doublet faced with elaborate stitching and his hair elaborately curled and perfumed. Physically he was impressive, with wide shoulders that tapered to a nipped waist and long legs that showed well in silk hose. About him was an air of nonchalance, as if none of his finery mattered.

The room was dark-paneled and windowless except for a beautifully detailed oriel where Northumberland sat on a cushioned seat, possibly to take advantage of the exterior light. "Simon Maldon, your master requests that you be included in this matter. I agree, provided there is no tattling to your fellows of what you see and hear."

Simon glanced once at Carthburt, whose face pleaded that he acquit himself well. "Your Honor, I am your servant."

"I am told that your father is a respected physician and therefore you have knowledge beyond that of most apprentices." As Simon tried to guess why the Lord President explained his reasoning to a lowly apothecary's assistant, Dudley continued, "Lord Amberson dined with His Highness yesterday, as did several other council members. He was found this morning as you saw him." He shuddered slightly. "Poisoned, your master believes, with arsenic."

Simon agreed, although it was not his place to offer an opinion. He had noted on the corpse telltale discoloration of the fingernails that accompanied the convulsive, painful death from too much of the mineral. "Then it is murder."

Dudley shifted uncomfortably, rustling his oversized silk sleeves. "That possibility you will keep to yourself. No one else has become ill, but if there was arsenic in the food, it could have been meant for any one of us." So the duke feared revolution by poison. "The target may even have been the king himself," he added solemnly.

"God shield us from that, Your Worship."

"Yes," Dudley said automatically, apparently unwilling to wait for God to act. "Two things must now be accomplished. We must find the murderer, for justice demands his life for that of Amberson. But we also must prevent further incidents."

Simon's first thought was of Elizabeth. Was she, too, in danger of being poisoned? A second fearful thought followed. Might they accuse her of trying to kill her brother so she could take the throne? She and her sister Mary had the most to gain from Edward's death. Still, there was no proof the king was the target, not yet.

"Who benefits financially?" Politics caused many a murder, but so did greed.

Northumberland's frown indicated that he had stepped wrong. "That is not the concern of an apprentice. You will bring to us the items necessary to protect His Highness and the council from poison. Carthburt here lacks the physical strength, but he will direct you. We require every means available, and quickly."

Simon was tempted to protest that they were not alchemists, but Carthburt frowned in warning, and he kept his peace. "We will do all in our power, Your Honor," he said meekly.

"Good. My son Robert will oversee this matter, for he has my complete trust, and that of His Majesty, of course." Simon glanced again at the well-dressed young man. So this was Robert Dudley, Elizabeth's friend Robin! He felt they were acquainted, so often had she mentioned him. "Robin says sailing the ocean is wonderful" or "Robin claims that if the Scots can't find anyone else to fight, they fight each other." John Dudley was obviously pleased with his fifth son, for his chin lifted when he glanced at Robert, who nodded amicably to Simon.

Then apothecary and assistant were dismissed. A servant at the door opposite the one they had entered motioned for them to exit that way, and Carthburt shuffled out, one leg dragging slightly on the thick carpet. The day's unaccustomed activity had tired him, but he seemed anxious to begin the tasks they were assigned.

As they left the room, a man brushed past them, hardly noticing their presence in his haste. About thirty years of age, he had strong features and a compact, sturdy frame. Black hair swept back from a face of contrasting planes: flat forehead, triangular cheekbones, and a jutting, squared chin. Simon got an immediate sense of power, a feeling that such a man would obtain whatever he set his mind on. Mud-stained boots and an expensive but bedraggled cape thrown back carelessly from his shoulders indicated recent travel. The door closed behind him with a solid thump.

Crossing the inner courtyard at Carthburt's slow pace, Simon noted the bustle common to wherever the king was. Carts of goods proceeded steadily through the gates after scrutiny from the guards: a sack of strong-smelling leeks just dug from the wet spring earth, dried and salted fish in barrels, and a dozen other deliveries to keep the crowd at Whitehall fed for another day. When Court was elsewhere, London became a much smaller town, but when Court was there, everything expanded and moved more quickly.

At the wide outer courtyard, archers practiced marksmanship on one side of the pathway while chickens squabbled over insects on the other. Carthburt limped on, lost in planning what they would need to satisfy the king's demands. Staring up at the windows of Whitehall, Simon found himself wondering if Elizabeth might be looking out one of them this very moment. Would she acknowledge him if she were?

Carthburt spoke, and he turned his thoughts to the business at hand. "They'll want Venetian goblets, powdered emerald, toadstone, and bezoar stones. A unicorn horn would suit, but where to find such a thing at this time of year?"

"Master, you don't believe in unicorns. I've heard you say it," Simon chided.

Carthburt stopped. "If the king orders it, lad, we provide it.

He is afraid, is young Edward. I know not if Northumberland believes in amulets, but he does what he can to keep the king calm."

"I've heard that excitement brings on fits of coughing."

"And when that happens, he spits up blood, phlegm, and bile."

"So we soothe with the illusion of protection, which may prevent some of his symptoms."

"Yes." Carthburt's voice took on a familiar, pedantic tone. "With the talisman, the medicine, and the amulet, we give peace and hope, which the mind and the soul require. At the same time, we tell them what to look for, what to avoid, and what steps to take if poison is suspected. It is all we can do, for God decides the matter."

Simon knew from the leech-books that the cure for poison was often as dangerous as the poison itself, and he shuddered at the thought of what such physic might do to a sickly boy. Fear of assassination, murder, and execution was the price one paid for position in society, and it did not surprise him that the nobility were a different sort. Better, they thought, but he doubted it. Such an existence, though glamorous, could not help but take a toll on all but the most wise, and he often pitied the gentle folk for their hectic, fragile lives.

On their return to the shop, Carthburt went to work. He began with a medium-sized emerald Northumberland had provided, grinding it to a fine powder. "A dusting of emerald over His Majesty's drink should neutralize any poison within."

That, however, was too expensive for the fifteen remaining members of the council. In the shop, they had half a dozen bezoar stones. The "stones," found in the stomach of deer, were said to neutralize poison when dropped into a glass of liquid. Carthburt chose several toadstones as well, said to accomplish the same feat, although he admitted they were merely white pebbles. "I once tried to procure genuine toadstones," he said with an ironic smile. "The instructions were to put a toad on a red cloth and wait until he spit up the stone. After a night of waiting, all I had was a grumpy toad and one less night's sleep."

Simon returned to Whitehall that afternoon with the collected items, asked to see Robert Dudley, and was told to wait. The anteroom still hummed with the sounds of hopeful favor-seekers. The sad-faced man in brown was there, his manner even less optimistic than it had been in the morning. How many waited to see the duke or some other person of power each day? How many went home unsatisfied?

The happy thought struck him that Elizabeth might be with Robert, and he would see her as well. Would she speak to him if they met face to face? The thought turned bitter when he imagined that she might not.

It did not matter, for Dudley was alone in the room. He accepted the packet with no ceremony. Simon recited his master's instructions on how to use the stones, his caution to hire food tasters, and his advice that council members eat fruit, which could be washed and was therefore harder to poison. Dudley's expression implied that he did not need to be told that, but he thanked Master Carthburt solemnly by way of Simon, who then returned to the shop.

"Now, go and find Venetian glass goblets," Carthburt ordered. "Men say they explode if poison is placed in them. And I fear we must look for a unicorn's horn, or something like." He made a wry grin at Simon's grimace of distaste. "If we disappoint the duke, he will consult someone else, one who might cause actual harm." There being no regulation of medicines or those who practiced physic, only reputation counted. Carthburt would neither cheat the king nor supply harmful substances. Another apothecary might not be so knowledgeable, or so careful.

Procuring the items caused no great trouble. Simon found

Venetian goblets at a shop near his home, and he bought powdered unicorn horn from a wise woman his father sometimes dealt with. She was as honest as one who sold such things could be, and if it was not truly the horn of the beast, neither was it harmful.

Again he entered the palace to seek out Robert Dudley, but this time the atmosphere was different. A crowd blocked the way to the stairs, and muttered comments and constant shuffling to gain position revealed that what the crowd saw was shocking. A woman sobbed, some whispered to those behind them who could not see, and a man shouted, "Guard, ho! We need help here."

As guardsmen pushed their way through the crowd, Simon got a brief glimpse of a body sprawled at the bottom of a long flight of stairs. From the clothing, he surmised it was a servant. Like the figure he'd seen earlier, complete stillness indicated absence of life.

"What happened?" he asked a man who pushed his way out of the crowd, apparently having satisfied curiosity.

"She must have tripped, poor soul. Her neck is broken. Now move aside. I must take the news to the king." He disappeared down a hallway, important for the moment due to the tragedy he had witnessed.

Because of the accident, Simon had to wait over an hour to see the younger Dudley, but he was unwilling to leave the materials he had brought with anyone else. Since poison was suspected, he would deal only with those the Lord President trusted. Dudley was as calm as before, although he asked what Simon had seen. "I arrived after the poor girl fell, Your Honor. I saw only the aftermath, those who crowded around."

A well-formed lip curled slightly. "For some, the day's entertainment, and the week's gossip as well." He turned to the matter at hand. "You have found the rest of the items, then?"

"We have." Handing them over, Simon began reciting Carthburt's instructions, but a woman burst into the room. She was both pregnant and distraught, but he had seldom seen anyone look more beautiful in either state. Tall and graceful, she had hair the color of copper and a face poets might spend months trying to describe. Beyond her arresting physical appearance, there was a hint of something more, something indefinable and deeper than physical attractiveness. Her slippered feet made no sound; she seemed to glide toward them like a dream-image.

"Ellen!" Dudley said in surprise. "I thought you had gone."

"The duchess wanted some packing done and asked me to stay a bit longer and see to it. We were at that work when they came with the news. Is it true that Marie is dead?"

Her hands fluttered like tethered birds, and he took them into his. "She fell on the stairs."

She swayed slightly, and Dudley put an arm around her for support. "Your lady mother is away," she said in a faint voice. "Her strength would be a great comfort to me now."

"I'm sorry I did not come and tell you myself. I would have, given time. Take care that your distress does not harm your child."

At the gentle reminder, she put her hands to her belly and breathed deeply, reaching for calm. "How did it happen?"

"She fell on the stairs. No one saw it, but they heard her cry out and found her at the bottom, her neck broken." He added gently, "No one seems to know why she was in this part of the palace, so far from your rooms. Do you know?"

She shook her head. "Lost, I suppose. She came from France only a fortnight ago. I hired her to go home with me to Rochdale, to help with the child when he comes. Being unfamiliar with Whitehall—" Her eyes filled with tears. "If she had not been here—"

Dudley's reply was reassuring. "There was nothing you could

have done to change things. Our destiny is in the stars and cannot be avoided."

"Still, she was a sweet girl." The lady made a visible effort to control her emotions. "I thank you for your kindness."

"I wish I could do more. You return home soon, I understand."

"Yes. I promised Andrew I would return before the child arrives."

"Although we will miss you here, that is best. You will forget this unfortunate accident once you are reunited with your husband."

"Of course. Andrew is always a comfort, so strong, so sure of himself."

As Simon stood, wondering whether he should slip away discreetly or wait to be dismissed, the woman seemed to sense his unease. "I've interrupted. I'm so sorry." She smiled at him directly, and he blushed at the attention.

"I was just leaving, madam." He turned to Dudley. "If there is nothing else, sir?"

"We have done our best for the nonce."

"I have kept you too long from your duties," the woman said.

"Time spent with a beautiful baroness is never ill-spent," he said gallantly. "I will see what must be done for your Marie."

As Simon left the room, he passed the same man he had seen that morning as he and Carthburt left the audience room. The sense of pent-up emotion noted earlier still emanated from him, along with a strong odor of horse, suggesting he had not had time to refresh himself after a recent journey. As he peered through the doorway impatiently, Simon sidled by, noting up close that one eyebrow was exactly halved, possibly by a small scar, giving the appearance that he was always on the verge of asking a question. If he had a question for Dudley, Simon thought, today was probably a bad time to pursue it.

"Do you work here at Whitehall?" Simon turned to see the woman named Ellen, whose path apparently paralleled his. Like many pregnant women, she rested one hand on her belly as if protecting the child within.

"No, my lady. I serve as apprentice to Thomas Carthburt, who had some business with the Lord President."

"I am sure you serve him well."

"You are kind to say so." He hesitated, unsure how much conversation was called for between people of such different stations with a common destination. "I am sorry to hear of your maid's death."

"Thank you. I did not know her well, but she was a merry girl." The lovely face went sad for a moment, and he wondered what he would do if she began to cry again. He could not take her in his arms and comfort her as Dudley had done, but she seemed genuinely sorrowful. They went on a few steps, and she regained control. When they reached a parting of their ways, she asked, almost shyly, "May I tell you something?"

He looked directly at her in surprise. She asked his permission to speak? Warm eyes met his, and he blushed deeply. "Of course, my lady, if you will."

"It doesn't matter as much as you think." His mind was confused for a moment, though his heart knew immediately what she meant. His arm, of course, the arm that did not do his bidding, would not hold its share of weight or grasp small objects. How did she know? He took great pains to conceal it, priding himself on the fact.

"Each of us has a weakness," she said, her voice flat and her eyes downcast, "some part that fails us. Those with visible weakness are best served, for they must learn to face them. You are stronger for having done that, are you not?" He nodded, in awe not only at her perception of his infirmity but her intuitive understanding of how hard he worked to overcome it. "What a weakness does to make a person grow is much more important than the weakness itself. So I say again, it does not matter."

"I—I thank you, my lady." Without further word, she turned, leaving Simon to proceed outside alone. In the courtyard, the sounds of manly pursuits assailed him: practice with swords, drills with pike and lance, wrestling moves and countermoves. He glanced at his withered arm. It really did not matter in any important way, he realized. He had achieved what he wanted in life so far despite it, and he would continue to grow stronger. The baroness was wise as well as beautiful.

Back at the shop, Simon told Carthburt about the French girl's death. The old man listened intently and asked when he finished, "Was this servant housed in the same area we visited this morning?"

"I do not think so. Dudley mentioned that her presence in that area was curious."

Carthburt glared at his workbench. "Odd, two deaths in one day."

"But the second death was an accident."

"According to whom?"

Simon went over what he had seen, reconsidering the possibilities. "You think she was pushed down those stairs?"

"She was young and carried nothing, you said. Those who fall are usually overburdened or elderly. It could be an accident, but one wonders, coming so soon after a murder."

"Northumberland believes the murder was aimed at the king and council. What would a servant have to do with that?"

"Amberson and Northumberland are chambered next to each other, according to what I was told. If the maid was from the duke's household, she might have seen someone entering Amberson's chamber or leaving it."

"Then the poison was administered there? Amberson was the target?"

"Likely, given the timing." Carthburt stoppered his jars and returned them to their proper places on the shelves with soft thumps, restoring order to the world in which he had control. "I don't comprehend it, though. His Lordship was no threat to those in power."

"His family then. Does someone gain from his death?"

"He has only two children living: a daughter and the son you saw, who is illegitimate and therefore will not inherit. The girl, Madeline, only eleven years or so, is the heir."

"Who was the man who went in at the last this morning? I saw him again this afternoon, waiting to speak to Dudley."

Carthburt rubbed his forehead as he dragged the name from memory. "Charles Beverley, if I recall correctly. He once had rooms near here but has since moved up in the world."

"What do you know of him?"

"Much concerned with advancement, they say. He holds some post at the palace and made himself useful to Amberson of late in hopes of rising even higher."

"Might he kill His Lordship, hoping to take his place on the council?"

"Little hope of that. Beverley has no money, no friends other than Amberson. In fact, he may suffer at his mentor's death, since his hopes for the future were built on him."

"Someone meant to benefit."

Carthburt grunted agreement. "And killed one of the more honest advisors the young king had. One more tragedy in the story of our poor nation."

They were silent for a while, considering the years of uncertainty England had endured with no sign of better days to come. Finally, Carthburt rose from the table, pushing gnarled hands onto it to ease his body upright, and patted his apprentice's shoulder. "Close the shop, Simon, and go home. This day has been long enough. I will spend time with my daughter."

With that, he shuffled through the curtained door, to where a fragile kind of peace awaited him.

CHAPTER THREE

On his way home, Simon stopped at Hampstead Castle to see Hannah, his future bride. Busy with her work, she did not see his approach, so he paused to watch her for a moment. He was surprised, as always, by her loveliness: abundant dark curls, deep green eyes, and a face like the angels that graced the altar at church. Equally surprising to Simon was the love she had for him. They awaited, not very patiently, completion of his apprenticeship with Thomas Carthburt so they could marry.

Simon's mother, Mary, had been at first aghast that her son chose not to become a physician like his father, but even that determined lady had to admit that her son was better suited to the work of an apothecary. His aversion to inflicting pain, even in the cause of healing, was a hindrance, and his withered left arm made many of a physician's tasks difficult, even impossible. Simon entered his second apprenticeship rather late but was relieved to have a trade in which he could serve his fellow man without dealing with amputations and bloodletting.

"Simon!" Hannah said when she turned and saw him. "I had not thought to see you until later." She tucked stray curls into her cap self-consciously, and he reached out to touch one that sprang back with a will of its own to dangle over her forehead. While he wondered at her love for a cripple, Hannah, a penniless orphan, had once believed her lack of education made her an unfit companion for Simon, who read several languages and understood complicated mathematical problems. At the urging of Elizabeth Tudor, she had revealed her misgivings, and Simon had in turn revealed his. When private fears faded, love blossomed and marriage plans resulted.

"I cannot visit this evening," he told her. "I must speak to my father at some length."

"It is good of you to come out of your way to let me know."

Simon grinned. "No trouble. You know I love this place!" Hampstead, where Hannah lived and worked, was a drafty, miserable castle in great need of renovation. The only thing that brought Simon to it voluntarily was her presence, and Hannah longed for him to have his own shop so she could leave the place forever.

They moved to a quiet corner, stepping out of the bustle that dinner preparations occasioned. A footman passed with a tray of fragrant pastries, nodding to Simon, who was familiar to everyone there. Simon returned the greeting and then sobered. "I saw Elizabeth this afternoon."

Upon hearing the story, Hannah was sympathetic. She felt no jealousy over Simon's affection for Elizabeth. Part respect, part admiration, it was completely unlike the love they shared. "I don't understand it, but she has endured much these last years."

"Yes. Mother, who thrives on Court gossip as you know, claims old Thomas Seymour seduced Elizabeth under his wife's very nose. I doubt it, but such talk must embarrass her."

"I often feel sorry for them all, caught in the web of betrayal that costs so many their heads." She pressed her lips together briefly. "Even her mother."

Simon said a silent prayer: *Not Elizabeth! She has too fine a mind to die simply because she might pose a threat to someone, sometime.*

As usual, Hannah seemed to read his thought. "I wish her well, though what will happen if Mary takes the throne, none can say."

"God grant that sisterly affection overcomes fear and distrust." He kissed her cheek chastely, aware that others watched. "Now I must be on my way."

At home, Simon found his mother elbow-deep in meal preparations. His sister Ella rushed around trying to please her in a dozen tasks at once. "Have you finished the sallet, daughter?" Ella, now ten, showed her mother the mixture of spring greens she had prepared, setting it on the table next to the cheese and freshly baked bread. Mary took the rabbit from the hearth and set it on the table, completing the meal preparations.

After supper, the Maldons sat at the back door of their modestly comfortable home. Spring warmed the evening and insects were not yet a problem, which made for a pleasant hour. Simon kept his peace about the day's events; he meant to speak privately to his father later. His sister entertained them with a song she had learned, her sweet voice soothing the cares of each family member's day. Just as she finished, a rapping came at the front of the house, and Jacob, one of the twins, went quickly to see who was at the door. He returned with a rolled parchment, sealed with wax. "It's a letter for Simon," he said in an awed tone. "A servant in livery brought it."

"Whose livery?" Mary Maldon demanded, but the boy shrugged, unable to say.

All eyes were on Simon as he took the letter and opened it. Glancing at the signature, he felt his face flushing and hoped the fading daylight covered it. The message was simple: "Richmond Park tomorrow noon, at the huntsman's cottage." The precise "E" at the bottom told him his earlier impression was mistaken. Something was afoot, and Elizabeth wanted him to be part of it.

"What is it, Simon?" His mother's face lit with curiosity.

Although he could play a role and wear a disguise with great

success, Simon could not lie effectively to his mother. Only eva-
sion served, and that was hard enough with her probing questions. His mouth worked, but no suitable explanation formed.
His father came to his rescue. "I suppose Hannah prevailed
upon someone to deliver a message for her?"

Gratefully, Simon accepted the help, muttering, "We cannot
meet tonight."

Jacob rose. "Then why don't we walk together for a while,
since you have no lovemaking to attend to for once?" Deftly
and with his usual perception, he had provided his son with two
things he needed: an escape from his mother's curiosity and
time for the two of them to talk.

Once away from the others, Simon related the events of the
day, ending with the message from the princess. Jacob listened
carefully, his upper lip pressing down onto the lower one in an
expression characteristic of both father and son. When Simon
finished, he was silent for some moments in careful delibera-
tion. As he waited, Simon noticed for the first time that he now
stood taller than Jacob. And to think he had once feared he
would forever be stunted!

"You say the dead man was Lord Amberson of the king's
council? A man of moderate views, I understand." They walked
on in silence for some moments. "And he supped with the boy
king. They fear, then, that the poison was meant for Edward?"

"Of course they told us little. Carthburt believes Amberson
himself was the target."

"And what is your role in all this?"

Simon smiled ruefully. "To provide protection from poison to
the king and his council."

Jacob sniffed derisively. "As if amulets and magic goblets will
protect them!" His pace accelerated as emotion stirred. "Poison
is all too convenient. A dose of 'inheritance powder,' and the
way to wealth is clear. A dram of 'bastard killer' from the yew

tree, and an unwanted child is no more. A little powdered antimony in wine, and the 'stepmother's poison' leaves no heir in the way of ambition. Without the means to prove murder, we too often see such crimes go unpunished."

"If Carthburt had not been consulted, they might have assumed His Lordship died of natural causes. I mean, he was—" Simon stopped before he said *old*, since the dead man had been about his father's age.

Jacob did not notice. "The princess wants light shed on the matter. Why else would she summon you except past association in her mind with the solving of murder?"

"But here is no bloodthirsty madman. This reaches the highest levels of government."

"Then you must step carefully, for you can be removed from this earth if someone in power feels threatened." Jacob's voice held an unaccustomed note of fear. "What does Carthburt think?"

"He's doing as ordered," Simon answered thoughtfully, "but he was suspicious about something else that happened." He told of the servant girl who had fallen on the stairs. "The second death unsettled him, I think. He sent me home early." Simon shrugged at his father's questioning gaze. "I stopped at Hampstead."

"As well you should. Your patient Hannah will someday make you a good wife." He sighed. "The help I can give for your start in life will not be much. I have William, the two younger boys, and Ella, who will require a dowry." Only Simon's sister Annie was settled, having married a young tailor. The two, poor as church mice, happily awaited a child at midsummer. Thoughts of her must have reminded Jacob of Carthburt's daughter. "How is Rachel?"

"She spends her days with pigeons and the household chores she can manage." Simon asked something he had often wondered about. "Was she always as she is now?"

"Only since her mother's death." From Jacob's tone, Simon sensed a tragedy long past.

"What happened to Rachel's mother?"

"She died when the girl was perhaps twelve or thirteen." As usual, Jacob's mind ran to his profession, and he wandered away from the question. "Martha was a medicine woman. From her I learned much concerning traditional remedies. Of course, some are mere superstition, and one is hard-pressed to understand the thinking behind them. Starve a cold and feed a fever, or vice versa?" He swatted the confused advice away impatiently with a gesture. "But others are time-tested, and those who cannot afford my services do as well or better with them than some who have all of modern medicine at their command."

Simon thought of the woman with fine clothes and decayed teeth. "For all their wealth, gentle folk do not escape illness and disability."

Jacob grunted. "They have too much of everything. To my mind, the diet of the poor is more conducive to good health, being simpler. Henry himself showed what too much food can do, and at the end no doctor could help him." Simon recalled the time he had seen the king, huge and in need of assistance in order to walk. Jacob had counseled dietary restrictions and been dismissed as a charlatan. "There was naught to be done for him by the time I was called in."

Simon grinned. "But Mother still blames you for the loss of royal patronage."

"She cannot forgive my inability to conform." Jacob smiled thinly. Although Mary Maldon undoubtedly loved her husband, she did not understand him, and he was not one to explain himself. Not that she would have comprehended anyway.

"I am lucky to be taught by you and Master Carthburt, who

are guided more by wisdom than precedent."

Jacob brushed away the compliment. "Our ideas are not new. The Arab Al-Thahabi suggested a plan for optimal health five hundred years ago: good air, good food and drink, plenty of physical movement, enough sleep, regularity of body functions, and moderation in all things. Care for the body that God creates for each of us is simply good sense."

Simon could not resist a playful argument. "But the priests tell us sin causes illness. God's unhappiness with a person's disobedience results in disease."

"Nonsense and you know it." Jacob sailed off on his favorite subject. "The priests know where their benefit lies! When a poor man contracts leprosy, they claim he is impure, perhaps having performed the sex act during a holy week. But if a nobleman becomes leprous, the sin is blamed on more general evil, such as national pride or widespread debauchery."

The son chimed in, knowing well his father's litany, "Since illness comes from within, we must learn as much as possible about the workings of the body."

"Today, men of learning discard superstition, but the untaught cling to amulets and signs."

Simon glanced up at the stars, controllers of men's destiny and predictors of their fate. They seemed cold and far away. "Carthburt says we cannot discount magic entirely."

"And he is correct. The soul, the mind, and the body are indivisible, each depending on the other, so nothing that the patient considers helpful can be discounted."

Simon grinned. "Still, I've never seen you turn over a stone on the way to a patient's home to see if the presence of living things under it predicts recovery."

"It would be below my dignity," Jacob said with a chuckle. "And you have no doubt heard it said that I hold dignity dear. Even old Henry Eight could not make me surrender to lies."

Thoughts of Henry brought Simon back to Elizabeth. "I wonder what the princess wants with me. I have nothing to do with palace affairs."

"That may be precisely what she needs." Jacob put a hand on his son's shoulder. "Consider how hard it must be for her, unable to trust anyone completely. She might seek to put her trust in you again, since you proved yourself before."

CHAPTER FOUR

The next morning Simon excused himself to Carthburt, saying he had an important errand, and walked toward Richmond, one of the king's hunting grounds. Though the city itself was crowded and overbuilt, on its outskirts were fields, woods, and open country. Following the river Thames' course, he soon spied Richmond Palace, built by Henry VII and surrounded by a large park where kings hunted at their pleasure. The huntsman's cottage sat at the edge of the wood, and he made his way toward it.

The day had begun with rain. Now the spring sun prickled his neck and steam-dried his damp shoulders. As he walked, Simon found himself wondering what Elizabeth would be like as a young woman. After the scandal a few years ago over her stepfather's supposed seduction, she remained out of the limelight as much as possible, living at Hatfield House with such quiet demeanor and appearance as to be of no interest to gossips. Now she had returned to London, probably to be near Edward, whose condition grew steadily worse. *What does she want with me?*

A member of the King's Guard, an impressive physical specimen with frizzy black hair untamed by the jaunty uniform cap, questioned Simon when he approached the cottage. Clearly unimpressed with the visitor, he nevertheless gave Simon permission to pass when handed the letter he carried.

The cottage, nestled in a copse of ancient elms, almost

seemed part of the landscape. On the far edge of the garden, a figure in a green riding outfit sat on a bench. Her skirts spread softly around her, but the jacket above them was brocaded and stiff. The lace that spilled out at the throat was only a little whiter than the skin above it. A large hat tied with a matching length of green silk protected fair skin from the sun's rays. Around her, the trees formed a frame, the setting perfect, down to the call of a melodious bird and the smell of spring-fresh greenery. A charming picture, and Simon wondered briefly if it was arranged for his benefit. If so, he was flattered, although it also served to remind him of the gulf between them. Elizabeth lived in a world of appearances, but under it all was constant danger. He wondered if she ever longed to be just a woman.

A young maidservant with a shy smile led him to the bench, murmured, "Your Grace," and backed away. Only when the girl was gone did Elizabeth turn and meet his gaze directly.

She had been thirteen when they were first acquainted, and their passing the day before had been brief. Now he saw that she was taller, more womanly in shape, although formal clothing hid most of her figure. Her face was unchanged yet somehow older, the eyes less readable, the mouth less soft. She had suffered, and it had changed her from a precocious child to a woman who guarded every expression.

"Master Maldon," she began in a formal tone, "it is some time since we met. Are you yet married?"

He paused before replying. What possible interest could the princess of England have in his marital state? Daring a reference to the past, he said, "Despite your best efforts, I am not, Your Highness. It is neither my fault nor Hannah's, but our purses that are to blame."

"Yes, the current state of England's finance makes things difficult. I suppose you hope for some reward from John Dudley as you assist in protecting the king."

Simon's face warmed at what he took for an insult, but he answered calmly, "I work for His Majesty's good, Your Highness, no more."

Her gaze went to the red blotches that stung pride brought to his neck. In an instant, the formal manner dissolved, and he saw his old friend behind the mask. "You are offended." Although she would never apologize, there was regret in her tone. She hesitated, unused to speaking honestly, to acknowledging emotion. "I have had a multitude of experiences since we last met in which men looked only to their own advantage."

"Yes, Your Grace."

Elizabeth sighed. "There are few like you at Court, Simon. But seeing you now, hurt that your motives are questioned, I am reminded that honest men exist." She looked away for a moment. "What of your master, this Thomas Carthburt?"

"A man of integrity."

"I guessed you would not attach yourself to an avaricious sort, nor would your father allow it." She put out her hands in an unconscious plea for understanding. "When I saw you yesterday, I had just learned of Lord Amberson's death. I did not let on that I knew you but noted the shop's location, suggesting to Dudley that he might find honest men there to confirm what he feared."

"So you were responsible for our being called to the palace." How quickly she had contrived a plan, letting no one know of their acquaintance but managing to get him involved, at least tangentially, in the investigation of what could be a threat to more than one old man.

She watched his face, waiting until he put it together, her nervousness betraying itself in the scuffing of one dainty boot-heel on the paving stone beneath the bench. "The king must be protected. If anything happens to Edward—" She left the thought unfinished, but he knew. Fond of her brother she might

guard his life. He is their assurance of continued power."

She smiled at the forthright statement. "Logic indicates that Dudley needs Edward alive, but the man is ambitious, and none can tell where his schemes will lead. Another reason I cannot go to Robin for assistance. I need someone removed from, hopefully uninterested in, the machinations of power."

Beginning to see the scope of the problem, Simon felt both excitement and fear. To be important to Her Grace was exciting, to be close to her, dangerous. As if in response, his senses picked up movement in the trees nearby. Someone was there, listening! He signaled for quiet, and she obeyed with quick understanding. They sat silent for some time, Simon sweeping the area with his gaze and Elizabeth listening carefully. No bird called, no movement flickered in the trees. All was still. "Nothing."

Her eyes slid left to right in concern, but she, too, saw nothing and went on, her voice lowered. "We could work together, as we did before. I will learn what I can within the palace. You will use disguise, subterfuge, whatever means you can devise, to discover the killer. I thought your friend Bellows might help, but I have not seen him of late among the guardsmen."

"We have not met in several years." Simon, Hugh, Elizabeth, and Hannah had once hunted down a murderer together. Simon recalled now that he felt more alive at that time than ever before or since. He immediately began planning to steal an hour to find Hugh Bellows. A thought interrupted, though. "How would you and I meet without raising suspicion?"

The princess stared out over the grassy expanse before them. "That is why I asked if you had married. Hannah can serve as go-between."

Simon was surprised that she remembered Hannah. "She is still at Hampstead."

"Well, then. I believe I am about to develop a need for a new maidservant. Send her to me—if she is willing to leave her Utopia." Here Elizabeth quirked pale brows, knowing the dreary castle too well. "I will remain at Whitehall for at least two weeks. As Hannah's future husband, you will visit her, and she will communicate between us." She rolled her eyes. "If I can somehow convince Kat that she will not poison me. This business with Amberson reminds her of how easily such a deed is done."

Simon had not met the fiercely loyal Kat, Elizabeth's governess, companion, and staunchest supporter, but he believed Hannah could charm her way into anyone's heart. "I will speak to her today." Knowing that Elizabeth liked women of learning around her, he could not resist boasting a little. "She reads now and writes a better hand than I do myself."

"If memory serves, that would not be difficult," Elizabeth replied drolly. "Your handwriting was ever poor. But I am pleased to hear it, for she felt the lack of education keenly." She rose, and he followed suit. "It is good to see you again, Simon Maldon. I have missed our talks and our shared adventure, frightening as it turned out to be."

"And I have always enjoyed your company, Highness. You have but to call and I will respond." As he bowed and backed away, he could not banish the feeling that someone watched. He supposed Elizabeth was always under observation. Did one ever get used to it?

When Simon left her, Elizabeth sat for some time, listening to the silence and wondering if she'd done the right thing. Was Simon capable of what she asked of him? And Hannah. Was she putting the girl in danger by bringing her into her household?

The answer in both cases was very likely affirmative. She had to depend on her judgment of people. It was all she really had. Simon was blessed—or cursed, possibly—with strong curiosity.

He would not stop until he found out all there was to know about Amberson's death.

And Hannah? Elizabeth promised herself that she would watch over her. She did not want anyone to suffer on her behalf, but she knew that protecting Edward was vital. Between Simon and herself, Hannah would be protected. All she had to do was relay information, after all.

This is what being a leader is, she thought. *Weighing the life or well-being of this one against the needs of the whole. It is a weight on the heart, for certain.*

After a while, the princess rose and turned to where her maid and the guardsman stood chatting amiably as they waited. "I am ready to return to the palace, Daniel," she told the young man, who moved somewhat reluctantly away from the pretty young girl. *That is my fate,* Elizabeth thought grimly. *Always to be in the way of someone else's goals and desires. God grant that I may truly be in the way if someone plans to murder my brother.*

Hannah was not nearly as pleased at Elizabeth's invitation as Simon had imagined. Her vegetable chopping speeded as he described the proposal, reaching such agitation that he feared a bloody result. "The palace?" she squeaked. "To work for the princess?"

"I have said," he replied patiently. "It is a great honor."

"A great terror!" she corrected. "I am a kitchen maid, Simon. How should I behave in the king's own palace? Even if Elizabeth were indulgent, which she is not, will others not notice my mistakes and demand my dismissal? Then how would I get another post? Hampstead is cold and drafty and antiquated, but at least here I know the people, the procedures, and my place." She ended with a plaintive, "I'm not ready for such a step."

"But the princess asked for you by name."

Her eyes widened. "She did?"

"It was she who suggested the plan."

"Only so she can meet with you." The knife clattered to the table as she abandoned her task in earnest argument. "Simon, I am not jealous, I swear it. But you and your royal friend overlook the possibility that I might not want to do this, might not be able to."

Simon sensed fear, not inability, held her back. "What if I ask Sir George to give you a week's leave to try the post? Then if you do not like it, you can return to Hampstead."

"If I don't *like* it? If I am tossed out for saying or doing the wrong thing! If I am beaten for offenses I won't even know I've committed! If I am jailed for pretending to be a lady's maid when I am nothing like it!" Her voice rose as she imagined her terrifying future, her disquiet at leaving the place she had called home for most of her life. Hampstead represented safety in Hannah's mind, its damp walls and gray ugliness comforting in its enfolding strength.

He took her hands in his. "Hannah, do you trust me?"

"Y-yes." Her face cleared and she seemed to absorb from him some confidence.

"I believe you can succeed. The princess would not suggest it if she did not."

Hannah sighed. "All right. Speak with Sir George, then. I should not keep the princess waiting." She managed a grin as she added, "As we both know, she is not known for patience with those who attend her."

CHAPTER FIVE

The Yeomen of the Guard of the Body of Our Lord the King, apparent in all areas of the Court, were charged with the personal protection of the royal family. To curb criticism of the cost of their maintenance, yeomen performed household duties as well, so guardsmen in striking uniforms might make the royal bed at one point in the day and serve as armed escort to the king at another.

Hugh Bellows, one of many petty captains, had been one the old king trusted to do special, sometimes secret, tasks. During one such assignment, he and Simon had become acquainted, learning to trust and admire the other. Afterward, life intervened, and they lost touch.

Simon's search for his old friend began at St. James Palace, where they had last met, but he was told there that Hugh had left the guard. That was a surprise, but the man on duty knew nothing more. Simon tried the names of the two other guardsmen he knew, Calkin and Gooderich. Recognizing Calkin's name, the guard went to see if he could find him. As Simon waited, he watched two off-duty guardsmen play at dice, throwing the cubes against the nearest wall with audible clicks and making noisy comments on their luck or lack of it. From somewhere nearby the smell of cooking cabbage emanated, promising vegetable soup for the guards' next meal and reminding Simon how long it had been since breakfast.

Within ten minutes, the heavily freckled Calkin appeared

through a doorway, his expression curious as to the identity of his visitor. After a moment of uncertainty, his homely face split in a wide smile, and he lurched forward to clap Simon on the shoulder. "Simon Maldon! Lad, you've grown a foot, I trow!"

The guardsman looked exactly the same as when he'd patiently taught Simon the use of the throwing knife, a skill he had maintained since then, since it compensated somewhat for his withered arm and made him feel less like a cripple. "You have not visited for some time."

Simon hung his head, ashamed that he had neglected old friends. "I am apprenticed to an apothecary in Hampstead and have almost completed my training."

Calkin nodded. "A master takes a good deal of a fellow's time, but you'll have a steady income when it's done. Come, sit!"

They moved to a table and took seats at the benches alongside it. Simon knew from earlier visits that the guards' quarters consisted of this hall, a sort of commons area, and a barracks down a short hallway to his left. Around the hall hung the trappings of the trade: weapons, belts, hats, and other accouterments of the guard, but the walls seemed somehow less cluttered than before.

When Simon commented on it, Calkin lowered his voice. "We are weakened, though our duties remain the same. They expect us to protect the king with fewer men and less money each year." He glanced around to see that no one took note of his words. "Hugh protested the reduction and in return for his honesty was told he was no longer welcome in the guard."

That was a shock. Hugh, the quintessential guardsman, had been discharged for speaking the truth? Imagining his friend's distress, Simon asked, "Where has he gone?"

"The Earl of Pembroke hired him to manage his London

estate, and Hugh is content there, though he would not have had it so."

As soon as was polite, Simon was on his way to Hugh's new posting. It took the rest of the morning to find Pembroke's house on the Strand and then locate Hugh himself, but Simon's reward was a glad cry from his old friend.

"Simon! Why, lad, is it really you?" Hugh's forehead had grown taller and his face more lined from the sun, but he seemed in good health.

"I am sorry to have stayed away so long, and sorry to hear you have left the guard."

Hugh's plain face sobered. "Well, it's the way of things, is it not? I have a good posting here."

Simon looked around him. Pembroke's estate, Wilton House, was in Salisbury, but like most noblemen, he maintained a town house to facilitate his service to the king. The earl's status was evident in the size of the household that buzzed around them. Men in Pembroke's livery were everywhere, one busy hammering at a piece of metal, another grinding an edge on some tool, some at their ease. A few females moved among them, some flirting while others kept their eyes on the ground as they traversed male territory.

The house stood near the riverbank, allowing use of the Thames for travel. Simon noted a barge with the earl's colors tied at the dock. A neat wall separated his territory from homes on either side. The house itself was half-timbered, the wood dark against white daub that covered bricks beneath. The upper story extended farther than the lower, front and back, providing convenient shade from the unusual warmth of the May afternoon. Hugh took up a stool and kicked a second one away from the wall for Simon.

"What have you been at, lad?" Again, Simon felt guilt at neglecting a friend. Life had pulled him in other directions.

"I've almost finished my apprenticeship and hope to marry next year."

Hugh grinned. "I've often said to myself, 'Hampstead is north of Simon and I am south.' I knew which way you'd go." His voice held no trace of reproach. "I meant to visit you, too, but my life changed as well. Aside from this"—he indicated his new surroundings—"I have taken a wife."

Simon's jaw dropped. Knowing that Hugh supported his widowed sister's family, he had not expected he could ever afford to marry.

Obviously enjoying his surprise, Hugh explained. "Bridget found herself a husband, a good man with a trade, dropping my status to doting uncle. Then I met Constance, a widow with two grown sons, and such a cook, lad!" Hugh smiled and patted his belly, rounding incongruously from his lanky frame. "With my new post I have more free time. When the earl returns to his estate, things become very quiet here. Now, as you can see, we are overrun with folk, but at least the hours pass quickly."

Simon gathered from all this that Hugh was content, as Calkin had said, but he knew his friend's dismissal must have rankled. Soldier-for-hire to an earl was not the same as king's confidant. That brought him to the point of his visit.

"I have fallen into a situation in which I could use your help." Briefly, he outlined the events of the last two days. When he finished, Hugh shook his head in wonder.

"Will the princess launch herself into danger yet again?"

Simon defended Elizabeth. "There is no danger. She will merely learn what she can."

"She has a positive lust for gossip and secrets," Hugh countered. "Like old Harry, it is said she encourages all around her to tell every scrap of information available."

"As does Princess Mary. For their own protection they must always know which way the winds blow."

"That may be so." Hugh shifted his legs to a more comfortable position, setting an assortment of tools attached to his belt jingling. "I heard of Amberson's death, of course. They are all concerned. If His Lordship, mild as milk, had an enemy, any of them could."

"Can you find out more about who might have killed him?"

Hugh puffed out his breath slowly as he considered. "My position here gives little access to such information. You'd best go to Calkin."

Simon was disappointed. He had pictured the four of them working together as they had before. Still, he understood Hugh's removal from palace affairs in his new position.

"I will do that." With sudden inspiration he asked, "Can you give me your impression of some people I have encountered thus far, to give us a starting point?"

"Willingly, if I know them."

"Lukas Seawell?"

"The old man's bastard son? They say he is a zealot Protestant who will bring trouble on himself with his insistence on a purer church."

"Robert Dudley, known as Robin?"

"Ambitious, like his sire, but passing honest, I'd say."

Simon searched his mind for others he had heard of in connection with Amberson. He could think of no names, so he asked a general question. "Is there someone on the council who might commit murder to advance himself?"

Hugh swatted him playfully for the naive question. "All of 'em, lad. Such men crave power over others, and only caution keeps them as honest as they are." He pulled his earlobe in thought. "What you must discover is who thought he could kill and get away with it."

That brought the servant's death to mind. "Do you know a woman named Ellen who is friend to Robin Dudley?" He briefly described the woman and her obvious pregnancy.

Hugh considered. "Baron Rochdale's wife is called Ellen, I believe. She carries his child, an heir some thought would never be."

"Who is Baron Rochdale, and why should he not beget heirs?"

"I know him only by report, but they claim he refuses all other pursuits for love of hunting, even his attractive wife. She was sent to visit Northumberland's wife, who is the baron's cousin."

"That must be the one I saw, since she would know Robert Dudley well enough to seek him out for information. Was this Baroness Rochdale connected to Lord Amberson in any way?"

"If you're thinking of a liaison between them, I doubt it. Amberson was long past such things. His one youthful passion, a serving girl in his father's house, produced Seawell. He remained true to her, and only after her death married as his family desired."

"And produced his only legitimate issue, Madeline."

"Yes. Madeline's mother is dead, so the king will decide what becomes of her." Hugh sighed. "There is likely to be a scramble for guardianship, since whoever controls the daughter controls her sizable fortune. She will someday be bartered like beads at a bazaar, but that is the fate of noble girls." He made an abrupt turn in thought. "Speaking of girls, how is Hannah?"

There followed some catching up as Simon told of her newly created post with the princess. "She will do well," Hugh said once he understood the plan, "but believe me, Simon; you will be in debt to her for the rest of your life over this."

"I only hope she and the princess are both satisfied."

Hugh's sniff indicated that was a vain hope. "Anyone else I can slander for you?" The stool squeaked as he leaned back against the wall.

Simon paused in thought. "The only other man I have come

in contact with in the matter so far is a knight named Beverley. I think he was friend to Lord Amberson."

Hugh's voice became a growl. "Beverley! That monster has no friend but himself."

Simon sensed Hugh's dislike of the man was deep. "You know him."

"When Charles Beverley managed to ingratiate himself with the council and was named to oversee the king's guard, we in the guard soon learned to watch our backs."

"Carthburt says he pursues his own advancement more than most."

"There is no end to which he will not go to increase his wealth and power. Beverley is the worst of a kind we have plenty of in this world."

"Is murder within his scope?"

Hugh hesitated. "I believe he has done it ere this."

At Simon's wide-eyed expression, he raised a cautionary hand. "I have no proof, but here is what I know. Two women Charles Beverley married brought modest wealth to the union, and both died young." Leaning forward, he lowered his voice. "I suspect he killed his second wife, but my witness disappeared before I could act on the information. At about the same time, I was called in, branded a malcontent, and dismissed from the guard."

"And then you could do nothing."

"Having a wife requires some discretion. Luck brought the offer of this post, and Beverley was apparently content to have me gone from the palace."

"If he has killed before, might he not try another time?"

Raising a hand, Hugh cautioned, "I say what I believe, not what I can prove. A man with two dead wives is not so uncommon."

"How did they die?"

"One died slowly of a stomach ailment. The other complained of a headache and became sleepy. Shortly afterward she convulsed and died."

"Arsenic and cyanide." Simon shrugged at Hugh's questioning gaze. "That would be my guess, if their deaths were murder."

"Amberson died of poison." Hugh put a calloused hand on Simon's shoulder. "Tread carefully, lad."

"Drink carefully is more like," he replied, rising and skidding his wooden stool back against the wall. "I'm not a likely candidate for poisoning, since I will never dine with Beverley or his ilk." He sobered. "I will warn the princess, however."

"We would not want to lose that one," Hugh agreed, "though she will always be a trial to those around her."

After promising to visit Hugh's home soon and meet his wife, Simon returned to St. James and again sought out Calkin, who was serving himself a cup of soup. He ladled out a second portion, welcome considering how early Simon's breakfast had been. As they ate, he explained his mission. The guardsman's brow knit in consternation, and he surveyed the room to see if anyone was listening before answering. "I'd like to help the princess, but things are not as they once were. No one knows who will be in control tomorrow, so we in the guard must be careful to offend no one."

"I understand." Those with power could be ruthless, and a man risked his career, freedom, even his life, if he trusted wrongly. Elizabeth's own servants had been harassed and threatened when her stepfather's plotting threw suspicion of treason on her, but they had stood firm.

Calkin stared into space for a moment then shrugged, signaling a decision. "No harm in a drink with an old friend, says I. If over a mug of ale I report what I've seen in the course of a day, you can do with that information as you will, provided my name is never attached to it."

"We can meet at any place you choose."

Calkin considered, scratching his nose vigorously. "In the Savoy there's an inn where I often have the noon meal on my off, which is four days hence. The Stag and Stalk, it is called."

"I will find it."

"And what shall I tell you there?"

"Anything you learn about the dead man, to begin with."

"All right, then." He took up the now-empty bowls and replaced his spoon in its hook on his belt. "Now I must be about my newest task."

"And what is that?"

"Training new troops as harquebusiers." At Simon's puzzled look, he explained, "We have been provided muskets and ordered to train the men in their use."

"And is this a good thing?"

Calkin shrugged dismissively. "To my mind, the individual firearm will never become a practical weapon. The things are useless in damp and often don't work even under perfect conditions." He shrugged again. "Still, I have my orders."

They parted then, Simon following the murmuring river as it bent northward before continuing east. With the resignation of the career soldier, Calkin turned to practice with the harquebus, useful or not.

CHAPTER SIX

When Simon reached the shop, Carthburt limped out from his living quarters, visibly upset. "It is good that you have returned, for Rachel needs us both."

"Is she ill?"

The old man looked down at his hands. "Not ill. Unsettled."

"What happened?"

"She took one of her frights, worse than ever. She needs your help, if she will accept it."

"Let us see what we can do." When Rachel was afraid, she climbed as high as possible, taking refuge in the rafters of the loft where she had slept as a child. Oddly enough, she was as terrified of heights as of everything else, so that once there, she froze in fear. Twice before Simon had coaxed her down, holding her steady as she descended the ladder to the main floor.

Carthburt entered the living area first and spoke to his daughter in soothing tones. "The man is gone, my dove, and only Simon and I are here. You can come down, but you must let him help so you do not fall."

"Yes, Father." Her voice was weak and shook with tears. "Is he truly gone?"

"He is. Simon is going to come in now. He will steady you so that you can return to your papa. Won't that be best, sweet one?"

"Yes, Father. Are you sure the dark man is far away?"

"Far away, my dear. Come in now, lad." Simon entered

through the curtain and looked up. A crosspiece of the building's frame ran from the edge of the loft to the opposite wall, and Rachel crouched at its center, eyes wild and breathing rapid, clutching the upright post in the apparent hope that no evil could reach her there. As usual, fear had clouded her judgment, and the place of safety she had fled to was now her prison.

Simon's weak arm hindered him in these instances, and he considered his path for a moment. He would have to climb up and make his way across the beam to the frightened girl, steadying her return to the loft and the ladder while finding a way to anchor himself so they did not both fall. Sure of his own balance, he made it up easily enough. When he reached Rachel, she reacted with unexpected trust, throwing her arms around his neck with such force that he teetered for a moment. "The dark man! He will hurt me again!"

"No one is here. Look down. There is only your father. Can you cross to the ladder with me?" Below them Carthburt looked up, one gnarled hand swiping anxiously at his beard.

Simon continued to speak soothingly, copying his father's tactic for calming fearful patients. He told her in advance what would happen and at the same time assured that he would do his part. "We will cross the beam together. You know I will keep you from falling, do you not?"

"Y-yes." She sounded uncertain.

"Hold on to my belt, here." Taking one of her warm, damp hands gently from its stranglehold around his neck, he set it on his waist. "Now we shall stand up together."

Trembling, Rachel did as instructed. When he felt her hand tighten on his belt, Simon stood, moving slowly so that she could grip the post with her other hand until she felt stable. Reaching up, he grasped a rafter with his good hand, steadying himself. He stepped sideward, waiting after each step for the girl to do the same. When she could no longer touch the upright post she whimpered, but he spoke again in calm tones. "You are very good at this, Rachel. Put your other hand on my belt now. This time when I step I will smile, and you must smile as well."

Her eyes were wide and the smile she managed a mere tightening of her lips, but she did as he said. "Very good. On this step you must say, 'I am coming, Father.' Tell him."

"I am coming, Father."

Silent, Carthburt moved beneath them, making himself available as a cushion should she lose her balance. "With this step we will listen for the doves. Do they call for their supper?"

Rachel's face lost some of its rigidity at the thought of her pets. "I hear them."

"Then we will take another step, for we are almost to the end."

Finally, they reached the loft's edge, and Simon stepped onto the plank floor, putting his good hand back to steady the girl. She stepped lightly off the beam, her face suddenly free of fear. "My birds," she said. "I must feed them."

He held the ladder as she backed down to where her father waited below. He took her in his arms, holding her tightly as Simon made his own way to the packed-earth floor.

"Rachel, my love, what frightened you so?"

The child-woman looked at him in surprise. "I am not frightened, Father. And my birds are waiting." With that, she pulled herself free and went out the back door, leaving both men looking after her in consternation.

"You say a man came into the shop and caused this?"

"Yes."

"Was it someone you know, one she might have seen before?"

Carthburt hesitated, his gaze focused on the opposite wall. "No. He was a foreigner, a Spaniard from his accent." He gestured upward. "When he left, I found her up there."

"Do you note that men with black hair and dark eyes send

her into these states?"

Carthburt's face closed and his tone became abrupt, signaling that he wanted no more discussion. "She is calm now. Return to your work, and I will join you shortly." Hobbling toward the door where his daughter had exited, he paused. "I thank you, lad. Lately it seems you are more savior than apprentice."

Simon waved a hand dismissively. "I owe you much more than I can ever repay, master. It is little enough I do in return." He reentered the shop and went to work pounding mandrake bark, but his mind remained on simple, beautiful Rachel and her fears, real and imagined.

Hannah did not know how she had managed to make it this far. She presented herself at Whitehall and asked to see Katherine Ashley, as instructed. Waiting in nervous agitation, she hardly noticed the detail in the room's trim and the elegant furnishings, so superior in quality and quantity over Hampstead. Had Elizabeth told Katherine why she was here? Surely, "Kat" would have her own opinions about who should serve the princess for whom she had been responsible for fifteen years.

Interrupting her thoughts, a door opened behind her with a small squeak of protest. A woman entered, frowning briefly at the hinge as if promising it would not have voice for much longer. She was neatly dressed, her movements brisk, creating the impression of businesslike efficiency. Her hair had gone gray in front; the rest hid beneath the cap she wore. Hannah curtseyed correctly, not too low but respectfully looking at the floor between them.

"You are Hannah?"

"Yes, madam."

"I hear that you were of great service to Elizabeth at Hampstead, when I was indisposed."

61

"I tried to be, madam."

"I know a bit about those events." A tightening around her mouth signaled disapproval. "I got most of the story from Mary Wood, who believes the princess was more involved in certain matters than was ever revealed."

"I wouldn't know, madam. I only worked in the kitchen."

"I see."

So what did she think when, after all this time, Elizabeth demanded that Hannah be brought to Whitehall? She would know the princess was up to something. To accommodate a new girl they would have to send someone away, since their budget was strictly controlled. In addition, Hannah knew little about serving royalty, which required competence in a dozen areas as well as the ability to keep silent about household affairs. Required to take her on without knowing the full reason, Katherine had every right to be resentful.

Her new superior seemed to read her mind. "I'm not sure what your purpose is here, girl, but I long ago gave up arguing when the princess makes up her mind. Since you are at least neat and clean, I will accept your presence. If at some point you feel inclined to tell me the truth of it, I will listen, for everyone knows that Elizabeth is my first concern, always." She waited briefly while Hannah continued to examine the floor. It was not for her to tell. Kat gave an irritated sigh. "Let us discuss what your duties will be."

They were simple chores at first, things that kept her under Katherine's watchful eye. Mindful of that, Hannah observed the behavior of those around her, copying them so that if she was not perfect in compliance, at least she did not stand out. Elizabeth's maid Blanche, the other person likely to be offended by a new servant for "her" princess, had apparently been given some explanation. While she was not friendly to Hannah, neither was she openly antagonistic.

That is not to say that the new girl was welcome. Among the fifteen hundred people at Court were hundreds of servants. Service to royalty was an honor, and a girl plucked from obscurity and installed among them so suddenly caused some resentment. Within an hour Hannah had more jobs than she'd thought possible. She was to tend to the fires, empty the slops, clean the princess' shoes, wash soiled underwear, and a dozen other tasks someone thought of to keep her busy. In return for all of it, few so much as gave her a smile. She was, however, pleased to be able to give an affirmative reply when asked, rather condescendingly, if she could read. Simon's tutelage paid off there, for the women around Elizabeth were better educated than most, and she won some grudging respect.

To her embarrassment, the princess insisted that the new maid attend when she visited her brother that afternoon. Eyebrows rose, and Hannah guessed that she would pay for the privilege. The prospect was both exciting and frightening. One day in the palace, and she would see the king!

After much bustle and preparation, the two set off. Carrying an assortment of items the princess might conceivably need for the visit, Hannah followed Elizabeth through the confusing mass of rooms that comprised Whitehall. There were few hallways. Most rooms led to other rooms, so that one passed through the lives of dozens of other people on the way to almost anywhere. Some rooms were noisy and smelled of wine or beer; others merely hummed with subdued conversation. In some, children frolicked as their nursemaids looked on. In most cases, the inhabitants hardly looked up as they bustled through.

At Edward's door, Hannah looked carefully at the face of the guardsman who admitted them, but he was not one of Simon's friends. The man's uniform was slightly shabby, reflecting, she supposed, the sad state of England's economy. He stood strictly at attention, though, and ushered them into the room with dignity.

The room was overheated and stuffy, with the acrid smell of medicine hanging in the air like a mist. Edward half-reclined on a velvet couch, his manner listless and dazed. Aside from two bright spots of red on his cheeks, he was pale as death. From across the room they heard his ragged breathing, but he smiled as they entered. "How good of you to visit, Sister."

"Majesty." Elizabeth began the required obeisance imposed by the council. She had to kneel several times during each visit and could not sit anywhere that placed her on a level with her brother. Hannah did as her mistress did, although no one paid any attention to her. Her obligation ended, the princess seated herself on a cushion, careful to keep her head below Edward's. Once she had confirmed again her understanding that she was not his equal, everyone relaxed somewhat. Brother and sister behaved like family, beginning a game of chess as attendants gossiped in a far corner of the room. Hannah did not know what she was supposed to do. Certainly, she should not appear to be listening, but no one offered any distraction. Taking a stance against a wall, she turned her eyes to the floor. She could not help but hear what Elizabeth and her brother said, but she supposed that was the reason for her being there.

"What do you know of the death of Lord Amberson?" Edward asked, eagerness in his tone. He was a boy, king or not, and wanted to compare knowledge with his older sister, to whom he could speak freely on most matters. Left alone, the two seemed comfortable together.

"His body is being prepared. They will soak it in spices then wrap it in cloth that has been tarred and covered with molten lead." He gave her a questioning glance. "It is the way when one of importance dies."

Edward's sense of humor peeped through for a moment as

he raised an eyebrow. "I would wager they needed a good deal of lead for my father!" Elizabeth smiled, but Hannah, glancing up at her, sensed sadness. Grossly fat in his final years, Henry ended life vastly different from the athletic, handsome figure he had been in youth. He also suffered great physical pain, as Edward now did. In contrast, Elizabeth was seldom sick, though it was said she used illness as an excuse at times. Looking from the languishing king to his vibrant sister, Hannah remembered Simon saying once: *She should have been the one. She has the strength, the determination, the intelligence England needs at this moment.* All she lacked was masculinity. Heaven decreed that women were secondary to men, no matter their strengths.

"Have they a suspicion concerning who might have poisoned His Lordship?" Elizabeth moved her knight into jeopardy to draw Edward's bishop out, but he quirked an eyebrow to indicate that he saw her strategy.

"No dishes from the meal were discolored, so the poison was not administered there." Stained metal serving-ware was a sure sign of poison. "He returned to his apartments after dinner to work on some matters for ourselves. According to the servants, no one visited him there."

"The servants have been considered?"

"All have been with him for years." Edward studied the chessboard then slid his bishop forward, taking a pawn with a soft click. "Someone may have poisoned a glass cup he kept in his room. It was well-known that age had left him with a dry throat, and he sipped at some liquid throughout the day. The wine bottle he poured from was half full and contained no poison."

"But traces of poison remain in the cup?"

"No one knows what happened to it."

Elizabeth considered. "Then the killer visited the room twice, once to put poison into the cup and again to remove it."

"That would take both planning and daring."

"It seems difficult but need not be. When we are at dinner, the apartments are virtually empty. A patient person could slip in and poison the wine. And it would be easy enough to remove the goblet the next morning in the uproar after the death was discovered." She glanced at the outer wall. "One could toss it out the window and retrieve the pieces later."

"You have a devious mind," Edward said with a teasing smile. "I must never make you angry, for you will slay me in my bed and hide the evidence so cleverly as to go free."

Elizabeth paled. "I would never harm Your Majesty. In fact, I would give my life to save yours, were it necessary."

The king smiled again, but now his eyes held a hint of sadness. Although hyperbole was the language of the age, Elizabeth seemed sincere. Did that rueful smile reveal the truth of a current rumor: that he had decided neither sister would follow him to the throne?

No one had any illusion that this king would live to be an old man, including Edward himself. Illness piled upon illness, and his doctors could cure none of them. According to Henry's will, Mary would rule if Edward died. But Henry was dead and Edward was not, not yet. Mary made no secret of her Catholicism, and if she took the throne, everything done to make England a Protestant nation would be undone.

Yet could they disinherit Mary and leave the throne to Elizabeth? There were those who insisted she was not Henry's daughter, although how one could make such a claim upon meeting her, Hannah did not know. Each sister had proponents, and whichever one did not inherit was likely to make trouble for the other, whether she chose to or not. The wise thing, Edward's advisers counseled, was to look elsewhere for England's next ruler.

The problem was there were only girls. Henry Fitzroy,

Henry's bastard and only other son, was dead. Rumor claimed Edward leaned toward choosing his aunt's granddaughter, Lady Jane Grey, who had been playmate to him and Elizabeth as children. Devoutly Protestant, she was one of only a few in the world the king could call friend.

Hannah guessed that Edward would take the easiest way out of a bad situation, and having seen his condition and felt the pall of death that inhabited this room, he would have to act soon. If Jane were his successor, he would not have to choose between his sisters. Neither Elizabeth's Protestant followers nor Mary's Catholic ones could claim Jane was illegitimate. With a strong husband, some said, Jane would be the perfect candidate for queen.

"I know you love me, Sister," the king said carefully, "and you will do what is best for England when the time arises."

"Of course, Majesty," Elizabeth replied, but her voice was tight, and Hannah sensed that she too had heard the rumors and rebelled at the thought of Jane on the throne, as well she might. The woman lacked Tudor fire. Jane's husband would rule, would control her and therefore the nation. And as Simon had said so many times, the nation needed much more than a figurehead in these perilous times. England needed a ruler.

CHAPTER SEVEN

When Simon told Carthburt that he needed to leave again for a while that afternoon, the old man regarded him closely for a moment before nodding permission. Simon promised himself he would make up for it, easing his master's burdens more than usual for the rest of the week.

Later, the servant who answered a knock at the door of Lord Amberson's apartments found an odd-looking young man literally draped with fabric, all of it black.

"What is it?"

"Charles Copper, the tailor, sends cloth for His Lordship's funeral." Simon coughed from the smell of dye and the dust buried in the depths of the fabric he carried.

"Wait here."

He hoped it would not be long. It had been difficult convincing a friend who really was a tailor's apprentice to let him present the goods at Amberson's apartment. It was vital, he reasoned, to meet His Lordship's daughter and discern whether she might have been in some way involved in her father's murder. There was more time to survey the outer room of the apartment today than there had been earlier. The place still smelled faintly of paint, but repairs were complete and draperies now hung in place over the window. Both doors to the other rooms were closed. Simon wondered if anyone would sleep in the one on the left, where a man had so recently died.

A tall window stood open ahead of him, and he moved toward

it, apparently idly. Stepping out onto a small balcony, he saw below it a sheer drop. No trellis, no vines or handholds: no way to climb to this height unassisted. On either side were additional balconies. Leaning out, he judged the distance. Too far to cross from one balcony to another without support of some kind.

A sound came from one of the side doors, and he quickly stepped back into the room. A man entered whom he recognized from his first visit. Lukas Seawell, Amberson's son. He pulled in his chin, hoping the disguise was good enough. In an oversized cap, cheeks stuffed with wax, and freckles dotted on his nose, he counted on the fact that people seldom really looked at apprentices. "What's this, boy?"

Simon repeated his request, lowering his voice and changing the cadence of his normal speech. Seawell cut him off before he was half done. "We'll have no popish ceremony for my father's death. He is with his God already, and there is neither need to mourn nor need to impress those who remain on earth with extravagant expenditures and brass ornaments."

Definitely a reformer. There was great difference of opinion in the nation as to funeral observances. Reformers held that death was an immediate, joyous reunion with God, and therefore mourning should be minimal lest men offend Him. They preached the elimination of wakes, funeral sermons, elaborate homage, and "minds," traditional candle-lighting services held one month, one year, and seven years after the death of a loved one.

For a nation once steeped in Catholic beliefs, however, it was hard to let go of the idea that conspicuous funerals helped speed a person's entrance into Heaven. They also served to demonstrate a family's importance and the extent to which the deceased would be missed. Anglican churchmen rarely discouraged extravagant rites, since the church profited. The poor looked forward to the largess associated with them, the pomp, the break in their monotonous lives, and most of all, the charitable acts done in remembrance of the dead.

The door behind Simon opened to admit a man he had seen twice before, now carrying several official-looking pieces of parchment. Charles Beverley took in the situation at a glance and observed, "Mourning clothes, Lukas?"

Seawell flushed and his brow descended. "I was telling this boy we have no need of—"

Beverley raised an admonishing hand. "None of your tired sermons on religion and thrift. Your father will be given every honor." He turned to Simon, who added to his earlier impression of the man. There was about him an even stronger sense of power today, perhaps fueled by recent success. Simon kept his face impassive but decided Charles Beverley was not one he would like to know better. The man was too certain of his own importance to the world, too convinced that only he knew the right way of things.

"Tell your master we require one hundred blacks for the poor made of—" Beverley reached out to feel the thickness of one of the less expensive fabrics. "This will do. Madeline will need a suitable dress in yellow, as will several women of the Court, and suits, of course, for the family." He paused. "Including Lukas, if he will."

Seawell spoke calmly, though anger flushed his neck and flared his nostrils. "I take it you have achieved your goal."

Beverley regarded him with faint amusement. "If you mean that I am appointed guardian to your sister, you are correct. The fact that I am executor of your father's will convinced His Majesty that it is proper."

"And you will not desist from an overblown display of funeral rites? My father is this moment at the right hand of God and needs not your pageantry."

"But the world wants it." Beverley made a half-hearted attempt at argument. "Think of the benefit to the poor, Lukas. Blacks handed out at such events are the only new garments some of them ever receive, and the dole during a funeral procession provides relief to the suffering. Your father's will stipulates the cost, so we can judge that he wished the observance substantial."

"And you will no doubt line your pockets at every opportunity." The other tried unsuccessfully to keep the snarl from his voice. "I want no part of it."

"You *have* no part in it, Lukas. You alienated yourself from your father with your fanatical ravings. He chose to limit your inheritance and leave you no role in managing his holdings. An annual sum is your portion, and I will administer the rest for your sister." Beverley's tone betrayed both contempt for Seawell and pleasure at his own good fortune.

It was apparently too much for the other. "My philosophy teaches that mourning more than one day is arrogant selfishness. In practice of my faith, I will absent myself from further obsequies." With that, he left the apartment, his careful closing of the door behind him speaking much more of his anger than slamming would have.

Beverley behaved as if the recent unpleasantness had not occurred. He spread one of the papers he held on a nearby table and began making notes, looking up every few moments at the display Simon wore. Once his brows met in a frown, and Simon felt a pang of fear, wondering if Beverley recognized him. Apparently, however, Madeline's new guardian was merely making a decision. "We shall have hoods and cloaks for the honor guard, and hoods for the horses as well." He jotted down a notation, the pen scraping on the thick parchment.

The other door opened, and a girl put her head out timidly. "Uncle, is someone angry?"

Beverley gave Simon a glance before answering, "No, my

dear. I think you heard your brother telling me a story about his friends and their antics."

"Has he gone?" She peered around as if Seawell might hide behind a chair or a drapery.

"Yes. He has returned to his own kind. Come, my dear, and see what the boy has brought." He took the girl's arm, drawing her into the room. Madeline Amberson seemed even younger than her eleven years, tentative in both speech and movement. Beverley motioned Simon nearer, inviting the girl to examine the fabrics he had brought.

She touched a velvet swath tentatively. "What are they for?"

"Why, for your father's funeral, my dear. We pay him honor, for he was a good man."

Madeline's brow furrowed, and it seemed to Simon that the word *was* concerned her. Her guardian saw it, too, and said softly, "You remember that he is dead, do you not?"

"Yes." Her tone did not reinforce the affirmative word.

"We will see him again in Heaven. Do you understand?"

"Yes." Again, the underlying message contradicted the word.

Madeline was soft, Simon thought, like a pillow. Her face was white and pudgy, her arms bulged within her sleeves, and her waist was twice his own. He sensed her mind was pillow-like as well. Any impression was easily shaken off, and the fluff returned to its original shape.

Beverley was patient. "Will you choose the fabric for the honor guard's cloaks?"

"Will there be many of them?"

"How many would you like?"

"Twelve, I think."

"Then twelve it is. I will make the arrangements."

"What must I do?"

He patted her arm. "Go to your nurse. I will tell you exactly what to do when the time comes. Will you like that?"

"Yes." She pouted. "I don't like new things. I only like what I already know how to do."

"You needn't worry. I will take care of everything, and this afternoon my sister will help you choose a new dress for the occasion." He turned to Simon. "Can you bring something suitable and let her choose?"

"Either I or the other apprentice, Your Honor."

Again, Beverley gave him a long look. "Good then. Come after the midday meal. Now, Madeline, you will be well cared for, despite that your papa is gone."

"Thank you, Uncle." The girl sidled out of the room, giving Simon a shy glance.

Watching her go, Beverley muttered, "That one will always be a child." Remembering Simon's presence he admonished, "See that you return with good stuff for her dress. None will say that I stinted on my ward or her father's honors."

By the end of the first day, Elizabeth had devised a clever reason for Hannah to accompany her almost everywhere, although it undoubtedly caused comment among those who knew the princess well. Early on Hannah remarked that she loved dogs, so after the evening meal Elizabeth sent her to the kennels to choose a pet. Declaring herself thrilled with the little creature, a spanielle, she announced that it would accompany her everywhere. Although the rest of her household seemed surprised at her sudden inability to be without a lapdog, the pretense allowed Elizabeth to include Hannah most of the time with the claim that only she could adequately see to the dog's needs. Of course, the whole matter did nothing to endear the newest maidservant to the others.

To make things even worse, Elizabeth insisted that they spend time alone together that evening, getting acquainted with the dog. "How goes it?" she asked when even Kat was shooed away with the excuse that the princess had a headache.

"Very well, Your Grace," Hannah lied, knowing it was no good to complain but at the same time vowing that one week would be enough of this.

"Does Simon come this evening?"

"He said he would try, Your Grace."

"You must meet him in the courtyard. It would seem odd to allow him up here." She switched topics, confirming Hannah's suspicion that she had been meant to eavesdrop on her conversation with the king. "What do you think? Was the cup thrown out the window?"

"It would be convenient, if it were the means used to poison His Lordship."

"You must tell Simon to inspect the ground below Amberson's chamber."

"Perhaps I could go, madam, if you tell me where to look. It will be dark when Simon comes, and he might be arrested prowling about the walls."

"True." Elizabeth thought a moment. "I will give you a pillow I embroidered, which you will take to the king's barge. If you are stopped, it will give you a reason to be walking along the wall." She chose a cushion with a rose motif from several in an oaken trunk and shook it, dispensing the scent of dried lilac throughout the room. After giving Hannah directions to the spot, she ordered, "Return quickly and tell me what you find."

Hannah recited in her mind the directions as she followed them. Once outside, she counted windows to determine the correct location. Amberson's closet had been on the second floor, six or seven windows down from the doors, by Elizabeth's reckoning. Since the path to the river took a different direction, there was little traffic along the wall itself.

At first, she saw nothing, but bending low, she caught a glint of glass and picked a sliver about two inches long from among the stones. Holding it up, she thought it might well have been part of a goblet. So intent was she that she jumped when a voice behind her asked, "Digging for gold on the palace grounds, wench?"

Whirling in surprise, she found a handsome youth standing behind her, apparently enjoying the view of her upraised bottom. He was well dressed and well favored, with light brown hair and eyes with a golden tint within brown depths. He regarded her with a teasing grin, obviously unashamed to have been caught ogling.

"Oh, sir," she began, spinning a tale as she went, "I was sent to deliver this cushion to His Majesty's barge, but I saw a reflection and found this piece of glass. I will dispose of it in the earth closet lest it cut someone."

He evinced no interest in her story, but his eyes revealed interest in Hannah herself. "I have not seen you before."

"No, sir. I serve the Princess Elizabeth, who is visiting His Majesty for a time."

"Lucky princess! I would offer half again what you are paid were you to serve me."

Hannah was surprised. Did people actually steal each other's servants? She supposed so, since good help was required to make an impression in society. She mistrusted the young man's motives, however, and doubted he sought only a competent maidservant.

Putting on an innocent face, she replied, "I could never leave the princess, Your Honor, though I thank you asking."

"If I can't hire you—" She never learned what came next, for a voice interrupted.

"Giles, what are you about? The boatman is waiting."

They both turned to where a rail-thin, dour-faced woman waited impatiently. Behind her, a manservant literally teetered, stacked with the paraphernalia of his mistress' visit to Court.

"Anon, Mother," the young man called out.

"Who is that with you?" She peered nearsightedly at Hannah. "Is it Madeline?" Her voice echoed against the river and returned, wavering like the waters themselves.

"No, Mother. I was giving directions to a serving girl who lost her way." The young man, Giles, winked at Hannah.

"No wonder. The place is a veritable maze." She stepped closer and lowered her voice. "But what if Madeline saw you consorting with maidservants? You must be particularly careful of your behavior now." She approached, footsteps crunching on the gravel path.

Without appearing to do so, Hannah studied Giles' dominating mother. She was dressed well, in all the layers, frills, and other additions that fashion at Court required. Still, a practiced eye noted refurbishments that indicated economy: clumsy attempts at taking the dress in, a sleeve shortened to hide frayed cuffs. The woman's hair was styled elaborately and adorned with jeweled pins, braided-in extensions, and a brocade hat, but again, one pin had a missing jewel, and the feather on the hat drooped slightly with age.

The woman herself had once been beautiful, but now her face was shrunken, and she took pains to speak without revealing her teeth. Ignoring Hannah as all servants were ignored, she demanded of Giles, "How will you win the girl if you do not meet with her?"

"I tried to see her," he answered. "They said she is in mourning and will see no one. But Beverley was there. I heard his voice."

"You see? He will petition to be her guardian, and we will be lost. You must—" Her gaze slid to Hannah, boxed in by the two of them and the wall behind her. "What are you doing, girl?"

"I—nothing, madam. I will go if you excuse me."

"Go then!" She backed up a step and Hannah hurried away,

remembering just in time to deliver the cushion. She found the royal barge, placed the pillow among a dozen already there, and returned up the path. The two boarded a red and yellow ferryboat, Giles gallantly taking his mother's arm. He turned as she passed and murmured, "I hope we meet again, lovely!" Hannah lowered her eyes, feeling the cold gaze of the mother on her back as she retreated.

At the entry, she asked the guard on duty, "Who are they who took yonder boat?"

"Why, that is Lady Fuller and her son Giles."

"Are they important?"

The young man's lips curled in an ironic smile. "Not as much as they would like to be." He stopped abruptly, having said more than he should to a pretty girl he did not know.

Sensing it was worth some time, Hannah lingered, explaining that she was new to the castle and needed to learn who was who. She listed a number of palace luminaries seen so far, letting her tone betray awe of their exalted position and letting the young guard enjoy her apparent admiration of the nobility. She finished with, "That young man spoke quite nicely to me, but his mother seemed less friendly."

By now, the guard judged her no threat. "The mother hoped her son might win Lord Amberson's daughter. I could tell you stories of their scheming to get young Giles inside the castle at all hours so he could 'chance' to meet the girl."

"And his mother encouraged this? What of the lady's reputation?"

"I doubt she cares if the maid is won. Of course, it is all changed now."

"Will she not have him?"

The guard chuckled. "Madeline is now a great heiress."

"I see. She may not marry as she likes."

"Not likely. The king will name a guardian to control her estate."

The legal age a girl could marry was twelve. Giles' luck had apparently run out. Or was there something else going on? Had he come to see what she found because he knew what was there? Someone threw the goblet out Amberson's window, but what had become of the other pieces? Was it an accident that the man who wooed the murder victim's daughter had interrupted Hannah's search for evidence of poison?

CHAPTER EIGHT

Early the next morning, when Simon knocked at the door of the house where Lukas Seawell rented rooms, the scent of cinnamon accompanied the answerer. Seawell's landlady, a crisp but cold woman in a flour-speckled apron, directed him to a small meetinghouse. "He's at the church, as always. You could return here at sundown or find him there."

The meetinghouse was a plain, square structure with one window and a door of solid oak. Simon waited outside for a while, unsure of his welcome in such a place. Finally, a man came along and noticed him. "Are you interested in our fellowship?"

"I wish to speak to Goodman Seawell. I don't wish to disturb his worship, but it is a matter of some importance."

"Come in, then," the man urged. "You may find more than what you seek, for within is true faith and godliness."

Inside, a group of perhaps a dozen men studied in various positions: some stood, some leaned, some sat on whatever was available. The room had almost no furniture and the wood was stark, unvarnished and unpainted. Several held books and followed with their fingers as the reader's voice echoed across the empty space. "I will lift up my eyes to the hills. From whence cometh my help? My help comes from the Lord, who made Heaven and Earth."

It was Seawell himself. His forehead furrowed briefly as he noticed Simon, but he went on. When he finished reading the psalm, he launched into an explanation of what he thought it meant. Several others added opinions of their own, and a lively discussion ensued.

In spite of himself, Simon was fascinated. He had never heard people arguing religion, giving their own interpretations of scripture, or presenting varied opinions of what the Bible says to men. To him, religion was what the church leaders said it was. Wise men had already wrestled with such things. Their answers, most agreed, should be the common man's answers.

The Church of England rejected the idea that a priest stood between man and his God, granting or withholding salvation, but the new church was uncertain how much freedom the individual should have to interpret scripture. Reformers claimed the Bible should be available to everyone, that each man should form his beliefs through his own study.

At a whispered alert from the man who had invited Simon in, Seawell approached. "We have met before, but I cannot say where."

Swallowing hard, Simon spoke the half-lie he had decided on. "My master was called by the Lord President to the scene of your father's death. I was asked to aid the duke in the matter."

The carefully phrased answer seemed to satisfy Seawell. After all, he had seen Simon in the palace, escorted by the king's man to the murder scene. "You seek his killer?"

"I do." Simon let him assume that the investigation, too, was at Dudley's order.

"And you are come to ask if I am guilty?"

"I am come to ask if you know who might be."

Seawell met his gaze squarely, his eyes intense. "Look to the man who now controls my father's estate."

"Charles Beverley?"

"Him. He wormed his way into my father's business with a

well-oiled smile, asking nothing in return. But I saw the serpent in him at first glance."

"How did he gain Lord Amberson's confidence?"

His lips tightened. "I hold myself to blame, for we had disagreed, and I turned away from my father for over a year. In that span, his mind began to fail. If I'd been there, seen the signs, I might have prevented that monster from insinuating himself into our affairs."

Monster. Hugh had used the same term for Beverley. Simon knew that monsters were sometimes able to hide their evil faces, for he had seen it before. "So when he signed the will that named Beverley as executor, your father was not fully competent?"

"There were times when he could not tell you our names. I was 'that boy' and Madeline was 'the girl.' Other days he was almost himself. It made my heart ache to see it."

"Now Beverley controls your father's wealth, not you."

Seawell actually laughed aloud. "And you think I care? The scriptures say it is easier for a camel to go through the eye of a needle than for a rich man to reach Heaven. The priests will not tell you that. They speak only in homilies handed to them by those who seek to control our thoughts."

"Your philosophy rejects wealth, then?"

Seawell grasped the doorframe beside him, running a hand over the rough board as if replacing emotional pain with physical discomfort. "I wanted nothing from my father except his love. Although God must come before family, I had tried to establish peace between us despite our differences in philosophy. It is my biggest regret that our quarrel gave Beverley the chance to weave his spell, since I see now that my sister will suffer for it."

"You fear Beverley's treatment of her?"

He folded his hands almost as if in prayer, but they would

not remain still, and his palms rubbed against each other in nervous agitation. "To secure her fortune he will do anything."

"What will you do?"

His face tightened. "Nothing. My interference will not bring my father back to life."

"What of Madeline?"

He spread his hands, palms upward as if in petition. "Her fate rests in God's hands." He glanced at the waiting men. "I must return to devotions." Apparently forgetting the whole matter, he moved to rejoin his companions, who conversed in low tones as they tapped significant passages in their Bibles. The group parted to let Seawell in, and immediately, one of them asked what Simon had to say. Simon was surprised until he realized that the Simon they meant was not him. It was a Simon who lived fifteen hundred years earlier, also known as Peter.

On the street, he turned back once to look at the meeting hall and reflect on Lukas Seawell. If he suspected Beverley had killed his father and seized control of his sister, could he really turn away from the matter and forget it? Was he even now plotting revenge? Or were his accusations against Charles Beverley a clever deferral of blame from himself?

So preoccupied was he with thoughts of murder that he stepped into the street just as a rider on a huge black horse came galloping by. A woman behind him shouted a warning, and Simon spun out of the way, losing his balance and falling hard on one hip. The rider went on without even a glance backward while the woman hurried to help Simon up.

"Are you hurt, young man?"

"I think not."

"He should be ashamed, riding pell-mell through busy streets that way!"

"It was my fault, too. I was not watching."

The woman moved on, muttering about dandies with no

regard for others. Simon could not have said a thing about the rider's social state. All he recalled was the horse's black muzzle bearing down on him. Dusting his backside off, he discovered that it hurt. A bruise to remind him to look before crossing the street.

Elizabeth spent the day attempting to ascertain the movements of everyone close to Thomas Amberson on the day before his death. Madeline was the easiest to trace, for she had been on an overnight visit to the family of her companion, once her nurse. It was both a mercy and a tragedy, people said, for she had not had to see her father die, but if he had not been alone, he might have been saved. Elizabeth doubted that was so, but watching them at dinner, she rejected the idea that either woman was capable of murdering Madeline's father. Their interchange consisted almost wholly of the companion trying to curtail Madeline's appetite while the girl downed overlarge portions of everything offered. In the end, the woman contented herself with periodically wiping grease from the girl's face and clucking like a nervous hen.

Manipulating dinner conversation with ease born of long practice, Elizabeth learned what she could about the rest. Lukas Seawell had been absent from Whitehall in the days before his father's death. He had come early that morning, apparently to confer with his father, and met the agitated manservant as he ran for help. That meant he had the time to dispose of the goblet before the guards arrived, even if he had not himself administered the poison.

Next to Amberson's apartments, the Dudleys lodged in a relatively expansive apartment. The Lord President claimed the servant's call for help woke him. He in turn woke his son Robert, and the two of them arrived on the scene within moments. "It was horrible," Robin told Elizabeth. "Only the day before he'd teased me by calling me John and pretending I was my father."

"He was a jokester, then?"

"Not as a rule, no. But of course he well knew who I am."

"Who else was in your father's apartment that night?"

Robin gave her a long look but answered willingly enough. "Well, my mother has gone a-visiting, so there are fewer than there were last week. Three ladies remained behind to pack her things and send them on to Warwick, where she will spend the summer months."

"And which ladies are they?"

"Ellen Rochdale is one. She stayed behind to help but will return to her own home when the others leave for Warwick."

"I remember her," Elizabeth said. "Very lovely, very pregnant."

Robin nodded. "And very upset right now. It was her maid who fell down the stairs."

"How terrible." Elizabeth stayed focused on Amberson's murder. "And the others?"

"The Carlson sisters. I can't say which is which, but they are called Anne and Betty."

Knowing them slightly, Elizabeth dismissed the Carlsons as possible murder suspects. Neither could stop giggling long enough to do anything stealthy. "Can you think of anyone who might have slipped into the apartments and put poison in Amberson's cup?"

Robin raised his eyebrows. "Your Grace, your interest in this crime is unnecessary. My father will investigate, and he needs no assistance."

Here was the thing that infuriated Elizabeth when dealing with men. They wanted to put her into a box and keep her there, at least until they wanted something of her. "Robin," she began, knowing it was useless to argue but unable to resist, "who will people say is likely to perform murder in the king's own palace? His evil sister, the child of the Boleyn witch. Do you think I do not know what is discussed in council? Gossips will babble that I plan to kill them all, one by one, so that they cannot disinherit me again."

His face revealed distress. Although she believed that Robin truly liked her, the Dudleys cared first about themselves. The father would do what benefited him, and the son would follow orders. "Elizabeth," he said softly, "you will be well, as long as you accept what the council decides."

It was as close as he could come to saying Edward did plan to disinherit her. Questions about the murder faded briefly into the background. She had hoped in her innermost heart that as the Protestant princess, she might follow her brother, but that was not to be. Once more, she was the unwanted heir, and it did not help a bit to know that Mary was in the same position.

Would Northumberland go so far as to frame her for murder so that his plans for Lady Jane Grey's ascension to the throne could go forward more smoothly? If so, she could count on Robert for nothing. Like all men, he underestimated her.

No, not all men. Simon Maldon wanted nothing from her, never patronized her, and recognized her as his equal in intelligence. Simon never told her to go away and be a good little princess. He believed she could affect England's destiny, and that was what she wanted to do more than anything, though she could not admit it, even to him.

The hour was late, and his mother would surely comment on it, but Simon went to the palace after supper. On the way, he pondered what he had learned thus far. Although those who benefited financially from Amberson's death were his children, neither seemed likely to commit murder.

The killer might be the man who now controlled Madeline's

future. With Amberson's death, Charles Beverley for a third time gained control of a woman's fortune, and Madeline was certainly no stop to his ambition. Hugh claimed Beverley was capable of murder, possibly had done it before now. Hugh's assessment was good enough for Simon.

The gardens were coming into glorious bloom, and the scents of various flowers drifted toward him on the evening breeze. His heart leapt at the sight of Hannah waiting beside a pink-tipped witch hazel bush. Instead of her usual faded brown shift, she wore a crisp, cream-colored apron over a deep blue dress. While Simon thought her beautiful in whatever she wore, he was pleased to see her blush of pleasure when he complimented her attire. Taking her arm, he noted the softer stuff of her dress, so different from the coarse wool provided to Hampstead staff. He vowed to himself that as his wife, Hannah would have the finest clothes the Sumptuary Laws allowed for their station.

"This will be our meeting place," she told him. "It is normal for a man and his sweetheart to walk in the courtyard, but it would be hard to explain you visiting the princess' apartments." He felt a stab of disappointment, for he enjoyed any chance to talk with Elizabeth. Knowing her curiosity, however, he guessed she would sometimes find ways to join them.

He quickly related what he had learned that day, ending with, "It is doubtful the daughter has a hand in anything. She is more child than she should be and no doubt a pawn in the schemes of others. And the son claims no wish for his father's money."

"Her Highness' questions brought the same result. But if His Lordship was poisoned in his chamber, as we now suspect, he was the target, not the king or some other council member."

"The motive might have been his position on the council, to create a vacancy or to change the balance in some way." Simon took out his knife as they approached a wooden target. With skill and speed, he flung it at the center circle so that it spun in the air and landed with a "thunk" in the center of the thick wood slab. Hannah shivered, possibly from old memories, but he felt a rush of pride at his accuracy. He retrieved the knife, and they walked on. "I suppose Lukas Seawell might have killed his father for some reason other than money."

"Some grudge, perhaps?"

"They quarreled over Lukas' dedication to reform."

"Would it not require a great deal of anger to kill one's father?" Hannah, an orphan, knew little of mothers or fathers.

"The passions that arise at home are greater than any other, whether good or evil," he replied. "Family is either our greatest blessing or our cruelest bane. Sometimes both."

Without comment on Simon's gossipy mother and taciturn father, Hannah returned to possible murder suspects. "So we cannot rule Seawell out. Who else?"

"One must include the Dudleys when there is any sort of scheme afoot."

"Why would they murder His Lordship?"

"He might have opposed them on some matter or learned something that cast a poor light on one of them." Simon frowned at his own words. "I think it unlikely, however. Murder seems an extreme measure."

Hannah was more cynical. "If the Dudleys thought Amberson might jeopardize their position with the king, and if poison would solve the problem, I doubt the extremity of the act would concern them."

"There is also the maid's death to consider. Did she see someone entering that room? Did she know the reason for the murder?"

"Or did she herself have a hand in it? We must find out more about her if we can."

At Simon's request, Hannah related what Elizabeth had gleaned from questions asked here and there. "There was wine already poured into a green glass cup. It is likely someone entered while he was at the midday meal and added poison to it, since he did not leave the room or have visitors for the rest of the day. The wine remaining in the bottle is untainted."

"So it was someone who knew the old man's habits and the way of things at Whitehall. Seawell might know the former but not the latter.

"Everyone was downstairs during the meal except Ellen Rochdale, who was ill and stayed upstairs with her maidservant, this Marie who is now dead. Ellen and her maid had a small room in Northumberland's apartment, next to Lord Amberson's. She could have slipped into his closet unnoticed at that time."

"We must consider it, though I see no benefit to the baroness in Amberson's death. Hugh says her husband has no aspirations to be part of the council."

"I hear she is quite lovely, even in her present condition."

Simon nodded more enthusiastically than he intended as he pictured Robin Dudley taking the baroness into his arms. What man would pass up the chance to comfort such a lovely creature? Recalling her words to him, he warmed slightly. Not only lovely, but insightful as well.

"The princess could find no one who ever saw Baroness Rochdale even speak to Lord Amberson," Hannah said. "She says the woman is extremely timid and seldom speaks at all."

"The man who is now Madeline's ward might have killed Amberson." Quickly he explained Hugh's opinion on the current commander of the King's Guard.

"We thought of that as well when we heard he controls the estate, but Beverley was not in London at the time," Hannah replied. "When first you saw him at Whitehall, he was newly returned from a fortnight in the north."

Simon blinked. "He was gone from London?"

"Apparently, he went to his estate, where he oversaw the planting." That brought Simon to an abrupt halt. He had begun to focus on Beverley as the killer. "The princess wants you to see if he really left the city," Hannah continued, and he sensed she had been leading up to this point.

When she finished explaining, he looked at her in disbelief. "She is not serious!"

"If I can play a princess' maid, you can do your part," Hannah replied. Retrieving a cloth bag from under a bush, she pressed it into his reluctant hands. Simon liked playing roles, but this one stretched his abilities. Aware of his doubts, Hannah spent some time relaying instructions from Elizabeth. When he tried again to speak his fears, she merely patted his hand. "She says you must. It will advance the investigation." Reluctantly he took the bag. He would have to try.

Reminded of her own contribution, Hannah showed him the green shard found under Amberson's window. "We think it is a piece of the cup to which poison was added." She explained how she had found it at Elizabeth's order.

Simon carefully touched the sharp edge. "This could have lain against the wall for a year," he objected.

"But Her Highness sent me to look for broken glass, and it was exactly there," she rejoined. "She believes someone threw the goblet out the window and retrieved the pieces later. That left no proof of poison, no matter what is suspected."

"I suppose it could be as she says." He tried to picture the way Amberson's chamber had looked, as his friends in the guard did at the scene of a crime. "All a man has is recall when later he tries to put the clues together," Hugh often said, and it was true. One had to notice and remember, and that required practice. "The window was open when we saw the body. That is unusual, since nights are cool this time of year."

Hannah almost remarked that night air was unhealthy but

remembered that Simon did not believe it. Although he rejected many things she had been taught as pure silliness, it was hard to forget what she'd heard from the cradle. "So someone opened it."

"For a dozen possible reasons: light, fresh air, or to dispel the odor of death that permeated the room. But it could have been to dispose of a murderous drink, too."

"Someone was interested in what I was looking for under the window." Hannah related her meeting with Giles Fuller along the castle wall. At her description of the mother, Simon frowned. "Is there a large mole on her chin, off to one side?"

"I believe so, now that you mention it."

"She came to the shop recently, and I felt sorry for her, since it is obvious her teeth hurt terribly. Does the princess know them?"

"They have a small holding near Lincoln but need money badly, she says. Lionel, the husband, works to make a success of farming on the estate, but his lady has put her hopes into finding an advantageous match for Giles."

"And why did they believe Lord Amberson, one of the Privy Council, would align his family with a penniless knight?"

"The Fuller name is old and respected. They undoubtedly hoped Madeline, apple of her father's eye, would insist on having Giles."

"Then their scheme is ruined by Amberson's death. Madeline has a guardian now, and her fortune is under his control."

"Unless they have worked out another way." His view of her face faded as the light failed, but she grasped his arm in excitement. "The mother warned Giles to mind his behavior with women 'under the circumstances.' What if he somehow convinced Madeline to marry him in secret? With her father dead, he could announce their elopement and take the chance that the king will countenance the union."

"I suppose that could be so."

"He *is* handsome, though he thought me a flirt-gill." Her voice revealed irritation.

Simon frowned. Virtue was not always enough to protect servants from molestation by noblemen who thought them easy prey. "What did he say?"

She blushed. "Things as such men often say to girls like me." As Simon's muscles tensed under her hand, she rushed on, "And he offered employment. Of course he has no money to pay what he offered, so it was merely sport."

"Stay away from him!" Simon ordered. "Such men have little enough to hold them back when they see a wench they fancy."

"It was but play," she insisted. "You must forget it."

"I begin to regret your presence here. Two people have died, and your questions might well be noticed." He did not add that a pretty girl such as she encountered hundreds of men at White-hall, whereas Hampstead Castle offered only a few. "Perhaps I should tell Her Highness you are required elsewhere." It would put his mind at rest on one score, at least.

Surprisingly, Hannah disagreed. "This was your idea, Simon Maldon, and you set a week as the trial period. We can give her that much, poor thing."

He was baffled. She had been reluctant to come, still feared making some dreadful public error that would embarrass both her and the princess, and yet she would not make an excuse and escape. He cursed the contrariness of women as he cursed his own ingenuousness. His desire to help Elizabeth had blinded him to the consequences, and now he had involved Hannah. And her sense of loyalty to the princess, it seemed, was every bit as great as his.

He decided to leave both the topic of murder and the idea of her leaving for tonight. Escorting Hannah to the doorway, he ended their meeting with a kiss that left them both weak. "Our wedding cannot come too soon," he whispered.

"But houses do not simply appear rent-free." She caressed his face, her smile warm in the torch-lit doorway. "When you finish your training, when your master judges you ready, that is the time to speak of a wedding."

Neither acknowledged that even when the apprenticeship was over and he was legally able to marry, England's sad financial state meant he probably could not afford a house, a shop, and the things necessary to begin a business. It was hard to wait, even harder to have no way to know how long the wait would be.

It was late when Simon returned home, but his father was just getting in as well, his doctor's cloak reeking of blood and worse. He left it on a peg outside the back door to air and ate a cold supper as they sat before the fire, unwinding from the day's events before attempting sleep. Jacob related the details of his present case, not so much for Simon as for his own comprehension. Medicine was his greatest love, but he knew how inadequate his efforts were in many cases. Simon listened patiently, understanding his father's frustrations. Often he and Carthburt, too, felt challenged by their inadequacies.

Finally, when Jacob was silent and it was his turn, he reported Rachel's reaction to the stranger who had visited Carthburt's place of business. "Apparently she panicked when this man entered the shop. Carthburt doesn't want to admit it, but I fear she grows worse and may endanger herself or her father." He remembered the old man standing below, offering himself as a sacrifice. "Was she always thus?"

Jacob remained silent for some time before answering. "I told you that Thomas' wife died tragically three years ago. What I did not say was that she was murdered."

Simon turned to look at his father. "Murdered!"

"Carthburt was away, and Martha was minding the shop. When he returned she was dead, the shop a shambles, Rachel gravely wounded. She survived but never recovered."

"Did they learn who did it?"

"No. It was apparently a robbery, for the moneybag was gone. At first, Rachel muttered bits and pieces about what happened, but it was hardly intelligible. Apparently she was asleep in the loft, heard noise, and looked down to see a dark-haired man attacking her mother."

"Yes, she greatly fears such men."

"She climbed down, tried to help her mother, and was struck and left for dead."

"Poor Rachel!"

"Carthburt found them, Martha dead and Rachel bleeding from both ears. She was very confused and in time retreated to a world of her own. Now she remembers nothing but her fear."

"A double tragedy, to lose a wife and see a daughter so changed."

Jacob shifted his feet away from the fire. "At first I thought Thomas would lose his mind. Only caring for her kept him on this earth. Only Rachel."

"And she saw someone today who brought her fears back."

"I doubt there's much logic to these fits of hers."

"Except she most fears men who are dark."

"Like the one who killed her mother. But she shies from the rest of mankind as well." He reached forward to stir the ashes with a metal rod. "At the time Carthburt tried to discover the killer, but in the end he put the matter behind him, at least as much as a man can do in such a case."

"It must plague him that the crimes were never avenged."

"Life on earth promises no justice. We must believe that the next life balances things." Jacob leaned forward, putting his hands on his knees and rubbing the fire's warmth into the joints.

"But your task is more current. What have you found in the matter of Amberson's death?"

Simon answered, but a part of his mind stayed with the trembling girl who whispered when he reached her lofty place of refuge, "The dark man! He will hurt me again, I know it."

CHAPTER NINE

Hannah was a pariah among the servants, although she had much to do and little time to notice. Some went out of their way to add to her burdens; others simply ignored her. Most of the guardsmen were cheerful, however, and greeted her whenever they met. Early on her third day, as she returned from emptying the chamber pot into the midden, she encountered a woman who seemed most offended by her presence. Waiting until Hannah was just inside the entry, she took a step back, bumping her roughly backward. As she flailed to avoid falling, the pot fell from her hands, shattering into a hundred pieces. With a smug look that said she had accomplished her purpose, the other continued on, leaving Hannah to clean up the mess.

"Here, let me help." It was one of the guardsmen. "I saw what she did, the cow."

"It was nothing. An accident." She tried to speak casually but at the same time wondered how much trouble she was in for breaking palace goods.

He bent down and helped her pick up shards of pottery, tossing them into her apron for disposal. "I know where the store is kept," he said. "No one needs to know what happened."

She met his eyes, gratitude overcoming shyness. "I thank you. I am new here and would prefer not to be known as the clumsy one."

Retrieving a piece that had skidded under the door, he

surveyed the floor for others. "You serve the princess, do you not?"

"Yes." Hannah had learned to elaborate as little as possible until she got a sense of a person's view of Elizabeth.

"I am Daniel Mann. I sometimes escort her when she goes out. She is ever kind to us, says the government is more secure because of the guard."

"I am sure she is correct. My name is Hannah."

He tossed a last shard into her apron with a dull clink. "Your princess is fair, as are you."

"You are kind to say so." She examined him discreetly. Tall and broad through the shoulders, he was physically impressive, as Edward liked his guardsmen to be. His thick, black hair that seemed to have a will of its own, and his face was pleasant, with gray-blue eyes, even features, and good teeth.

Guiding her to a storage room on an upper floor, Daniel showed her a stack of chamber pots. As she chose one similar to the broken one he watched idly, apparently unwilling to end their conversation. "Do you like it here at Whitehall?"

"It is a beautiful place." She grinned as honesty broke through. "I haven't gotten over the fear that any moment I'll do something unforgivable and be dismissed."

"Yes. It can be hard, pleasing those above us. But it is a great opportunity as well. You may rise even farther if your princess becomes queen."

Hannah feared it was a test. "She has no aspirations to the throne, being a loyal subject of His Highness in willing obedience to the decisions of the council."

He waved a dismissive hand. "I accuse her of nothing, but it is possible she may someday take the throne, and you would benefit, being close to her." He smiled to forestall further objection. "We take what is offered us. It is how life goes."

Hannah replaced the pots she had displaced to reach the one

she wanted. "It is a wonderful opportunity to see Whitehall," she said, avoiding the topic of personal advantage.

Leading the way down the narrow stairway to the main floor, he said, turning to watch her face, "Did you know there was a murder here?"

"I heard something of it."

"I was one of the first to see His Lordship's corpse. My captain called me to the old man's rooms and there he was, dead as a duck."

"Oh."

"He was in a state, I can tell you. It was not a pleasant death." Seeing the enjoyment his retelling provided him, Hannah began to sense why Daniel sought her out. Gossips live for telling, and he relished finding someone who had not heard his tale.

"It was sad, I'm sure." She tried to hide her distaste at his enjoyment of violent death.

His eyes searched her face, aware that his revelation had failed to impress her, but apparently confused as to why that would be. "Have you ever seen a murdered corpse?"

"No," Hannah lied. She knew she was supposed to flutter and turn shuddery at the thought but could not force herself to do it. If Daniel was one of the first there, he might have seen the goblet that was now missing. "What did you notice about the room? Was there any sign that someone had been there who should not?"

He frowned. "What do you mean?" His tone turned pejorative. "Do you think to join the guard and seek out murderers and such? That would be a rare thing!"

Too fast, she warned herself. She had played it wrong, should have let him tell it in his own way. *Simon,* she berated him mentally, *I am no spy. I do not have your gift for drawing people out, making them gladly tell what they know.* "They will wonder where I've gone."

Daniel locked the door behind her and led the way down the narrow stairs, taking up their original topic. "They don't like you coming to work for the princess. The others."

"No."

He replaced the storeroom key on its hook with a clank. "You must not mind their insults. They are jealous that you are pretty and that you serve Her Grace, who may yet be Her Majesty."

She took a middle path, polite but not affirming. "I suppose you are correct."

"Do you ever walk in the gardens on your free hours?"

Hannah thought on it for only the briefest moment. In order to learn what she could of those near Amberson, she had to start somewhere. A gossip was a good source as long as she sorted fact from speculation. Besides, no one else would have anything to do with her. "I might."

He grinned with pleasure. "I must return to my duties, but we could meet on the practice grounds after supper."

The area was open, always populated, and therefore quite safe. She would certainly not accept food or drink from him, in case he was a murderer. Simon would not like it, but Simon didn't have to know. "I will be there."

At about the same time that morning, a young groom in a stable near Whitehall started in surprise when he climbed down from the loft and found a well-dressed young dandy waiting. Dressed in fine clothes, silk stockings, and a rather ridiculous hat, the youth leaned at a jaunty angle against a post. "Good morrow, fellow," he called out as the groom reached the dirt floor.

"Good morrow, sir." His tone was polite, but Simon read his thought. Not even a chance at breakfast before he had to see to some nobleman's demand!

"I heard there is a horse for sale here." After learning where Beverley stabled his horse, Simon took the chance that they had at least one horse for sale in these uncertain times. "Can you direct me to the animal?"

The groom obligingly led the way to a stall where a chestnut gelding waited. "A fine example of the breed," Simon said, making his voice significantly louder and more forceful than usual. He was nervous about this impersonation, having never before tried a role above his station. Donning the garments from the bag Hannah provided had made the physical transformation. Now it was a matter of acting the part Elizabeth had . . . *suggested* was too weak a word: ordered. From his two female friends, Simon now knew that he did not stand quite straight, had a tendency to mumble, and often failed to meet the eye of those he spoke to. "The princess says a good deal of being noble is awareness that you are noble," Hannah had said firmly the night before.

"That's just it. I'm not."

"Then you must believe that you are, at least for a while." Recalling her words, Simon tried to emulate gentlemen he'd seen in the shop, to think of the groom not as a fellow human being but as one put on earth to serve him. "The animal is sound? I require a beast with stamina."

"The owner is very proud of him, always cautions me to comb him and feed him just the right amount." The groom's tone hinted that he knew his job and had not needed tutoring.

"You would say it is a worthy animal?"

"Oh, yes, sir, I exercise the beast every day, but, truthfully, he needs a good long run."

"That is just what I intend. I go north, to Beverley. Do you know it?"

"No, sir, but Charles of Beverley stables his horse here."

"Yes. He has mentioned his fine horse to me, more than once or even twice." Simon allowed his tone to suggest irritation at a friend's boasting.

The groom hid a smile behind a fist. "His Worship likes a mount with spirit, likes to know that the beast is his and no one else's, he says." There was a trace of resentment in his voice. A man might enjoy owning a beast that required delicate handling, but grooms probably did not enjoy dealing with it. "His would not be a good mount for one uncertain of his skills."

As uncertain of his riding skills as anyone he knew, Simon tried to look confident anyway. "I'll have a look at this one, then, and let Charles keep his stallion." He almost choked on the informal "Charles" but had to appear the man's equal in status. He pretended to examine the chestnut, prolonging the conversation, asking questions and listening with apparent great interest to the groom's answers. Like most who feel flattered, the man became expansive, giving advice and bits of equestrian wisdom gleaned from his experiences.

When finally he judged the foundation laid, Simon asked, "And where is this paragon of Charles Beverley's? Since I am here, I'd like to see him." The groom led him to a large black with lines even Simon recognized as unusually fine. "A magnificent animal, as you said."

"You should have seen him when he came in after their last trip. He was—" The groom stopped, remembering his place. "He'd been through a lot."

Simon watched the restive horse, quailing inwardly at its size and power. He had a natural aversion to horses, and his recent experience with one similar to this had not made him any fonder, but he kept his tone even. "He seems to have recovered, due, no doubt, to your care and attention."

"He'd been pressed, I can tell you, and not stabled well along the way."

"I knew Charles was away, but I have forgotten where he went," he said, looking away from the groom as if still interested in the stallion.

The man scratched at his head with some diligence. "Well, he said he was heading home to oversee the planting, but he was more interested in the way to Chester, where I come from. Wanted to know which road I took when I went home to visit." He gave a rather phlegmy snicker at the idea. "I never go back there. London's the place for me."

"Did he ask for directions to a specific place?" The groom looked up in curiosity and Simon improvised. "I have family near there."

"Do you! Where?"

He cast about for a place in the vicinity but far enough away that the groom should not have firsthand knowledge of it. "Salford."

Luck was with him; the groom looked disappointed at not knowing the place. "He didn't plan to actually go to Chester. He only asked about it 'cause he knew I was born there."

From what Simon had learned of Charles Beverley, he was not the type to make small talk with servants. If he asked the way to Chester, he had a reason. "When did he leave London?"

"Right after the full moon." Three weeks ago. There was no way Beverley had poisoned Lord Amberson, then. But he could still have arranged the murder.

Something bothered Simon about the trip, and now he put his finger on it. "I wonder why he didn't take a ship north. Easier on both man and beast, I'd say."

The groom smacked his thigh in agreement. "I said that very thing! Roads are nigh to impassible this time of year. The landowners are responsible for marking and maintaining 'em, but who sees that they keep the way open or the ruts filled?"

"No one." The government had neither the funds nor the organization to see to such things. "What did Charles say when you suggested he travel by boat?"

"Said him and the black needed exercise after lying about the

101

castle all winter."

"And he returned the day His Lordship was found dead."

The groom's head shook like one of his charges banishing flies. "A sad homecoming for Sir Charles, to find a friend murdered."

"Yes," Simon replied. "It changed his life, I'd say."

When Hannah went down to meet Daniel that evening, she hoped no one noted her turn with a man other than her intended husband. There was a murmur of objection from one of the other maids, but to her surprise, Kat Ashley stopped it with a word and a look. Suspicious she might be of Elizabeth's motives in bringing Hannah to Whitehall, but Kat was loyal to the princess and apparently would further her causes even when she did not know what they were.

Daniel turned out to be a fount of information, although she soon learned that he had his own reasons for cultivating friendship. What he wanted was gossip about Elizabeth, and he was more than bold in his quest. "When did she last bleed?" was one question. "Does she take any sort of physic, anything at all?" Protesting that she had not been there long enough to learn any secrets, Hannah passed along snippets of interesting but innocent information, substituting Elizabeth's liking for chestnuts and dislike of brown dresses for real revelations.

Once he was comfortable with her, Daniel freely admitted to spying, peeping through keyholes, and listening around corners to learn what he could of his betters. "They think themselves superior, but when you know them, you see their human side. Ones like you see even more than I, so close to the princess. Has she ever had visitors you were not allowed to overhear?"

"No."

"Of course you are newly come to Whitehall. I will wager she dreams of becoming queen someday. Who in her position would not? Then you would be confidant to Her Majesty." He broke off a branch of apple blossoms and offered it to Hannah with a courtly bow, as if she were already a woman of importance.

Daniel, Hannah saw, was not only a gossip but also one who longed to be part of the glitter of royalty. His interest in the lives and deeds of the upper class had a ring of envy to it, a longing to be close to those at the top, to bask in their reflected glory. He assumed she wanted the same thing. It was not treason Daniel spoke, merely wishful thinking.

She held the sweet-scented petals to her nose. "The princess seems content to let others decide how such matters turn out."

He nodded. "That is wise, for she is a woman and easily led astray." Hannah's tongue almost rebelled, but she maintained silence and what she hoped was an agreeable expression. Daniel squeezed her arm. She had already discovered that he was one of those who hold on to their listeners, perhaps in unconscious recognition that they would prefer to keep their distance. "A clever man I know says she must be very careful who she visits and what she says."

Hannah almost huffed in derision. As if everyone in London did not know that! "Good advice, I suppose." She tried to encourage further confidences. "This man is an admirer?"

"Not precisely," he admitted. "He says it is unwise to attach oneself to a single cause. But if the princess keeps to herself and stays out of palace affairs, she may yet prevail, being so much younger than the other one. She will only be allowed to live if she does that, he says."

Hannah began to take an interest in the "clever" man who guided Daniel's opinions. "So this man would advise the princess to spend her time at tapestries and tatting."

"Exactly."

"He sounds wondrous wise." Her mouth could barely form the words, but Daniel seemed pleased that she understood the benefits to Elizabeth of quelling both curiosity and intelligence.

"Yes. He thinks far into the future, like a chess player. Always planning ahead, he is."

"And since this man is your friend, you will rise as he rises."

He looked satisfied. "I do my part, though I have not his scope and understanding."

Hannah wondered if the man Daniel spoke of was Dudley, the council's Lord President. As nosy as the guardsman was, he had undoubtedly heard more than he should of discussions about Elizabeth's future. What else could she learn from him?

Carefully she drew him out, mixing questions about unrelated matters with inquiries about those she was interested in: Amberson and his two children, Charles Beverley, Giles Fuller and his mother, and the Dudleys. Daniel reported scraps of gossip about them all, some of them ridiculously improbable. She was most successful with questions about Amberson himself. Daniel had approved of the old man, mostly due to his generosity. "He got confused sometimes. Gave me a silver coin once for taking him back to his rooms. I know all the ways through Whitehall.

"Simple," he said when Hannah mentioned Madeline's name. "Still, he loved her."

"And his son? What did His Lordship think of him?"

"Took up with reformers, them that don't think the Anglican Church went far enough to stop the Catholics. They had harsh words over it, since the old man was no fanatic."

"They quarreled?"

"Something awful."

"Often?"

"Oh, no. Only once I ever heard of. Of late they had reconciled, agreed not to speak of religion so they could tolerate each other."

That was as far as Hannah felt she should go on that subject. She was thinking of returning inside when Daniel asked, "Were you here when Marie died?"

"Is she the maid who fell down the stairs?"

He huffed in disgust, and dark hair rose briefly from his forehead before returning to its original disarray. "Fell, my rump! Pushed, I say." He gave Hannah a tiny push as he said it.

"Why do you say so?"

He glanced around suspiciously. "I will tell you, since we're friends. You must not speak of it to anyone else, though. Her and me talked a few times, like you and me are now. My mother was from Calais, you see, so I speak French. The night before she died, she said something odd had happened. Said it was dangerous to speak of it, even to me. The next day, she suddenly become clumsy and fell down the stairs. I say someone pushed her so she could never tell what she knew."

"Do you have proof?"

He looked at her as if she were mad. "It ain't like I'm going to run to my captain and accuse anyone," he answered. "I'm just telling you, as a friend, to be careful in this place."

"You think there is danger?"

"For those who know too much, there might be." He stopped at Hannah's doorway. "Marie said a servant learns not to rush, for if a task is done quickly they simply find her another. Take her time, that is what Marie would have done. How, then, should she trip and fall?"

"Do you think this guardsman could be correct, or is he just a scandal-seeker?" Elizabeth asked when Hannah reported Daniel's contention that Marie had been pushed to her death. It was afternoon and their first chance to speak privately.

"I don't know. On one hand, he is almost frantic for gossip and might hope it was murder to make life more exciting. On the other, he is correct. There was no reason for her to fall."

"People fall every day."

"But he says she was not one to hurry about her work."

"I know that sort," Elizabeth observed dryly. "If she was pushed, and if she did indeed tell this man that she had a secret, it might pertain to Amberson's poisoning."

Hannah shrugged. "It could be anything, but so soon after the murder, her death is ominous."

Elizabeth sat back in her chair. "See what Simon has to say about it, and we will talk again in the morning. Tonight at the ambassador's I will perhaps glean more information as I charm those around me."

"You will certainly do that, Your Highness." Hannah liked the princess, but she also realized that part of a maidservant's duty was to assure and reassure with compliment after compliment. Royal folk had great need to hear how important they were to the world.

Chapter Ten

The ball was not as entertaining as Elizabeth had hoped. The king stayed away, since the Spanish ambassador was the host. Edward had decided of late that he disapproved of "foreign dances and merriments," probably meaning those given by Catholics anxious to heal the rift between England and Rome. The ambassador was sanguine, despite the king's absence. Word circulated of Edward's deteriorating condition, and he could afford to be patient.

Unsettled questions of succession made such affairs tedious. Every conversation Elizabeth attempted was stilted and inane, for no one wanted to be quoted later as saying anything that might be interpreted as support for her or for Mary either, for that matter. That left two topics: health and the weather. Once she had assured several dozen smiling faces that she was well, thank you, and commented that yes, spring was progressing nicely, she was sick to death of them all.

However, she had work to do. Making her way around the room, she managed to end up next to Charles Beverley, who appeared to have grown in stature since she saw him last. His recent good fortune, she supposed, made him swell with pride. Beside him, his sister Henrietta was even more puffed than he was. Her oversized appearance was partly due to her gown, obviously new, expensive, and grossly unbecoming. Elizabeth guessed the late Lord Amberson had paid for the monstrosity. He was quite probably better off for not having lived to see it.

"Your Highness," brother and sister said in unison as she turned to greet them. Their bows were respectful and well executed, and she pictured them practicing together.

"Master Charles. Mistress Henrietta." She knew Beverley only by sight. He was attractive in a general way, with a somewhat superior air that probably appealed to a certain type of woman. However, she had sniffed out his reputation, and it was less than favorable. A cold man, he had twice married daughters of wealthy citizens and without apology spent their money to further his career. He went to great lengths to gain influence and leveraged every scrap of power he managed into more through cunning, manipulation, and bald-faced flattery.

Mention of Beverley's sister brought more unflattering tales. Henrietta had come to London to run her brother's town house while he lodged at Whitehall, overseeing the King's Guard. She had an overblown sense of her brother's importance and a lack of subtlety that would have been comic had it not been so irritating. As Mistress Henrietta panted a breathy greeting, her brother eyed Elizabeth's chest, apparently unaware that she had eyes and could discern it. Henrietta was a simperer, a particularly odious trait in one so large. Her eyes were the same deep brown as Charles' but squeezed small by over-round cheeks so that they seemed tiny points of darkness in her fleshy face. It would not be a pleasant conversation, but Elizabeth was used to being pleasant when she would rather not be. After the usual responses: yes, she was feeling well, and yes, the spring was fine, she asked, "Have you seen to your planting, Master Charles?"

He looked up with a start. "I have, Your Highness. His Majesty allowed me two weeks' leave to do so."

"Beverley is to the north, am I correct?"

"Quite right, Your Grace. My lands are north of the Humber, near Kingston upon Hull."

"And you returned to find that your mentor was dead."

"Yes." He lowered his gaze, and she resisted the urge to hide her chest with her hands. "A shock."

"But you will look out for his daughter and find her a husband, serving Lord Amberson even though he is dead."

"Mistress Madeline is young, Your Grace. She will be with us for some years yet." He gestured at Henrietta without looking at her. "My sister is most fond of her and visits every day."

"Yes," the woman responded as if on cue. "Only this morning I took her to the kennel to see the newest batch of puppies. Such outings will not replace the poor girl's father, but we do what we can." No doubt they would do anything to keep Madeline contented and single, for in that state they controlled her wealth and could dispense it as they pleased.

"We must send Her Grace a bottle of mead, Charles," Henrietta said in sudden impulse. "You will find it quite good, I trow."

"Mead?"

"From our estate." Her tone implied grandeur, though Elizabeth knew Beverley was a small holding. "When I compliment our mead, I do not boast, Your Grace. Everyone agrees that our mead is superior, and we provide it for His Majesty's own table."

"How good of you."

"We do what we can. Quality stuff is hard to come by since the old church was banned."

In spite of herself, Elizabeth asked, "What does the church have to do with mead?"

Henrietta's face glowed with pride at being able to edify a princess. "Candles, Your Grace. The new church uses far fewer candles, and there are no monasteries or nunneries now to burn them. In the past, many, many candles burned on altars every day, so everyone kept bees for the wax. Now, no monks, fewer candles, less need for beekeeping."

Here Charles, obviously unwilling to let his sister have the limelight for long, broke in. "Less beekeeping led to a drop in the production of mead. Many estates have discontinued it altogether, but at Beverley, we continue the practice."

In her eagerness to regain Elizabeth's attention, Henrietta broke in with a truth she probably did not intend. "There is little else there, the land itself being poor. My brother hopes that his service to the king—and to his family—will meet with satisfaction." Her glittering eyes said more strongly than any words that the hope was for more than simple payment.

As soon as was polite, Elizabeth moved on, her impression of the Beverleys confirmed. They were a grasping pair, and Henrietta was hand in glove with her brother's plans. Could she have delivered the fatal dose of poison?

Moving through the room, she sought out those who had known the old man well. She spoke to a few council members, most of whom she had known all her life. Fortunes had changed dramatically with John Dudley's rise to power. To gain support he had doled out large land grants, so knights were now barons and barons, earls. It was often hard to keep track of the changing fortunes of English gentry.

On her left, Elizabeth noticed a startlingly thin woman who stared directly at her, the gleam of calculation in her eyes. Beside her, a handsome youth surveyed the women on the dance floor, unaware of his mother's intent until she pulled sharply at his sleeve. The two moved through the crowd at an oblique angle, attempting discretion but definitely headed her way. The Fullers, she surmised, recalling Hannah's description.

It took only a few minutes. "Your Grace?" She turned to find Anne Aldrich at her elbow and the two she had noted earlier close behind. Anne made the introductions and slipped away, the favor undoubtedly begged by Lady Fuller accomplished.

"Your Grace, I have so wanted to meet you. I was a great admirer of your father."

"As was I, madam."

Sensing there was nothing else to say on that subject, Lady Fuller cast about for conversation. "My son is a great reader. He has read every book in our house, some of them twice. And he can recall what he has read, which I could never do. I wonder where they get all those words. The writers, I mean."

Elizabeth glanced at Giles, who appeared as embarrassed by his mother's determination to portray him as a genius as by the admission of her own ignorance. The lady went blithely on. "I have said more than once that he and His Majesty would get on well together, being such scholars. They would have much to discuss, I tell you."

"I am certain of it," Elizabeth said agreeably.

"Of course, His Majesty's time is much taken with affairs of state, I know it. And Giles here"—she tapped her son playfully on the arm—"is busy wooing." She beamed at her son despite his glance of appeal. "Oh, he and a certain young lady are quite fond of each other."

Elizabeth asked the question Lady Fuller so obviously hoped she would ask, since she wanted confirmation anyway. "And which lady has stolen your fancy, Master Fuller?"

Giles could not bring himself to say it, but that did not matter, for his mother was only too willing. "My Giles and Madeline Amberson became fast friends almost from the first day we arrived in London. Were it not for the tragic death of His Lordship, I have no doubt the matter would be settled, for I believe Madeline has decided she wants to marry no other than my son."

It took all her royal control to maintain an expression of mild interest, but Elizabeth did it, despite an urgent desire to hurry from the room and report to Hannah and Simon what she had learned. Of course that would not do. Giving Giles Fuller a nod, she murmured, "Then I shall hope, sir, that you are deserving of the lady's affection, for she has had much sorrow of late."

As Giles formed a suitably flowery response, there was a stir behind them. Turning, they beheld the entrance of Ellen Rochdale, flanked by two other women who faded into obscurity beside her. Her costume suited her perfectly despite her obvious pregnancy, managing to call attention to her beauty without in any way appearing gauche. As Ellen smiled shyly in general greeting, Elizabeth surveyed the room, noting the reactions of the men. Judging from their faces, each man there felt certain the baroness' smile was directed specifically toward him.

She had seen the baroness before but had paid little attention. She was kind and considerate to all, people said, undoubtedly an excellent quality. What made Elizabeth less than interested in closer acquaintance was the woman's total lack of conversation. She seldom spoke except in reply to a direct question and seemed to have no interests at all. She did nothing, deferring politely when asked to dance or take part in a play or other amusement devised to entertain the Court. If she had not been so beautiful, she would have disappeared into the wallpaper. Still, the princess thought as men maneuvered into positions near her, a woman with so much physical attractiveness did not need much else to garner attention.

When the chance arose, Elizabeth approached, managing with practiced ease to discourage two men hovering near the baroness. "Your Grace," Ellen said, her curtsey perfect.

"We have had little opportunity to talk since your arrival," Elizabeth said, "but I have some knowledge of Rochdale, having been for some time at Burnley."

"How pleasant for you, Your Grace."

"I understand you will return home soon."

"Yes, Your Grace."

Elizabeth squelched a stab of irritation. This was what she had experienced the first time she met the baroness: a one-sided conversation with vapid replies. She tried again, taking up a topic most pregnant women would discuss at length. "Your child will arrive at midsummer?"

"Yes, Your Grace."

Was the woman shy, nervous, or merely stupid? Why did everyone speak glowingly of one who could hardly speak two words in sequence? Reluctant to give up without getting a sense of the baroness as a person, Elizabeth struggled to manufacture another topic. As they watched the dancers, the baroness surprised her with a question.

"May I tell you something, Your Grace?"

Elizabeth turned to her. "If you will."

Ellen's face was blank, her voice flat. "What they say will not always matter."

The words were a cipher, but she understood immediately, sensed their meaning without conscious effort. The whispers behind her back, the accusations that she was illegitimate, that her mother had been a witch, that she herself was a wanton and a schemer. They assaulted her very core, made her doubt her worth, her royalty. She presented to the world a confident image, but inside, she wondered if any of the gossip could be true. This woman, who appeared shallow, was quite the opposite. Ellen Rochdale saw into her soul, and somehow her words rang true. Elizabeth felt relieved, as if someone understood her past and foresaw a brighter future. But how did one respond when one's deepest fears were addressed in the midst of a dancing horde of courtiers?

Apparently, there was no need. Ellen seemed satisfied to have said it, like a Sybil completing the purpose of her existence. Elizabeth could think of nothing more to say. They had communicated on a level far above the mundane, and further conversation would only trivialize their exchange. She chose retreat rather than that. "My thanks, Baroness. I wish you a pleasant evening."

"Thank you, Your Grace."

After they parted, Elizabeth watched Ellen discreetly as she continued to trade thoughts on her health and the weather with other guests. The baroness initiated no conversations of her own, but many approached her, faces bright. Her answering smiles were shy, her eyes downcast, her responses brief. Her diffidence, her reticence, seemed to pull people to her. Word of the woman's insights must have spread, and that, along with her looks, drew others to her in the way great works of art attract: first by beauty but held by something deeper, something that cannot be described.

As Elizabeth watched, fascinated at how Ellen sought no company but was constantly surrounded, she noted an intriguing exchange. Crossing the room, the baroness came face to face with Charles Beverley, and both paused. He gazed directly at her, his expression signaling something like anticipation. Ellen lowered her face and moved on, too quickly, it seemed, and he turned to watch her go. Since her face was averted, it was impossible to judge the lady's response, but Beverley had communicated something to her, as certainly as if he'd shouted across the room.

The evening offered an opportunity to do some snooping. After the princess departed with a measure of fuss Hannah had never before witnessed, she scooped up the dog, announcing that he needed a walk. Minster was a convenient reason for her to be anywhere in the palace, since he was inquisitive, quick, and small enough to dart into unexpected places.

Whitehall had become less of a maze, and she knew how to get from place to place without too much trouble. Soon she was outside the Dudleys' apartments. The gentlefolk would surely attend tonight's ball, so it was a good time to learn what she could from the servants.

"Minster, do not fail me." After listening for movement inside, she opened the door a slit and pushed the little dog forward. Perfectly willing to explore new territory, Minster pushed the opening wider with his nose and disappeared into the room.

In seconds, she heard an astonished cry. "What are you doing here, Precious?"

Taking that as her cue, Hannah knocked on the door, calling, "Have you seen a dog?"

"Come in, come in," a voice answered. Stepping inside, she closed the door behind her. When she turned, a woman emerged from a side room carrying Minster, who licked her face happily. "Oh, he's a love!"

Hannah took him. "And a wicked scoundrel who will not stay where he belongs."

"Ah, not wicked," the woman rejoined. "Adventurous."

A quick glance revealed a room dominated by a raised bed. On each side of it were braziers loaded with charcoal to warm a chilly night. On one wall was a small desk for writing. Along the other sat three large chests, mostly empty. Various items lay stacked on the room's two chairs and the bed itself. The occupants, it seemed, were about to depart.

"And who might you be?" The woman reminded Hannah of Simon's mother, the same round shape, the same comfortable presence, the same curiosity about the business of others.

"Hannah. I serve the Princess Elizabeth."

"Our nation's great jewel."

"And this is her dog, Minster." Feigning ignorance she asked, "Where has the little scamp led me this time?"

"I serve Jane Dudley, Duchess of Northumberland, and these are her quarters. I am Charlotte, one of Her Ladyship's maids."

"Pleased to meet you, even by accident. You serve a great lady."

"The duchess is most gracious." Having exchanged obligatory compliments about their noble mistresses, they turned to gossip. "How does Her Grace this night?"

"Well. She attends a ball at the Spanish ambassador's."

"Our ladies are there as well."

"Ladies?"

"The duchess left to visit an aunt whose home is quite small. Accordingly, she left three ladies behind to pack her things and then take them to Warwick, where she spends the summer."

Glancing around, Hannah said slyly, "And shall I guess who must do the packing? You."

Charlotte grimaced in agreement. "Mostly they only watch and complain about how it's done." She waved an arthritic finger. "But they were pleased to be left in London without the duchess to watch over them, I can tell you." Her brow furrowed as she considered her situation. "I'm to have these trunks ready in the morning, and it's just as well they're out from underfoot. But how am I to know what my lady will need between now and fall?"

The problem was not the packing itself, Hannah realized, but deciding what should go and what should not. Setting Minster on the floor, she surveyed the items strewn about the room. "Let us see if we can sort it out together. When did the duchess last wear this?" By leading Charlotte to one decision at a time, Hannah allayed her dread of leaving something important out. Once they made their choices, she folded the garments neatly while the maid put them into the trunks.

"I think the duchess will be satisfied," Charlotte said as they worked. "You are a wonder at neat bundles."

Hannah steered the conversation to her purpose. "And the others, will they be glad you have done their work?"

She stuffed old stockings filled with cedar shavings into the duchess' shoes to prevent flattening and sweeten their odor. "Two will be happy to have more time to whisper secrets to each other." Charlotte's tone changed. "The third is different. She will see the worth of what we have done."

"Then your efforts will be appreciated."

"Yes. In fact, the baroness would have stayed to help me, except the other two insisted she go." She glanced at the filled trunks. "She will be pleased, and somehow that matters most."

"Why is that?"

"Her Ladyship is a woman one wants to please, to see her smile, though I fear there has been little merriment in her life of late."

"She is unhappy here?"

"Not unhappy, for she makes herself content wherever she is." Charlotte straightened her cap and retied the strings. "In truth, though, she is uncomfortable in this society."

Hannah supposed Court, even London itself, was a shock to one from the country. Inexperience would make it difficult to ignore the immorality, to speak the lies demanded by convention, to avoid the constantly boiling gossip pots. "It is hard to know whom to trust."

"Yes." Charlotte added with the slightly embarrassed air of one guessing at another's motives, "I think she holds back, being fearful."

"As beautiful as she is, some may seek to use her to their advantage."

"That's it exactly! Every man who sees the baroness wants to possess her. Every woman longs to find fault in her, though by my troth, they can find none. Sensing their motives, she seldom speaks her mind or shows what she is feeling." She struggled to put her thought into words. "She avoids notice because she is so noticed."

What the maid said made sense. A beautiful woman of rank and wealth could be manipulated a hundred different ways. Ellen Rochdale apparently kept to herself to guard against such a thing happening.

"Why does she stay here if she is so unhappy?"

"I could not say." Charlotte's tone implied that she could, and Hannah considered the best means for getting her to do so. It turned out the best means was silence, for when she did not reply, Charlotte went on in a rush of confidence. "*He* sent her here. He insisted that she come to London and then went his own way, leaving her to make her way as best she could!" Her contempt for the baron was obvious. What man insisted his pregnant wife travel and then left her to do it alone?

"What was his reason?"

"He said she should consult physicians here, but I have my own suspicions." She leaned toward Hannah as if someone might hear. "She says not a word against him, but here it is: his heart is set against her." She closed a trunk lid with a thud. "She never complains, of course. She is not that sort. But her true feelings slip out from time to time, and I note it. He is a harsh man, and he took against her from the beginning because her state was so far below his."

"The marriage did not please him?"

"The old baron chose her for his son, just before he died." She clicked her tongue in disgust. "An heir is important to him, so he tolerates her, at least until she completes the bargain." Hannah felt a stab of pity for Ellen Rochdale, despised by her own husband, adrift with no friends in the Court. No wonder she seemed timid and unsure of herself!

Charlotte had opened the floodgates of pity for the baroness, and the rest came out in a rush. "And hark to this: she must return to Rochdale to have the child, nowhere else."

"So she will have to travel soon."

"And in her condition, poor thing! One would think she should have her child here, where there are doctors of some learning, but *he* insists she return home." She shook her head, setting the strings of her cap swaying. "Traveling is unwise, but she says she will be well." Charlotte reached out to caress Minster's silky ears. "And to say truth, I believe her, for she has the Sight."

"Does she!"

"The baroness senses things about a person, things they don't say out loud." Charlotte hesitated before sharing her example. "Last week she told me, out of the blue, that I need not worry about my sister, that she is well. I had been worried, since Agnes was due to have a child and the last one almost killed her. Sure enough, not an hour later there came a letter from the village clerk, saying she is well." She sprinkled dried rose petals between layers of clothing, squeezing the scent from them with strong fingers. "It was good of her to ease my mind with her gift."

Hannah did not know what to make of the baroness' supposed gift, but it did seem an attempt at kindness, whether the Sight was involved or simple common sense. She moved on in her mental list of topics. "She recently lost her maid, I hear."

"Marie. Now she was a sweet little thing."

"You knew her well?"

"We couldn't speak much, because I have no French and she had little English. But she was a great help to me."

"She was new at Whitehall?"

"New to England. She and another girl came on a ship from France, looking for work. The baroness needed someone to help with the baby when he comes, and she spoke with both of them." Charlotte pursed her lips. "The other was older and seemed more competent, but the baroness took a liking to Marie."

"But then she fell on the stairs."

"Yes, poor child. I tell them to be careful, the young ones, but they are ever in a hurry."

"Someone said Marie seemed different that last day."

"Different? I don't think so." She started to dismiss the idea, but a memory stirred. "She did have a red mark on her cheek when we returned from dinner. Wouldn't say what happened."

"Were they both here when you returned?"

"I can't say if Marie was. She was such a quiet little thing, one hardly noticed her."

"The baroness was ill?"

"She suffers, as some do in pregnancy, with burning pain behind the breastbone, which kept her from the meal." Straightening, she twisted one shoulder and then the other forward, groaning. "I hope that she, nor you as well, never suffer with a weak back, as I do." She looked around distractedly for a moment. "I was searching for my pillow when you came in," she said. "I made it to ease a certain spot in my spine that plagues me of late." She frowned at the room's corners as if they conspired against her. "I hope I have not packed it in the duchess' things by mistake. Oh, well, it will turn up." Closing the third and last trunk lid and snapping the catches into place with twin clicks, she surveyed them with satisfaction. "Now take your lovely little dog and run along, dear. I thank you for your help, but it grows late, and my old bones want rest."

Wishing Charlotte goodnight, Hannah left the room and made her way through the almost silent palace. It was possible Ellen Rochdale had not been truly sick the day Lord Amberson was killed, possible that she crept away from Marie and poisoned his waiting cup. Still, she could think of no reason why the baroness would kill a harmless old man. Charlotte thought her kind and slightly pitiful, a beautiful bird in an expensive but confining cage. She was anxious to talk with the princess, but that would be at noon at best, after she rested from tonight's revels.

Elizabeth watched as dancers circled the floor, wondering where the Carlsons, the other two left behind to oversee the duchess' packing, had gone. They might know something about the day Amberson died. Finally, she located them standing in a corner, one whispering in the other's ear, so convulsed with laughter she could hardly speak. They watched one of the older dancers as he tried to keep up with the steps of a lively Spanish dance called the Canary. His dancing master would have been horrified, or at least should have been, to see the bumbling performance. It entertained the Carlson sisters greatly, however.

Moving through the crowd in a leisurely manner, Elizabeth stopped behind the two girls. They were not twins but might have been, with the same blondish hair, the same thin build, and the same superior expression on inferior faces. "You are enjoying the evening, I see."

They turned as one, eyes widened at the same time, and dropped into a bow as if joined together by wires. "Your Grace." One of them added, "A lovely night." They glanced at each other with the air of shared secrets common to silly people who have no secrets at all.

"I understand you leave soon to rejoin the duchess."

A grimace passed over the face of the one on the left, but the other, the braver one, spoke. "Yes, Your Grace. This is our last night in London."

"You will surely be missed by the gentlemen of the Court." They simpered at that, as she had guessed they would. "And the Baroness Rochdale? Will she travel with you part of the way?"

"Not with us." The second girl's tone indicated satisfaction. "She stays behind to seek out a new maid."

"Though what she needs a servant for, one cannot say," the other put in. "She is so shy she would not even let the girl help her dress."

"Some stay too long in the country," the first said, "and don't know how to behave among civilized folk."

The two, so much alike that it was difficult to learn which was which, obviously disliked Ellen. But people like the Carlson sisters often had trouble finding anyone to like.

"I hope tonight will be a lovely memory for you to keep," Elizabeth said as she moved away. Retreating, she heard one say to the other in a voice not quite low enough for privacy, "More enjoyable if the Lovely Ellen hadn't insisted on coming along to chaperone!"

Elizabeth smiled. The Carlsons would be glad to escape the company of the baroness, whose beauty and poise probably made them feel as plain and inane as they actually were.

CHAPTER ELEVEN

Elizabeth entered Edward's apartment the next morning and knelt, a cheerful smile pasted on her face, but her heart sank. He looked ghastly. His voice was so weak that she missed his first words.

"He says the Princess Mary is on her way from Kenninghall," said Robin, who stood beside the king as if on guard. "She will arrive in a few days' time, if all goes well."

She kissed Edward's cheek and felt the fever there, but his hands were cold in hers. "How good it will be to see her." In her brother's eyes she saw understanding of the lie, possibly agreement. Neither of them liked Mary much these days. Despite demands put upon her by the council to efface her own importance, her behavior clearly indicated she thought herself both wiser and more Christian than her siblings. When Edward directly ordered her to stop holding mass, Mary answered that she would obey the king in all matters except those dealing with religion, since he was too young to be her judge in such things.

"We will speak to her about the mass," Edward croaked.

And how would she answer this time? The king had outlawed Catholicism, but few believed in the permanence of the Church of England, most of them in and around London. In outlying areas, many clung to the old church, even after all these years. Knowing the king was loathe to punish her for her faith, Princess Mary flaunted it, growing more and more open in worshipping as she pleased. How could the king punish others when his own sister broke his laws with impunity?

Elizabeth glanced at Robin Dudley, wondering for a moment how much religion mattered to him. Although she conscientiously abided by the tenets of the Church of England, she had no strong feelings about how others should worship. It was difficult to comprehend why some needed not only to follow a certain ritual themselves but also to demand that others do the same, to observe the right rite, she thought with ironic amusement. Power over others must be the unstated, perhaps unconscious, goal. Mary believed that power was her birthright.

Elizabeth read to Edward for a while then spoke with his doctor, still musing over her sister's visit. It would be an uncomfortable one, for Mary was likely to shed tears when told she must abide by the nation's law. Tomorrow's dinner would be dull as well, because she disapproved of almost everything Elizabeth considered entertaining.

She took her leave after an hour, somewhat guilty at the feeling of relief that her escape from the closed, malodorous room engendered. Robin accompanied her to the door, leading her away from the others for a few words in private. "Do you recall the day His Lordship died?"

She gave him an ironic glance. "It was not so long ago that I would have forgotten."

"Were you in Amberson's room for any reason?"

She was shocked. "Of course not. Why do you ask?"

His face was a mask. "I thought you might have gone to speak with him."

"Someone says I was there." She met his gaze, and he nodded. "Who?"

"The maid who fell on the stairs told someone she saw you near Lord Amberson's door while everyone was at dinner."

"What exactly did this maid say?"

He seemed uneasy. "The message is secondhand, since the

girl herself cannot be questioned. It is reported that she was about to leave my mother's apartments on some errand when she saw you outside His Lordship's door, possibly leaving the room. She waited until you left, so you never saw her."

"Why would she say that, Robin? I was at dinner with everyone else that day."

"As many of us saw. It's just that no one can say—" He stopped, unsure of his wording.

"No one is prepared to swear I was there the whole time." Actually, she had left before the last course, bored to tears with the company of those seated around her that day.

"Exactly." His eyes sought hers. "Elizabeth, I would never believe evil of you, you know that. We have been friends too long, and I know you too well."

"But this maid's testimony, so conveniently beyond question, is problematic."

"Yes. Tread carefully, for there are only two possibilities. One is that the girl was mistaken and saw someone she thought to be you. And the other—" He paused.

She finished for him. "The other is that someone deliberately placed suspicion on me. Thank you, Robin. I will keep you no longer from your duties." She hurried away, the brush of her feet on the stone floor sounding like hissed warnings of doom and destruction.

As soon as she was out of sight, she paused for a moment, leaning against the solid wall of the palace for support as she fought the fear that shook her. She was under attack. Not for one minute did she believe that Marie mistook someone else for her. Someone wanted to destroy her.

In a room some way down, Hannah waited with Minster. The doctor had ordered him away from the king lest he cause fits of sneezing.

As they walked, Elizabeth told Hannah of Mary's impending

visit and Robin's warning. After she switched to innocuous subjects several times when they encountered others, they finally stepped into an empty solar so she could finish. The space was large and much brighter than other rooms due to a skylight high above and large windows all around. Balconies spaced every twenty feet or so leaned from an upper floor over the room. On either side of each was an earthen pot, the plants inside dropping graceful veils of green over the banisters.

Elizabeth was shaken, and Hannah searched her mind for some scrap of comfort. "Simon will discover the killer, Your Highness. Once he does, you will be safe."

"Safe!" The word came in a huff of disbelief. "I feared for my brother, but it is I who will never be safe. Too many want me out of the way."

Hannah shivered, thinking how precarious life must be for a person whose very existence thwarted the plans of others. "Was the murder planned to remove you from succession?"

"No." Elizabeth massaged her temple as if in pain. "Someone wanted Amberson dead and intended it to appear natural. Once his death was named murder, I became a convenient scapegoat, one whose ruin will appeal to Northumberland."

A grinding sound from above alerted Hannah, and she looked up to see a huge planter teetering on its pedestal. Forgetting ceremony, she grabbed Elizabeth's arm and pulled her toward the center of the room just as the pot fell heavily to the spot where they had been standing. Dirt spilled onto the white tile, and pot-shards skidded toward them, stopping harmlessly at their feet.

One of them, perhaps both, screamed, and people came from three different directions, gasping behind raised hands as they took in the scene. Questions began. Yes, they were all right. No, they did not know what caused the plant to fall. No, they had seen no one on the upper floor.

Hannah investigated, accompanied by a servant and a concerned courtier. What they found was five plants seated solidly on their posts, each with lush leaves flowing out of it. Where the sixth had been was a circle squarely in the center of the post. Hard to imagine how the pot could have tilted and fallen by itself. That brought more questions. In the end, Elizabeth presented a plausible theory. "Someone was above, perhaps lovers stealing a moment alone. When one of them leaned against the pot, it fell. They ran off, fearing punishment."

Sage nods were exchanged, and she thanked everyone for their concern. They need not mention the accident, she added, as it would upset the already ill king. Finally she, Hannah, and Minster escaped the clamoring little crowd with one more assurance that they were well. As they left, both added at the same time, "And we need not tell Simon, either."

Simon was unprepared for the tragedy that engulfed him as he entered the shop. He was late again, having spent some time determining at the docks that Charles Beverley could indeed have sailed to his estate in half the time it had taken to get there on horseback. Now he promised himself that he would make up for his neglect of his duties at the apothecary shop.

The place was quiet in an ominous way, and he paused a moment before calling softly, "Master, are you astir?"

The answering voice was Carthburt's yet not, the tone different, vacant. "Come, Simon. We are here."

Entering the living area, Simon released a moan of sorrow at the sight before him. The curtained corner was now exposed, and laid out on her narrow pallet bed was Rachel, still and pale. Beside it, her father, hunched to almost nothing, held her hand in his, speaking softly. "Do not fear, Little One. Your mother will care for you now."

"Master, what happened?"

Carthburt remained focused on Rachel but answered in the same odd voice. "This began some years ago. She was taken from me then, and only her shell remained. I cared for it as best I could, but she has chosen to leave us." He looked up at Simon. "He cannot hurt her now, you see. She took matters into her own hands."

The girl's garments were wet, her hair tangled, and the smell of algae clung to her. "She fell into the pond?"

"Yes." Carthburt seized on the words. "She fell into the pond. A terrible accident, and you must tell the authorities that."

From the odd response, Simon realized the truth. *She took matters into her own hands.* Rachel had so feared the dark man's return that she drowned herself. Her father, who would protect her to his last breath, did not want her buried in unhallowed ground.

"I will tell them." Rachel had been in no way able to comprehend that suicide was the ultimate sin, so he felt no guilt in calling her death an accident. But Carthburt, who had borne so much sorrow in his life, was now alone.

"She awoke in a fright this morning, saying the dark man would come for her today. I thought her fear would fade, as it has before, if I sent her to be among her birds." A single tear traced his cheek, and he brushed it away with a misshapen finger. "But when I went for her she was gone. I found her in the pond."

"You brought her home by yourself? How did you manage?"

Carthburt smiled grimly. "As I have managed everything since Martha died."

Simon took a moment to think. "I will go to the church and tell them what has happened." At Carthburt's pleading gaze he assured, "I will say that Rachel, the apothecary's daughter, fell into the pond behind her home and, being unable to swim, drowned." He saw gratitude in the old man's eyes. "What obsequies will she have?"

"Very few, I think. We have kept to ourselves these last years, and most of my friendships have faded. If you and your father come, Rachel and I will be content."

"Of course we will."

"Then let us have no other ceremony."

"I will arrange it."

"Good. I will sit with her a while longer." Carthburt turned to his dead daughter again. "She must know what I will do, now that she is safe from harm."

Simon spent the rest of the morning arranging for Rachel's funeral ceremony and burial. When he reported to Carthburt, the old man thanked him, his voice more normal and his manner, though sorrowful, more like himself.

"I will close the shop for a fortnight," he told Simon. "I surmise that you have some business that demands your attention, so you will not mind."

"But I should stay and—" Simon paused, not daring to say that he did not want his beloved master to grieve alone.

"There is naught you can do, lad," Carthburt assured him. "My sadness cannot be relieved by company, even yours, which I prize above all those living. You are a good man and deserve some time with your sweetheart . . . and whatever else occupies your mind of late."

Despite his sorrow for Carthburt's loss and Rachel's last despairing act, Simon recognized the benefit of extra time put into Elizabeth's quest for a killer. First, however, he found his father and acquainted him with the morning's events.

"I will go to him as soon as I can," Jacob said. "Sometimes an old man wants another old man to talk to."

Simon paused at that. Although he thought of Carthburt as

old, he did not see his father that way. Jacob seemed eternal, like the stones of the earth. Yet how quickly things changed. Rachel had been alive yesterday. He recalled the way her desperate fingers had gripped him tightly. Now she was gone.

Forcing his mind from his master's tragedy, he spent the afternoon considering what they knew and what they had yet to discover about the murder at the palace. Lukas Seawell, heir to a small portion of Amberson's estate, seemed not to care. Was he pretending? They would have to see if he needed money for any reason.

Elizabeth had expressed her intention to seek out those she could and get a sense of each one's character. Giles Fuller and his mother looked to join their estate with Amberson's. He could not see how killing the old man helped their cause, but there might be some unknown reason.

Charles Beverley, now Madeline's guardian and controller of her wealth, benefited most directly from Amberson's death. But Beverley had been away for a full fortnight before the murder. Had he arranged it and then left London to avoid suspicion? If so, he had a confederate who would kill for him. What sort of reward brought that much obedience?

That evening Simon told Hannah of Rachel's death, relieving the burden on his own heart by appealing to hers. He attributed the death to accident, keeping Carthburt's secret. Although Hannah had never met Carthburt, she knew of him from Simon, as the apothecary knew of her.

"Oh, the poor man!" Her voice wavered in sympathy. "Was she not his whole life?"

"Indeed." In fact, the thought had struck him that Carthburt might decide to close the shop for good. He had no need of money, having modest needs. With his sorrow, aching joints, and comfortable stack of gold, he need not ply his trade for one day more if he did not want to.

Where would that leave Simon? Admonishing himself for selfish thoughts, he prayed Carthburt would continue the trade at least until he was a journeyman with a salary. Who knew how long an apprenticeship a new master would insist he serve? He and Hannah had waited so long already!

He did not share his fears on that score with Hannah, whose thought had followed its own track. "Would Master Carthburt mind if I came to the funeral?"

"I think he would be honored."

"Then I shall ask Her Grace if I may."

Once they had exhausted the subject of Rachel's death, there was little time left for discussion of the investigation. Although Kat was willing to let Hannah meet Simon in the evenings, there was muttering from the others about privileges the new girl was afforded. Quickly she told Simon what Elizabeth had learned and what she herself had gathered. In return, he related his conversation with the groom and resulting doubts. "After announcing he would visit his lands to the northeast, Beverley asked for directions northwest."

"You think he lied about his destination?"

"Or added to it. In a fortnight of hard riding he might have accomplished two purposes."

"Maybe he went to meet some woman."

"That's possible."

She argued against her own premise. "Why leave London? There are women enough here."

He shrugged. "A special one, then, though they say he has no passion but advancement."

"Her Grace thought Lady Rochdale and Beverley might have some connection, judging from a glance that passed between them at last night's entertainment."

Simon reacted with disdain. "Beverley and Ellen Rochdale?

131

What would she see in him?"

"What do you mean?"

"She is—" Simon stopped, considering his audience. "She is most alluring."

Hannah felt a tiny twinge of jealousy at the awe in his tone but after a moment continued in a different vein. "You always say that knowledge is key, and you have time now to pursue that knowledge. We must not waste our opportunities, for Her Highness needs us." She did not tell him of Robin Dudley's warning, having been ordered not to, but she knew Simon would do his best for the princess, even as someone they could not yet identify did his worst.

CHAPTER TWELVE

Rachel's funeral was indeed simple, but there was one surprise for the mourners. When Hannah arrived, she came in a litter, stepping out self-consciously in a plain but becoming dress, her hair pulled back in a severe style that only showed her lovely face to better advantage.

As she alit, she turned and offered her hand to another. Simon almost choked. Elizabeth! She, too, was dressed plainly, but she was elegant nonetheless. Her eye met Simon's briefly, but she only nodded slightly before turning to Carthburt.

"I am come to give condolences for your grief," she said in a clear, low voice. "Hannah told me of your daughter's accident, and if you have no objection, I will join the funeral. It is a tragedy for us all when one so young dies."

Carthburt had never made Simon so proud, for he straightened his spine then forced it into a graceful bow. "Your Grace, I am honored by your presence. My poor child sees your kindness from Heaven, I am certain of it."

The service, held in a small, dark church unwarmed by sunlight or any other means, was brief, and Carthburt sat dry-eyed and composed. There were only a few there, Simon's parents and some neighbors. The homily was vague and dwelt on the innocent, for whom God makes special provision in His kingdom. Afterward, Elizabeth asked if Simon would accompany her and Hannah back to the palace. Jacob immediately suggested that Carthburt take the midday meal with him and his wife, and the two groups went separate ways. Elizabeth dismissed the litter-bearers, and the three walked along together with only a couple of yeomen as chaperones.

They were somber at first, as people tend to be after the funeral of a contemporary. Gradually, however, the mood wore off as they looked in shop windows and spoke of generalities. Elizabeth saw a tart in a bakery window that appealed to her, and on impulse, Simon went inside and bought three of them.

They sat down on a bench outside the bakery and ate the tarts, which were excellent but messy. Soon all three of them were sticky with the sweet fruit filling. A smear of berry clung to Hannah's lower lip, and Simon had to restrain himself from kissing it away. Instead, he wet his kerchief in a rain barrel and let the women clean themselves before wiping his own hands and stuffing the wet square into a pocket.

As they walked on, conversation wandered from topic to topic, a bit of literary commentary, a little silliness, and observations on mankind in general. Even the yeomen joined in when the subject of an upcoming fair arose. As they neared the palace, however, their manner again became more formal. Hannah and Simon slid half a step behind Elizabeth, and their escort straightened their backs and their expressions. As she turned to bid him good-bye, the princess said unexpectedly, "Thank you, Simon Maldon."

"Your Grace?"

"To you a pleasant walk, a whimsical treat, even a friend's funeral, is nothing extraordinary. But for me, it is a rare privilege to walk unnoticed in the sunlight, to talk of whatever comes to mind without wondering what is expected of me. I thank you for that." With one of her genuine smiles, seldom seen but nevertheless dazzling, Her Grace touched his arm briefly before returning to the world she inhabited, where everything she did was noted.

When Simon met Calkin at their prearranged time and place, the two spent some time recounting their activities in the years since they had seen one another. Calkin declared himself a confirmed bachelor, "Likely to lie with a maid but unlikely to stand up with her afterward." He had risen to captain in the ranks of the King's Guard, although he admitted that the guard was less than it had been. Reduced in number, held in strict account for every penny, and given ever more onerous duties in order to justify its existence, the unit that was once Henry VII's pride was now demoralized, veterans like Calkin somewhat bitter.

"These days we get few men of character," he complained, "only varlets looking for a place to sleep out of the elements. Only old fellows like me care about doing the job well."

"Were you called to investigate Amberson's murder?"

"Not called, no. But I heard the commotion and went to see if I could serve."

"Then you saw the room as it was, before others entered?"

Calkin took a drink of the ale bought with a small sum Elizabeth had provided for the investigation. Following suit, Simon found it better than expected, sweet, fruity, and cool in his throat. Calkin's gift was memory, and Simon had seen him recall in detail a scene he had only glanced at. "There were two there before me. Amberson's servant found him that morning and ran to find help. The man was literally shouting that his master was dead, which is how another guardsman and I came to the chamber. The son, Lukas, was there when we arrived."

"What was he doing in the palace so early?"

Calkin grinned. "Not my place to speculate on that, young friend. I tell only what I saw. The times are too unsettled to make an enemy of anyone, even a preaching peter like Lukas."

Simon understood. Hugh had lost his position, and Calkin intended to keep his. "Tell me exactly what you saw."

Turning his eyes upward and to the left, Calkin pictured the image in his mind. "The dead man was on the bed, and it was plain he'd died in distress. His night robe lay across the foot, his slippers on the floor beside it. On a small table in the far corner was an account book of some kind, a candle burnt down to almost nothing, and a goblet."

"You saw the goblet?"

"I did, but it was missing later, when we looked for it."

"Who came into the room?"

His friend snorted. "Half the palace, within minutes. You know how it is. They want to be in on the excitement. At least a dozen noblemen, several curious servants, even a few women. But"—he raised a palm—"I posted men at the door immediately. No one took that cup out of the room."

"Can you remember what it looked like?"

"It was glass, a greenish color, I think. Nothing unusual about its size or shape."

"Could this be part of it?" Simon unwrapped a piece of cloth, revealing the shard Hannah had found, and laid it on the table.

Calkin rolled it with a finger, letting it catch the light. "Maybe. But green glass is not rare."

Simon grimaced. "I know. It's just that we found it below Amberson's window."

"We?"

"Hannah, my betrothed, is maidservant to the princess."

"A lovely girl, I recall." He paused. "So you and the princess have again joined forces to solve a crime?"

Simon grinned weakly. "That is not public knowledge."

"Not to worry, lad. I will tell no one, but I knew she liked you. Elizabeth, I mean."

"And I admire her greatly."

Calkin cupped his chin in his palm and leaned his elbow on the table, coming closer so he could lower his voice. "They say she will be disinherited soon. The wolves around Edward don't want either of Henry's daughters on the throne lest they marry a Catholic."

Simon took offense at the notion. "Why would Elizabeth do such a thing? She is Protestant, and according to Catholics, illegitimate, since they reject Henry's first divorce."

"But she is a woman, you see, and women are ruled by their hearts, not their heads. Were she queen, Philip of Spain would come a-courting, and they say he can turn any woman's head."

Simon tried to imagine Elizabeth marrying a smooth-talking Spaniard but could not. He recalled a day long ago when she declared, "I shall never marry. Never." He'd believed her then and had no reason to think she'd changed her mind. If only the council understood the princess' character. She was truly Henry VIII's heir, and from what he heard of them, her siblings did not compare to her. Marry a Catholic, indeed!

Simon questioned Calkin in the same way he had quizzed Hugh, mentioning various people close to Amberson to get a general impression of their character. "Robin Dudley? A good enough sort, but that clan seeks power above all else. The old man will face the block yet, for he cannot curtail his ambition, and the son will be lucky if he does not go down with his sire."

The conversation paused as a man stopped to speak to Calkin. After some playful banter about a bygone game of darts and exchange of weather predictions, the newcomer made a comment that caught Simon's attention. "Do you know the name of the princess' newest maidservant, by chance? The pretty one with eyes that could drown a man?"

Calkin avoided Simon's gaze as he said casually, "I don't think I've seen her."

"You would not forget if you had. But I will find it out." The young man left, slapping Calkin's shoulder heartily and promising to beat him in the next competition at darts.

"And who was that?"

"Giles Fuller. He's a merry sort, not above a bowl of ale with the likes of us."

Simon's face flushed. Giles Fuller. The man who had flirted with Hannah. What had he gotten her into? He tried to forget his disquiet and resume normal conversation. "You are, I take it, as good with a dart as you are with a knife?"

Calkin sensed his desire to drop the subject of Giles Fuller. "I do well enough. Do you still practice your throwing?"

"When I can."

"I never had a pupil apt as you. And as you can testify, it is a skill a man can use."

Simon nodded. "Would I never have to use it again, but I am grateful for your teaching." Banishing the thought of a man he had killed to save Hannah's life, he returned to his questions.

"Beverley?" Calkin responded to the next query. "He is our commander, of course. At first, he was a trial, always interfering in matters that he knew little about. Now he has set his sights higher, and we are glad of it, since he leaves us petty captains to run things as we see fit."

"And as a person? What do you think of him?"

Calkin seemed torn, perhaps between loyalty and truth. "Those above Master Beverley see his public side, where he is efficient and helpful. Beneath is a less commendable man."

"What do you mean?"

Calkin hesitated. "I will not give specifics, but were I you, I would avoid him."

"The king has named him Madeline Amberson's guardian."

"Not surprising. He made himself indispensable to His Lordship these past months and appeared much taken with the child.

Amberson was not a weak man, except where his daughter was concerned." Simon thought of Carthburt, who had doted on his Rachel, but Calkin continued musingly, "He had become somewhat disordered in his mind, I think."

"What do you mean?"

Calkin again leaned forward, elbows on the table, chin on his folded hands, and softened his tone. "You've no doubt seen old ones whose minds lose the ability to focus and remember. His Lordship hid it well, but I have seen him make mistakes a person should not."

"Such as?"

"Forgetting the way back to the palace from a familiar location. Being unable to recall the names of people he knew well. And a general look of confusion at odd moments, as if he did not know where he was or with whom."

"Did others note this?"

"Possibly, but who would comment on it? Those close to such a man are more likely to cover for him than point out his failings, lest he lose his place on the council."

"So Beverley stepped in when His Lordship began to doubt himself."

"Once he gained the old man's confidence, he made himself indispensable."

"Then he would certainly not murder Amberson until his plans were secured."

Calkin took a long drink and set the tankard down with a soft thud. "Unless something threatened those plans."

That brought Giles Fuller back to mind. "That young man who just left us apparently sought to woo Madeline."

"It is not so much what he seeks," Calkin said with a chuckle. "Giles' wooing is driven by his harridan of a mother."

"Has he had success?"

"I can't say. Madeline is young, but stranger matches are

made every day. If her father was agreeable, Dorcas Fuller might have got her wish."

"She claims he had agreed in principle already, because Madeline wanted it so."

Calkin whistled. "They would have to have proof. And now that His Lordship is dead, I don't suppose there is any."

"Perhaps Giles will approach Beverley with his proposal."

The reply came with a huff of disdain. "I wish him much luck with that. He might have convinced a doting father that Madeline would be happy married to him, but Beverley will no doubt delay a wedding indefinitely or marry the girl himself." At Simon's look, he explained, "It would be the nearest way to complete control of her fortune, and according to rumor, he has need of it." Finishing the ale, he pushed the tankard away.

"Beverley is in debt?"

"His men have not been paid in months. It is expensive to entertain the Court, and he outdoes himself. They say his ultimate goal is higher than a knight should expect."

"You mean he wants a seat on the council?"

Calkin grinned as he rose and gripped Simon's arm in farewell. "They have a vacancy now, do they not?"

CHAPTER THIRTEEN

Elizabeth met Robert Dudley as she went in to the evening meal. "Your Highness, how goes it?" He regarded her closely, but she did not betray her fears. Blandness was essential, even with one she considered a friend.

"Well enough, Robin, and you? I think your father keeps you very busy."

"Only duty prevents me from spending the greatest share of my time with you," he replied in true courtier fashion. In an aside closer to the friend she'd known as a child, he added, "Better you than the dreaded Dorcas Fuller!" Taking her arm firmly, he led her to the table, smiling and nodding as they passed the lesser folk. From the side of his mouth he teased, "Turn on your smile, Princess. The people await your Tudor glow." Her heart warmed at his teasing. Dear Robin!

"So you have been dealing with Lady Fuller?" she asked as he seated her with a bow.

He made a grimace of distaste. "She has made claims that are . . . inconvenient."

"That Giles and Madeline Amberson are promised to each other?"

His eyes widened. "You really do know everything."

"She boasted about it at the ball, said Amberson was pleased with the match, wanting his daughter's happiness."

"The sad part is that it might be true. The lovely Madeline only giggles when asked for details, and Charles Beverley—"

"Is incensed."

"More than that, if there is a higher anger. He has asked to speak with my father tomorrow morning, to plead his case against the Fullers, I expect."

"What will you do?"

"I? I will listen, as I am trained to do, be diplomatic, as I am told to do, and reveal nothing, as I am glad to do. Beverley will not let the girl out of his clutches, so no matter how determined the lady is to secure her son's future, she will succeed only over his dead body."

Under her bland exterior, Elizabeth felt a shiver on her spine. If another dead body appeared, she was sure that someone, somehow, would find a way to attribute it to her.

Hannah made her way through the corridors to the apartment that had been Amberson's, where Beverley now resided, at least temporarily, as he cleared up the old man's affairs. During the midday meal, when most were in the hall for at least two hours, she intended to try the same tactic she had with Charlotte: find a servant who liked to talk and learn what she could, using the all-too-plausible excuse of being lost.

At the door she paused, unsure whether to knock boldly or wait for someone to come out and notice her. The decision was made for her. "What are you doing, girl?" boomed a voice. She turned to see a forbidding woman flanked by two maids, all with faces fit to curdle fresh milk.

"I am sent to deliver a message, mistress, but I'm afraid I've made a wrong turn."

"A message to whom?"

Hannah said the first name that occurred to her. "Constance Bernhaur, if it please you." She curtsied low, peeping through her lashes to form an impression of the woman. She seemed neck-less, a head apparently balanced on a wine tun of a body.

No waist was evident as her amazing chest met the equally amazing girth of her lower half. Her expression signaled an imbalance of humors, probably choler from too much bile. Hannah wondered briefly if Simon's physic might calm such an angry disposition.

The woman came closer, bringing with her the scent of anise. "A wrong turning brings you here? Nothing else?"

"Yes, my lady. The palace is confusing, and I am new here."

"I thought I had not seen you before. Do you know my brother, Charles Beverley?"

The knight's sister! She was almost as daunting as he was rumored to be. Simon had described him as burly, and she was no less so. What might have been attractive in a man was less pleasing wrapped in silk and starch. "No, my lady."

"Are you certain you did not come here at his bidding?"

"No, my lady. I do not know the gentleman, even by sight."

"Well, then. If you have no business here, be off."

Hannah left, stopping a few turns down to digest what she had learned. The daunting Henrietta seemed concerned about her brother's actions. Who was in control, the knight or his domineering sibling?

The three investigators managed a meeting immediately after supper in a section of the grounds planted entirely in spring-blooming flowers: snowdrops, primroses, and bluebells. As they breathed in soft scents, Simon and Hannah acted as if they were alone together, while Elizabeth pretended to read on a bench nearby. She listened, of course, and commented as the need arose.

"We know the poison His Lordship took was in a goblet in his room; therefore he was the target and not the king." Simon half-turned to Elizabeth. "We could let the Lord President handle the matter." He waited, unsure what he wanted to hear.

If the princess felt her brother was safe, Hannah could leave the palace and they could return to their lives. Still, part of him wanted to continue, wanted to know who poisoned a harmless, possibly senile nobleman.

In response, Elizabeth recounted Robert Dudley's warning. "I told Hannah not to tell you, but you see why we cannot end our efforts," she said calmly.

Simon's neck muscled tensed despite her calm. "She said you were there?"

"Someone reports that she did."

"Someone is lying," Hannah said. "Can we find out who reported this tale?"

"Calkin may be able to."

"Ask him," Elizabeth ordered. "We know I did not do this deed." She smiled grimly. "At least I hope you find in me no homicidal tendencies. But others are diverted from looking for the real killer as they consider my traitorous tendencies, and there still could be some plot afoot that threatens the king. We do not yet know why Amberson was murdered."

"The strongest motives are his wealth and his seat on the council."

"Madeline gains the wealth, but she is no killer."

"But the murderer may plan to control her."

"Which indicates Beverley or Fuller."

"The brother," Hannah interjected. "Might he petition to become his sister's guardian?"

"If he had such a plan, he missed his opportunity."

"But he was in the room that morning and could have tossed the goblet out the window."

"Are they plotting together?" Elizabeth spoke without eye contact, still apparently reading her book. "Half a fortune is better than none."

"That could be it," Hannah said excitedly. "He poisons his

father and Beverley rewards him from the estate, a larger share than he would get from the will."

"But they appear to detest each other," Simon objected.

"Some things overcome personal dislike," Elizabeth observed in a sardonic tone.

"Then one of them pushed Marie down the stairs, fearing she suspected them?"

"Beverley could have done the deed and disappeared before anyone saw him." She turned a page in the book she could not have identified if asked. "What if Beverley told Northumberland that Marie saw me upstairs? The captain of the guard has access to the duke, and if he is the killer, he would want to focus attention on someone else now that the world calls it murder.

"Everything comes back to Beverley," Simon said. "Alone or with someone else, he is responsible for His Lordship's death."

"I agree," she said without looking up from the book. "Now it is up to us to prove it."

CHAPTER FOURTEEN

"Your Highness, you cannot be caught spying on the duke!"

Since Elizabeth learned of Beverley's request for an early-morning, private audience with the Lord President of the council, she had been anxious to know its purpose. Accordingly, she had risen long before her usual time and now led Hannah toward the audience chambers.

"Simon believes Beverley is behind the murder of Lord Amberson. I want to hear what he says about me so that I can defend myself."

"Then let me go. If I am discovered, I can claim I'm lost, being new to Whitehall."

Elizabeth hesitated, and Hannah seized the opportunity. "Wait here." Realizing she had given an order to a royal princess, she added, "Please."

Hannah peered into the audience room. There was no one inside. Entering, she looked around for a place to conceal herself. Suppressing a shiver of dread at the thought of what she was doing, she noted two doors other than the one she entered, one on either side of the room. Behind the first a half dozen dour and silent men looked up questioningly, so she closed it again. The other door led to a tiny, empty area whose purpose she could not guess. Hardly large enough to be a closet, it had a second door that led to a large, well-appointed office where a clerk worked at a table. Concentrated on his work, he did not see her peep in. Deciding this in-between room was her spot,

Hannah closed the door on the oblivious clerk and left the other barely ajar.

It was some time before Beverley was ushered into the audience room. She heard him thank someone, probably Robin Dudley, for his courtesy. When Beverley was left alone in the room to wait, she was struck with terror, fearing he would start exploring and find her hiding there. Apparently he had no curiosity about his surroundings. She did not even hear him move about the room. In the absolute quiet, she forced herself to breathe shallowly lest she give herself away.

After some time the elder Dudley arrived, and Hannah leaned in close to catch every word. She could see little through her slit of view, but she did from time to time get a glimpse of the Lord President, who was apparently a pacer. He did not waste time with niceties. "Why the private conference, Charles? What secret have you to share with me?"

"First, let me assure you that I am as staunch in support of Your Lordship as was my mentor, Lord Amberson." Beverley's tone was pompous and self-conscious. "I was in his bosom and know he believed you to be the best man to guide His Highness until he is fully able to rule."

"I am gratified to hear it." Northumberland's voice revealed faint distaste.

"His Lordship believed that, although we have every hope that His Majesty will live a long and happy life, there should be preparation for every eventuality. Unfortunately, the nation is divided as to the rightful heir. Lord Amberson's support would have gone to one with as strong a claim as anyone to the throne, one who is not tainted with charges of bastardy."

"I know the person you refer to."

"As you know, I oversee the King's Guard. In that capacity, certain facts concerning the death of Lord Amberson have come to my attention, facts that need further investigation."

"You need not my permission to do the work you are given. I trust you will be thorough."

"Here is my point, Your Lordship. If it could be proven that one of the, um, other claimants to the throne is in fact a criminal, would it not, um, clarify the question of succession?"

Northumberland hesitated. "If it could be proven, yes. But the proof would have to be convincing." Hannah pursed her lips. The wily duke would not commit himself to a course, but he would let someone like Beverley construct a case against Elizabeth. If the attempt failed, he could claim he knew nothing of it. If Beverley succeeded, one of the two obstacles in his way disappeared. Since Northumberland was even now negotiating a marriage between his son Guildford and Jane Grey, it was an attractive prospect.

His response was enough for Beverley. "I will return when I have completed my investigation, Your Lordship. And I will count on your future kindness." Hannah wrinkled her nose at his obsequious tone and obvious bid for advancement.

The room went silent and she moved to the door, ready to make her escape as soon as possible. At that moment, a voice behind her demanded, "What are you doing here, girl?" Whirling around, she faced a barrel-chested man with bulging eyes and a short, squared beard that made his head look like a block of wood.

Hannah could not get a single thought to form, much less an answer. The man, not content with frightening her witless, repeated the question, louder and with more force, adding, "If you are spying on your betters, things will not go well with you."

"I—I—" Now thoughts formed. Thoughts of dungeons and boiling oil.

Suddenly Elizabeth was beside her, pulling on her arm and giving her a sharp slap on the face. "You wicked, wicked girl!

What have you done with that tart?"

"Your Grace." The man bowed, and Elizabeth appeared to notice him for the first time.

"Viscount Marle." She even managed a blush. "You must excuse my anger. This girl of mine has a love of sweets such as I have never seen. She took a tart from a tray in my room and came here to eat it undetected."

He found some amusement in the situation. "They are like children, are they not? I once caught a footman trying on my clothes."

"Well, this one will learn to resist petty theft or face branding." Elizabeth regarded Hannah with a scowl. "If you will excuse us, we will finish privately, in my quarters."

"Of course, Your Grace." He bowed courteously, stepped aside, and the two women left, Elizabeth dragging Hannah, still dazed by her near disaster.

"I would not have struck you, but I had to be convincing."

"I am grateful for your quick wit, Highness." Hannah resisted the urge to rub her stinging cheek. A small price to escape a charge of spying on the Lord President of the king's council.

Lukas Seawell's closest friend was a fishmonger who lived only a few paces down the road from their church. After careful thought about how to approach the man, Simon chose the role of a reformer looking for fellowship.

The shop smelled strongly of fish, of course, but it appeared to be clean, the dirt floor newly swept. The man who came out from behind a leather curtain was huge, with arms that bulged under his sleeves and a chest that would have made two of Simon's. His expression was forbidding, a scowl enhanced by dark hair and brows. The set of his lips suggested taciturnity. The sight of him relieved Simon's mind on one account; he had not been present at the meetinghouse and therefore would not recognize the lies he was about to tell. Still, he appeared distrustful. Doubtful of his chance of success, Simon nevertheless began his rehearsed speech.

"I am newly come from Switzerland," he said in response to a gruff greeting. "I heard that there are those in this area who might want news of John Calvin's latest teachings."

The change that came over the shopkeeper was both instantaneous and startling. Every impression Simon had formed vanished like bubbles in the air. The big man's face lit with joy, and he stepped forward so quickly Simon had to resist the urge to retreat. "You have seen him?"

"I have, and I am willing to speak of it to those who share my views."

The man patted him on the shoulder, a gentle gesture in intent but painful nevertheless. "You will find our group most interested," he said. "We study together as often as we can but welcome those whose view is wider than our own. Does Geneva's government go well?"

"It remains, though it has been sorely tested." Simon knew that much. Calvin's theocracy, though well established, resisted dissenters who disliked parts of it.

"We long for—" For the first time, the man seemed to realize that he might fall into a trap. "We regard those who seek to see God's face more clearly."

"I know that Lukas Seawell is one of your members. I was once acquainted with him through his mother, may God rest her soul."

"She was a wonderful woman."

"So you have known Lukas for some time?"

"Since we were twelve. It was his mother who—taught us many things." Lukas' mother, once a servant in the Amberson household, had apparently sown the seeds of reform in others.

"And now you seek True Wisdom."

He laughed. "I am a simple man, a seller of fish like those who followed our Lord, even named after Peter, who sinned but strove to do better. Now Lukas is wise. You should hear him argue points of grace and such as that!"

"And have he and his father mended their disagreement?"

Peter's face sobered. "Lord Amberson is dead. Killed, they say, by a poisoner's hand."

"God shield us." Simon bowed his head. "How has Lukas dealt with his tragedy?"

"He is much disturbed by it and fears for his sister, little Madeline."

"She may be poisoned as well?"

"Oh, no. But she must have a guardian, and Lukas likes not the man who is chosen. He says he is most likely to have poisoned His Lordship himself."

"And where was Lukas the day before his father died?"

"Why, with us at meeting. It were St. Cyril's day, and in recognition of his teaching we stayed together in the church from sunup to sundown, reading his twenty-three lectures." His rather slow wit finally caught up. "Why do you ask such a thing?"

"I only meant to discover if he is safe from suspicion. There is no doubt the authorities will look at him, but if he was all day with friends, then he is safe."

Peter nodded, apparently satisfied. "Lukas was no threat to his father." The door opened behind Simon, and Peter nodded to the customer who entered. As a parting observation he said, "I think Lukas would seek redress against the man who wormed his way into His Lordship's will if our beliefs permitted it, but we are taught, and must accept, that vengeance is the Lord's." With that, he turned to his customer's needs, and Simon left him to his work.

He had learned what he had come to learn: if Lukas' friends thought him one who might take vengeance into his own hands.

This man thought not. He was frustrated at not being able to eliminate even one suspect. Those who had the opportunity had no reason, and those with reasons to kill apparently had no opportunity.

Trying a different approach, he spent the afternoon visiting apothecaries in the city, asking at each shop who had bought arsenic recently. His luck was not good. "A person might collect small doses from a half dozen apothecaries without raising suspicion then put them together to make a lethal dose," he complained to Jacob that evening.

"Or simply find an apothecary who gives out larger doses than he should. There is little regulation and even less oversight of such things. Your killer might even steal what he wants from others, those who actually need physic." Jacob rose and began sorting his tools. "I don't think that line of inquiry will lead anywhere."

Simon joined his father, watching as he sorted the instruments his wife had rinsed for him and laid out to dry. He slid them into their places in his bag, the metallic resonances so familiar to Simon that he associated them with order in the world. "I was almost certain Beverley killed Amberson to get his fortune. But he was gone from London a fortnight before the man died."

"You say he traveled on horseback?"

"Yes."

"Odd. A boat would have been faster and more comfortable."

"I noted that, too. And the groom at the stable reports that he asked about the route to Chester, which is in a different direction."

Jacob finished sorting, closed the bag, and set it by the door, striking a final steely chord. "You have several more days without work. Perhaps you should retrace his lordship's journey and learn what he was really doing when Amberson died."

True to his nature, Jacob saw to the heart of the matter. If Charles Beverley was their most likely suspect, Simon should discover first, if he truly had left London, and second, why he had done so. Once they were sure of his actions and his reasons for them, they could either eliminate suspicion of him or work to figure out how he had committed murder from a great distance away.

CHAPTER FIFTEEN

A trip north was for Simon an undertaking fraught with uncertainty, since he had never been more than twenty miles from London in his life. He had never taken a journey on horseback, either, but figured the best way to track Beverley's movements was to travel the same way he had.

Calkin came to his rescue, offering to go along when Simon requested the loan of a horse. "I've been stuck in London for months," he explained, "and I'm ready for a bit of adventure." He arranged his absence with little trouble, calling on his old friend Gooderich to replace him on duty. Simon sent word to Hannah through Gooderich as well, and by mid-morning, the two started on their way with several days' provisions, equipment for life on the road, and the directions the stable man had given Charles Beverley. They planned to travel hard and return as soon as possible, since Simon was nervous about leaving Elizabeth and Hannah in an uncertain situation.

The groom had recommended an inn at St. Albans to Beverley, and they spoke first with the landlord there. He reported that his guest had stayed one night, asking directions to Leicester. After riding northward for several more hours, they spent the night, retreating to the shelter of a copse and spreading their cloaks on the ground. Simon had studied a map before leaving London and had in mind an image of the land. "We might be headed to Beverley, but I would not take this route," he said as they lay watching the stars above them.

"Maybe the roads are better that way," Calkin suggested. "Tomorrow will tell." With that, he turned and went immediately to sleep, in soldier fashion. Simon lay awake for a while, nursing sore muscles and pondering the cause of murder.

Elizabeth took on the task of talking with the French girl who had come to London with Marie, since Hannah spoke only English. It took a tedious visit to the wife of a viscount she hardly knew, but she spotted the girl, hired to care for the woman's two children, in the back garden as she exited the house. Using the children as an excuse to linger, she spoke to the girl in French.

"You are newly come to England, I understand?"

Without meeting her eyes, the girl responded, "Yes, Your Grace."

"I hope you are happy here."

"Yes, Your Grace."

How tiresome it was to get past social status and actually communicate! "I understand that the girl who fell on the stairs at Whitehall came with you from France."

"Yes, Your Grace." Her throat worked and her tone was strained.

"She was close to you?"

A pause. "My sister, Your Grace."

Elizabeth's heart went out to her. Had she been allowed any time at all to mourn, or had she been expected to see to her charges despite her sister's death? "I am sorry." Although it was painful for the girl, she had to ask, "Was Marie pleased with her new position?"

The girl looked up in surprise, and she realized her mistake. *Pleased* was hardly a word such as they would understand. Marie had agreed to travel far from London, far from the sister who was probably her only surviving relative. *Resigned* might have been the word to use. When she answered, the girl's face was again a mask. "She was content, Your Grace. I only saw her once after she went to the baroness. She said some of the other servants were kind and at least the baroness spoke French."

"And there was the child to look forward to."

"Yes." Her tone was odd, and Elizabeth waited expectantly. "Marie was a little afraid of that, since she had no experience with children."

"None?"

"My sister cared for our father until he died last year. It was I who lived with a lady in France and saw to her daughters until the family moved to Italy."

"So you had experience with babies and Marie did not."

"Yes, Your Grace."

"But the baroness chose Marie?"

Her chin lifted a half inch. "Yes, Your Grace."

She wanted to ask why, but the girl would never presume to know what a baroness was thinking. Wishing her well in her new post, Elizabeth left, the chorus of childish voices receding behind her. Why had the baroness chosen the inexperienced sister? Surely it would be an advantage to a first-time mother in a remote location to have a servant with some knowledge of babies and birthing.

Recalling Ellen Rochdale's intuitive message to her, she decided it must have been some sense she had of the two girls, some feeling that Marie was the better choice. Now that Marie was gone, they would never know what kind of help she would have been.

CHAPTER SIXTEEN

Simon and Calkin were on the road early, though the younger of the two suppressed a groan as he climbed onto the horse's broad back. Surely, the body was not designed to be stretched into such positions! As they rode, they talked of many things but seemed always to come back to the questions surrounding Amberson's murder: how it was done, why, and if the death of the serving girl related to the original crime.

Away from the city, Calkin seemed more candid concerning his superior, perhaps because trees could not report his words. "Beverley could have hired the girl to poison His Lordship then pushed her down the stairs to keep her from telling anyone about it."

Simon agreed it was possible. "He knew she was quartered with Northumberland's wife and therefore nearby. She could have waited for just the right opportunity and accomplished the deed when circumstances allowed it."

"Easy enough to slip away: the call of nature, an errand, something of that sort."

"But Marie seems an unlikely killer. 'Sweet' is a word often used to describe her, and I heard 'timid' and 'shy' as well. Added to that, she was newly come from France. Could Beverley or anyone else have convinced her to perform such a hideous deed in the space of a week?"

"Maybe he frightened her into it."

That brought another question to mind. "Does Beverley

speak French?"

"I doubt it. Barely reads and writes, from what I gather."

"Then they could not communicate, for Marie spoke very little English."

Calkin acknowledged the difficulty. "Hard to plot murder through an interpreter."

"Tell me what you know of Beverley. Everything," Simon demanded. "I need to understand him."

With a click of his tongue, Calkin urged his horse ahead so they could pass through a narrow spot on the trail. When they again could ride abreast, he had collected his thoughts. "Charles Beverley was raised in the north, on a patch of land too poor for profitable use. Not only is the estate rocky and unproductive, but the old knight, his father, drank his way through what money there was. When he died a few years back, Charles came to London to make his fortune. He doesn't mind whose boots he has to kiss to do it."

The story was not unusual. Plenty of knights lived on small holdings in genteel poverty. The more ambitious ones made themselves useful to noblemen who might drop income-generating positions in their laps. Managing the guard was modestly lucrative and prestigious enough, but apparently Beverley wanted more, hence his sycophantic attachment to Amberson.

"He is not generally well-liked, from what the princess tells me."

"Two-faced, is what he is. Those above him may sneer at his morals and his lack of subtlety, but they recognize his usefulness. He accomplishes much with little and can wring the last halfpenny of worth out of a horse or a tool or a man. To his superiors he seems efficient; those of us who work for him see little to admire."

"A difficult man to serve."

"Everything is show." The freckled nose wrinkled in disgust. "Everything is planned to his advantage, down to the last detail. He has no personal associations, nothing you or I would call a friend. He even hires his women, they say. Too much trouble to woo and win one, but he claims a man needs regular release in order to think clearly." He chuckled. "The sister makes it her business to stop him, claims it's a needless expense."

That might explain Hannah's account of her meeting with Henrietta Beverley. The knight's sister had been practicing fiscal responsibility! "So he is a man of no passions?"

"Only one—his own advancement."

Simon was silent for a while. It looked more and more like Beverley had decided that killing his mentor could help him move upward. Still, he did not seem like a man who would trust easily. So who had he trusted to poison Lord Amberson for him?

"A man of so much ambition should be feared." He thought of Hugh, who had dared to question Beverley's actions and lost his post.

"I saw him put in his place not long ago." Calkin grinned as he recalled it. "I came around a corner and found him with his hand on the arm of a certain lady of the Court. 'You would do well to consider it,' he tells her. Her face is cold as December, but she makes no answer, seeing me behind them. After he moves on, she says to me, 'It is sinful what a married woman must endure in this place.' I had to admire her, for she stood her ground with dignity."

"What lady was this?"

"The Baroness Rochdale. A beauty far above any Beverley should aspire to."

"So I have heard." Simon rode on for a few minutes in silence, listening to the plod of horses' hooves on soft earth. It was the second instance of contact between Beverley and the baroness, and both times, she had seemed unsettled by his attention. What could a man like him have done to upset Ellen Rochdale?

Elizabeth came to find Hannah that afternoon, her expression indicating important news. "Minster needs exercise. Leave what you're doing and come along."

Hoping Kat would not be too angry to see only one rug beaten clean, she scooped up the dog and followed. As soon as they were clear of the palace walls, Elizabeth turned to her. "Charles Beverley is dead."

"What?"

"It was poison for certain this time, mixed with mead from his own stock."

Hannah's mind raced with questions. How could the man they thought was a murderer be himself the victim of murder? Had someone else killed Lord Amberson and Beverley, or had a crime Beverley committed been avenged? If so, by whom? Seawell? Giles Fuller? Dudley himself? It was a lot to comprehend, but clearly, things were different than they had thought. Simon was in the north, tracing Beverley's route, which now seemed unimportant. If the knight was guilty, he had been punished, and if not, Simon was wasting valuable time when Elizabeth needed him here, helping to protect her name and her life.

Simon was miserable. His muscles ached from the unaccustomed position of horseback riding, and the mare he rode was as temperamental as any woman he had ever dealt with. Unhappy with second place, she continually nosed past Calkin's gray despite his best efforts to hold her back. His weak arm made him clumsy in dealing with her, which appeared to irritate her greatly. She was prone to biting, and he had to watch as he saddled or unsaddled her, for she could swing her head around and nip his ribs or his backside with amazing speed.

"Slap her nose," Calkin advised. "She needs to learn you are the master."

It seemed to Simon unwise to slap something as large as Bonnie, but he gave her a half-hearted blow the next time she tried to bite him. She turned her head forward again, but he sensed disrespect in her large brown eyes and knew the victory was only temporary. "I'm no horseman." Reminded of that subject, he told the story of his visit to the stables. The guardsman chuckled aloud when he recounted the disguise Hannah and Elizabeth had fashioned for him.

"A dandy! Those two will get you arrested yet."

"I had to pretend more courage than I felt," he confessed. "Not only in carrying off the role, but when faced with Beverley's horse. The beast is half-wild, with legs like tree trunks."

"A stallion. He likes the challenge of a restive horse."

"I for one would not take the chance of a mount so unpredictable."

Calkin thought for a moment. "His choice reveals his attitude toward life, I'd say. He is willing to take chances, even great ones, to appear to others the way he wants to appear."

"And to become what he dreams of becoming," Simon agreed. "However, if a man's mode of travel reveals his aspirations, I would as soon go afoot." He mounted clumsily, still stiff and wary of the horse's teeth besides. "Whatever Bonnie says about my status I would trade for the ground beneath my feet and a backside that does not throb each time she takes a step."

It was some time after Elizabeth announced they would go out before Hannah got up the courage to ask where they were going. "To pay a condolence call on Henrietta Beverley." A slightly raised brow betrayed excitement at the prospect.

When they arrived at a house situated in one of the more

fashionable neighborhoods, Elizabeth muttered, "No wonder he schemed shamelessly to get his hands on more money!"

The house was large and beautifully constructed, and lackeys rushed to assist the princess and usher her to the wide, columned entry. Inside were more servants and a large, open room with tasteful decoration in soothing colors. Hannah had a hard time imagining Charles Beverley in this house, or his sister either. Anything about the place that exhibited good taste had to have come with its rental. At least they had been wise enough to leave that purchased elegance in place.

Henrietta Beverley held a melodramatic pose at a window seat on the opposite side of the room. Beside her, a three-handled beaker sat on a small table, and the smell of fermented honey wafted toward them as they approached. The bereaved lady apparently intended to drown her sorrows with mead. She regarded Hannah for a moment with raised brow but had the good sense not to question the princess' choice of attendant. Instead, she said in a tone heavy with dolor, "Some refreshment, Your Grace? Our mead is very fine."

"I believe I will." A second beaker was brought and a portion served. Elizabeth pronounced it excellent, and Hannah thought she meant it, although it was early in the day for the princess to take so strong a drink. "I recall that you make the mead yourselves, at your estate."

"Yes, Your Grace. It pains me beyond saying that it was the means used to murder my poor brother. He always enjoyed it so much!" Here she broke down for some moments, sobbing into her sleeve. Hannah might have sympathized if her grief had been a bit more dignified, but Henrietta howled like a toddler with a skinned knee. Elizabeth was patient, however, patting her arm and murmuring comfort until she recovered.

When their hostess was more composed Elizabeth expressed formal condolences, choosing her words carefully to avoid overblown praise for a man she hardly knew, but conveying understanding of what his death meant to his sister. In answer, Henrietta began a self-pitying tirade that ran from the incompetence of the palace guard to a faint damnation of her brother for being so inconsiderate as to get himself killed and upset her plans.

Elizabeth made sounds of encouragement, letting the woman reveal her character, or lack thereof, in her own words. It soon became apparent that she fought with everyone she encountered, tried to run everything she was part of, and had probably made her brother's life a thousand times more difficult, since her ambition matched and perhaps overmatched his.

"I've told them at the palace that there must be a full investigation," she said, arching her back in unconscious reenactment. "And who will see to it, I asked them, since my brother himself was the one most qualified to take on such a task?" Gulping more mead, she went on. "And they will pay for his funeral, will they not? It should not be up to me, since he died in service to His Majesty." She put a plump hand over Elizabeth's, forgetting manners completely. "You will tell them, will you not? They will listen to you."

Hannah got an ironic glance, but Elizabeth replied, "I will see what can be done."

"Thank you, Your Grace. I am sure you have no idea how hard it has been for us. Charles had to maintain a certain standard, you know, but our resources are limited. And these London tradesmen are ruthless in their insistence on payment. They simply do not understand the concept of tomorrow, no matter how many times they are promised."

"What will you do now?"

"Return home, I suppose." She watched from under her lashes, apparently hoping the princess would insist London could not do without her. "Charles was dedicated to the king and moved here to be of use to His Majesty. Being a widower, he asked me to serve as hostess." Hannah guessed wild horses could not have kept Henrietta in the country when the prospect of a house in London appeared. "I have enjoyed my time here, but I must see to our affairs now that I am the last of the family." There was some satisfaction in her voice, although being in control at Beverley probably did not compare to the glamour of London's possibilities just a day ago.

"I am sure you will manage competently, despite personal tragedy," Elizabeth murmured. "Would you like to hold my little Minster? Hannah, bring the dog and then see if you can make yourself useful with the funeral preparations." Knowing what was expected, Hannah peeped into another room and found women braiding mourning armbands.

The change from one room to the next was drastic. While visitors saw a place attractive and genteel, this room was almost bare, the table battered and the chairs mismatched. Hannah understood: visitors saw the best of the house. The rest of it, where the servants and Henrietta herself lived and worked, had cheap furnishings and no warmth. Appearances were everything.

Hannah's offer of help was accepted, since the unexpected death of the master required the work of many hands. She soon proved her worth, twisting stiff black bands of ribbon expertly in a task she had performed many times. Sensing some hostility from the women, however, she said little. There were three of them: the two she had seen with Henrietta at Whitehall and a third, dwarfish and misshapen. Something in her eyes indicated wit, however, and perhaps even good humor. After a few moments, she broke her companions' disdainful silence.

"I am Joan. How long have you been in the princess' household?"

"My name is Hannah. I came to Whitehall less than a fortnight ago."

"You care for her dog?" The second woman's sneer made her even more unattractive.

Leaning back, Hannah looked into the main room, where Minster looked sadly in her direction, whining every few moments in distress at being abandoned to Henrietta's fawning clutches. "That seems to be my main duty."

"Can no one else care for the creature?" the third asked. "Odd to take a girl from nowhere."

It seemed that word had spread outside Whitehall about the princess' choice of an unknown serving maid. "Her Grace and I met many years ago. Lately we came in contact again, and she invited me to come to her, knowing how I love animals."

"Good for you," the tiny woman said, her tone separating her response from the others' snide observations. "Service far outshines making cloth at a workhouse or living outside the law."

The comment revealed that Joan, like Hannah herself, was an orphan, one of the "helpless poor" the government apprenticed in order to make them useful members of society. The "able-bodied poor," adults who could not be apprenticed, were sent to workhouses. "Rogues and vagabonds," those who chose not to work at all, faced branding on the tongue or even death if they did not mend their ways. Having in common similar backgrounds, Joan might speak freely to her if Hannah could find a way to get her alone.

When Elizabeth rose to leave, Hannah asked, "Do any of you know where I might buy some tea? I would like to present Her Grace with a small gift."

Joan seemed to read her mind, for she replied, "I can show you a place this afternoon, if you can find a free hour. It isn't far, and the prices are reasonable, even for folk like us."

The trail grew less and less certain as they headed northward, so narrow that they had to constantly duck branches that reached out to pull at their clothes and their hair. Simon was glad to discover that Calkin's talent for observation came to good use. He had an unerring sense of direction, for he noticed and interpreted things Simon would have missed completely: the track of a stream, the direction of birds in flight, the presence of specific plants in certain places.

They managed to find a farmer who had exchanged a few words with Beverley. "Headed for Derby he was. His mother's funeral." It was doubly satisfying: first, they were on the right track, and second, as Simon said as they left, "A man with nothing to hide doesn't lie."

"It may be something we haven't considered, though," Calkin pointed out. "He could have been on an errand for Northumberland, something requiring discretion."

"Would Northumberland trust him so much?"

Calkin shrugged. "The duke uses who he must to get things done." Brushing the hair from his eyes, he resettled his cap. "Beverley has a way of insinuating himself into the bosoms of the powerful. He collects information like a bee collects pollen and turns it into honey. I suspect the duke knows he can be counted on, whether to use his position with the guard to some advantage or to conduct some secret mission."

Simon had a new thought, one that Calkin would undoubtedly find uncomfortable. "You told me the guard is filled with lesser men these days. Are there those who might assist him?"

"I suppose there must be. Every group has members who may be threatened or tempted."

"Do you have any idea of who might be turned to his purposes?"

"They would not share their thoughts with me." Calkin's expression was stony, and he slapped away an insect that buzzed around his face.

Simon swatted the same bug farther on its way. "But a guardsman might have killed Amberson. They are almost unseen in the palace, so used are the inhabitants to their presence."

"Such a thing cannot be ruled out," Calkin replied. "We know Beverley lied about his purpose for this trip. He might have arranged things and left his confederate to do the deed."

"It makes sense. Guardsmen know the routines and would know when Amberson's room was empty." Simon's mind flew ahead. "And there was a guardsman with you when you discovered the body! He might have thrown the cup out the window, as Hannah says."

"No," Calkin said firmly. "That is not possible. The man with me, Daniel, never came into the room. As soon as I saw that His Lordship was dead, I sent him for more men. People were already rushing into the room, and I wanted to establish order. When he returned with others, I posted them in pairs outside the doors to both the bedchamber and the apartment itself, to assure that no one removed or disturbed anything. Daniel never set foot in Amberson's bedroom. I was there the whole time, and I can swear to it."

Simon was disappointed but not deterred. "It doesn't mean a guardsman didn't bring the poison in earlier. Someone else in the room disposed of the cup. Can you recall who was there?"

"I have tried," Calkin said, "but the room literally filled with the curious. They crowded in behind me and around the bed until Dudley ordered them all to leave." He made an effort. "Dudley and his son came early on, as I said before. Those two women from the duchess' household, the ones who giggle at everything, made pests of themselves, craning their necks and making odd noises. Seawell, of course, was there when I arrived. Members of the council, Russell and Talbot, for sure. I think Cecil came in as well." He stopped in frustration. "There were others, but I cannot say who. It was a muddle, as you can well imagine."

"At least we've got an idea. It's possible that Beverley used a guardsman, one he had some control over, to kill Amberson."

Calkin was less than enthusiastic. "I do not say that you are wrong, but it was a sad day for the guard, to have a man killed who should have been under our care. It only makes things worse to imagine that one of us might have been the murderer, thus doubly betraying the king's trust."

Henrietta Beverley's maid met Hannah outside Whitehall, where the day had turned gray as clouds gathered and humidity rose, threatening rain. Hannah learned immediately that Joan was both intuitive and direct. "You have some secret purpose," she announced. "I saw it, though the others were too busy being offended by your presence to consider your questions."

"True, I do not merely seek trinkets," she admitted. "If I could say more, I would."

Joan stopped and turned to her, brows raised. "So! You are a spy, then."

"Not a spy. One who wants to know who killed Lord Amberson and Charles Beverley."

"A noble effort." She moved on. "I cannot tell you why he died, or Lord Amberson. I know of no benefit in their deaths to anyone."

"Madeline seems to be the cause. Her father is killed, and then her guardian. Yet I understand she is a timid thing, not the sort to plot murder."

"Half-wit is what she is," Joan said emphatically. "If she is involved, she is but a pawn."

"The servant who died recently told someone she had a secret."

Joan looked up shrewdly. "You think she was pushed down those stairs."

"I have no evidence, but if I knew what her secret was, it would help. Could it have been that Lady Rochdale was involved with your master?"

Joan stopped dead on the street, causing a man behind her to swerve clumsily to avoid a collision. She barely noticed his irritated comment. "That pig? Not in a million years." Putting a hand over her mouth, she paused before continuing. "It's wrong to speak ill of the dead, I know, but Charles was no man for such as Ellen Rochdale. He had carnal relations with women as if it were breakfast or a haircut: on a schedule, at regular intervals, and with absolutely no passion."

"Your mistress seemed to suspect I was one of his women when I first met her."

"Oh, so that was you!" Joan chuckled at the thought. "Henrietta tries, um, tried, to make him give up his prostitutes. It was one of the ways she tried to avoid bankruptcy."

"What did your master say to her objections?"

"He had no time for her arguments. Once I heard him tell her, quite calmly, that he would take a wife when opportunity offered one, and in the meantime he would take for his pleasure such women as made the least amount of fuss."

A couple of passersby jostled them rudely, and they realized they were blocking the walkway. "So Henrietta feared I was one of the women her brother consorted with," Hannah said as they moved on.

"It must have been Tuesday when you met." She grinned at Hannah's questioning glance. "Charles was a man of routines, as I said. Every Tuesday, he hired a woman, and every Tuesday, Henrietta tried to prevent it. He argued that it kept a man's humors in balance to, um, relieve his tensions once a seven-night." She chuckled. "A man of lists and schedules was Master Beverley. Everything must be planned, every possibility accounted for." She glanced slyly at Hannah. "He did insist the

169

women be pretty. Though he had no real passion, he appreciated beautiful women."

Hannah suppressed a shudder at the thought. "Did others know of these assignations?"

"It wasn't common knowledge, but he would not kill to keep it a secret."

This news was disappointing. Hannah had theorized that Marie knew of an affair between the baroness and Beverley that might have offended Lord Amberson, but that seemed unlikely, listening to Joan. "What about your mistress? Has she behaved oddly in the last few days?"

Joan gave a whoop of laughter. "Difficult to define what is odd to our Henrietta." Realizing Hannah was serious, she hid her smile with one hand. "She could never kill anyone. She is a pot full of bluster and bother, but when all's done, she is harmless."

Hannah remained firm. "Was she at Whitehall the day His Lordship was poisoned?"

"She and I visited her brother's rooms that morning to see if he had returned from his trip," Joan answered readily enough. "She spoke with His Lordship, learned Charles was not yet back, and we went on our way."

"Was she alone at any time?"

Joan shook her head then reconsidered. "She answered the call of nature, but that is not unusual for her. She cannot go more than a few hours without visiting the commode. Although she would berate me for telling you, I prefer you know the truth rather than suspect her of murder. I say again, Henrietta is many things, but she is not capable of murder."

Hannah decided to retreat gracefully. "A good servant knows her mistress."

"But it is expected that we will keep silent." Joan fingered some lace displayed at an open stall. "I agree that this secret the baroness' maid spoke of might well pertain to the murder."

"I think she saw something that she later realized connected to the crime. She must have delayed, trying to decide whether to tell someone, and that brought about her death."

"Well, I'd stake my life it was not Henrietta, and Master Charles was up in Beverley. We know that because he returned with the mead your mistress shared earlier." So Beverley had indeed gone home. Simon would be disappointed to have gone so far for nothing.

"They seem quite proud of their mead."

"Truly, it is superior. Charles used it as gifts to impress those above him, but he liked it well himself, as does Henrietta.

Hannah had made note of that earlier. "How is it transported?"

"Usually by boat, of course, but on his return last week he brought a dozen leathern jacks with him." Hannah knew of the waxed leather bottles used by travelers to reduce weight and breakage. "He keeps good track of his stock, as he does with everything else." Joan stopped herself and corrected, "I mean, he did. It is odd to think of him gone."

"Now you will journey to Beverley."

Joan smiled. "It is no hardship to me, for I was born there and love its rocky fields and skinny sheep. All I regret of London is that we did not get the chance to become better friends."

"I feel the same." They parted then, Hannah thinking that she would never see Joan again. Even after only a day's acquaintance, it was a melancholy thought.

The threatened rain arrived just as she returned to the palace. To her dismay, she had to wait outside the entry as a litter blocked the way while the person inside made ready to exit. The fanfare required for the simple end of a journey intrigued Hannah. The litter-bearers set their burden down gently, and one of them took a small platform down from its storage place on the roof and set before the door. The other untied a small bundle at the back that turned out to be a waxed-leather canopy with poles on each corner. The two men stretched it between them, forming a shield from the rain, though not for themselves. When all was ready, one of them knocked deferentially to signal that they were prepared.

The woman who emerged was stunningly beautiful. She wore a cap that signified her married status, but the luxurious, red-gold mane beneath made it insignificant. Her simple costume draped cleverly, almost hiding her swelling belly. Every piece of clothing fit perfectly, and even the slippers that showed daintily as she stepped from the litter matched the overdress and were adorned with jewels of the same shade and shape as those on her bodice. The Baroness Rochdale: Simon's description had not done justice to her beauty.

The litter-bearers stood at attention, each one's face aglow with admiration.

She spoke softly to each of them, and in turn each blushed with pleasure. As Ellen Rochdale's gaze swept the courtyard, their eyes met. To Hannah's surprise, the baroness smiled self-deprecatingly, as if asking pardon for holding her up. The litter bearers moved with her to the castle entry. When she was inside, they rolled up the now damp canopy, replaced it and the platform, and took their lightened burden off.

Inside, the baroness halted to straighten skirts she had gathered to keep them from trailing on the wet cobblestones. Once again, Hannah had to stop inside the doorway, since the entry was too narrow to pass without offense. A man with a black armband tied to his sleeve had apparently seen the baroness enter as he came down the stairs, for he hurried over. "William, what has happened?"

With solemn expression, the man answered, his tone too low for Hannah to hear. She saw, however, that the baroness' spine stiffened. "You are certain?"

He spoke again, and Hannah caught the words, ". . . dead in his bedchamber."

"Poison?" She seemed genuinely shocked.

"The bottle he poured from was full of it." He excused himself with a bow, pleading an important errand. The baroness stood frozen, and Hannah wondered what she was feeling. Finally realizing Hannah waited behind her, she moved aside apologetically. "A second murder in the palace. It is a great shock."

"Yes, Your Grace," Hannah murmured as she sidled past. The baroness stood where she was, her expression conveying an emotion Hannah could not decipher.

"She seemed upset, but I can't say exactly how she took the news," Hannah told Elizabeth over a tapestry neither of them much cared for. At least the busywork gave her a chance to tell what she had seen.

"If she has been under some pressure from Beverley, it might be relief."

"And if she was involved with him, grief."

Elizabeth shook her head. "Nothing I can learn about Ellen links her to Beverley."

"If she's as kind-hearted as they say, any death might upset her. And certainly a second poisoning is ominous."

"Both victims were involved in government, which gives us poor females some peace of mind, I think."

Hannah thought of Marie, neither male nor involved in government, and silently disagreed, but she stayed on the current topic. "What is the baroness' husband like?"

"Andrew? Spends the majority of his time hunting stags and boars on his lands in the northwest." Elizabeth frowned, trying to recall what she knew of Rochdale. "The old baron was a heroic sort who received land in gratitude for some deed in defense of my father. His only son, Andrew, avoids the company of others, so no one seems to know him well. His father chose Ellen as wife for him two years ago. She comes from a poor family, but her beauty recommended her, and the old man hoped for fine grandchildren in his old age. They say it was a waste, for the baron hardly acknowledged his new wife, and the old man died soon afterward."

"Do you think the lady spends her time in London to avoid an unpleasant husband?"

Elizabeth stabbed her needle into the heavy fabric. "One can hardly blame her. She is quite shy, and men seem determined to make fools of themselves over her. For some time after she came, they spoke of nothing else. It is only her complete lack of response to social interaction that keeps her isolated here."

"She is lovely, even in her condition."

Elizabeth chuckled. "More graceful than most, despite her growing belly. I remember when Kat was pregnant. She walked leaning back, like a bear unaccustomed to standing upright."

"But the baroness is well-regarded despite her resistance to friendships."

"Perhaps because of it. She is the same with everyone, so one concludes it is her nature." Elizabeth bit the thread with her teeth. It looked for a moment as if she might say more about the baroness' character, but she did not.

"Still, her quarters were near Amberson's. She was there when the others were at dinner."

"Yes," Elizabeth said thoughtfully. "I've been thinking about that. If Charles Beverley somehow killed His Lordship, Ellen Rochdale might have seen something she should not. We can only hope that Beverley's partner, whoever he is, does not think her a danger, for we have seen how Beverley fared at his hands."

★　★　★　★　★

Hannah went to find Daniel that afternoon, feeling guilty that her purpose was not mere friendship. He was at his post, but he seemed frozen, face slack and eyes vacant. "Is something wrong?"

"Our captain was murdered. Did you not hear it?" He looked stricken, as if he could not fathom such a thing. Hannah paused to consider her response. It had not occurred to her that anyone in the guard would actually be sorry that Beverley was dead. Simon's report of Calkin and Hugh's opinions had colored her perceptions, but she realized now that Daniel saw things quite differently. He must have admired the man for some reason she did not understand.

"I was sorry to hear it. Was he a good man?"

"He was wondrous clever." Daniel struck a nearby post with a clenched fist. "He had such plans, and they would have been to the good of all."

So Beverley, not Northumberland, was the person Daniel had mentioned earlier, the man who knew what he wanted and made plans to get it. "How did he show his cleverness?"

Daniel's face changed, and she saw caution replace concern. "By doing well the things set for him to do." Something sparked his memory, and he glared at her, his sorrow for his captain forgotten for the moment. "You have a lover."

Hannah had feared Daniel's interest in her went beyond mere friendship, and she had dreaded having to admit that she could never be more than his friend. She kept her voice light. "Simon and I will marry when he completes his apprenticeship."

"He spies for Elizabeth. You befriended me only to learn what you could."

That was too near the truth to refute, and she hesitated. She could have sworn he had used her in the same way, but he would never admit it. Reluctant to lose contact, since his nosy nature made him a good source of information, she said, "Daniel, I do want to be your friend."

"What you want is naught to me." He kept his eyes averted. "I will do what I want now."

She sensed he was dealing with too much right now to think clearly. "I hope when we meet again you will think better of me," she said meekly, and went inside, leaving him glowering into the shrubbery.

"Your job will be to make us a fire," Calkin said as they chose a clearing in the wood in which to spend the night. "I will see if I can find meat for supper." He went off with a length of rope and, Simon thought, an exaggerated expectation. Still, he had never lived off the land, and Calkin had.

Simon built the requested fire, listening to the twigs pop and snap as they gave themselves up to the effort. He added fuel every few moments, until the flames were well established, then sat back to rest until Calkin returned. He stared unseeing for a while, lost in thoughts of murder and motive, but movement at the edge of his vision captured his attention, and he turned his head slightly to see what it was.

Not three feet away a spider had constructed a massive web between two trees and now waited patiently at one edge. Already the web was a success; a small insect struggled feebly in the sticky silk in a last, desperate attempt to save itself. The spider watched with no sign of impatience. When the victim finally went still, the web's creator moved in a businesslike manner to it, grasped it with two of its front legs, and carried it off. As Simon watched, fascinated by the scene, he noticed a second spider, a little larger than the first, waiting at the opposite side of the web. The first spider laid the insect before it, backing away in what seemed respect or even awe.

At that moment Calkin returned, carrying a rabbit he had

snared and killed. "Supper is on its way," he said cheerfully and knelt to begin the process of making game into meat. Simon pointed out the web, where both spiders had frozen due to the vibrations Calkin created. When he told what he had observed, Calkin grimaced in disgust. "Spiders! I hate the creeping things, though my father always said they do good work." He leaned in to examine the first spider. "That one is a male. He brought food to the other, a female, in hopes of mating with her and not being eaten afterward." He snickered. "It is ever the same with women, whatever the species." With a bloody hand, he reached out and swept away the spider web, crushing it into the ground and destroying both spiders. Wiping his hand on the damp grass, he returned to dinner preparation, leaving Simon to wonder at who kills whom, and why.

CHAPTER SEVENTEEN

Hannah loved visiting the kennels but disliked one section where a pair of mastiffs crouched in one of the more secure pens. The dogs were huge, bred and trained for fighting. When she passed, they lunged forward, apparently frantic to sink their jaws into her. The thick ropes that held them in seemed likely to break as they hurled their thick bodies at them, growling and snapping ferociously. She always breathed a little easier once she had moved on to the calmer dogs.

This morning her task was to choose a puppy as a gift for the Princess Mary, who would soon visit Whitehall. Elizabeth had decided on a lapdog, adding with a sniff, "It could benefit her to have something to love." Hannah sensed she thought her sister lacked some measure of humanity. Small wonder, declared bastard and ignored by her father for much of her life.

The puppies Hannah sought were housed at the end of a long, narrow row of pens, and when she reached them, she bent down outside the enclosure to watch their play. Spanielles, like Minster, blond and round with puppy fat, they squealed and yipped at each other, learning how to behave in dog society. One of the four, three times as lively as his siblings, ran around like a tiny tornado, nipping an ear or a tail, whichever presented itself. He would have been Hannah's choice, but she had to consider what the older Princess Mary might desire in an animal companion.

For a few moments, she lost herself in enjoyment of the puppies' play, ignoring noises behind her until a low growl caught her attention. She turned to see both mastiffs at her back, their heads low and their front feet set, ready to spring. How had they escaped their cage? There was no time to wonder, for two pairs of eyes focused on her. Hannah tried to remember what she knew of menacing dogs. Did one face them and stare them down, or turn and run? There *was* nowhere to run. The dogs blocked the exit; behind her were only more pens.

"Stay." The word came from her subconscious. She had heard the handlers use it to make the big dogs freeze despite quivering bodies that indicated they would rather not. It kept them in their pens when the handler went inside to feed them or do whatever else needed doing.

That was it! Pens kept dogs inside. Could the one behind her keep these dogs out? Rising slowly, she glanced sideways at the puppies' pen. It was lighter than the mastiffs' cage and only four feet high, that being sufficient for its occupants.

There was a moment of despair. She might jump into the spanielles' enclosure, but the mastiffs could clear the mesh fence just as easily, and then where would she be? Trapped inside with those gaping jaws and heavy, clawed feet.

It was better than nothing. With a repeated, "Stay!" and a loud cry for help, Hannah grabbed a supporting post and vaulted into the cage with the clamoring puppies. Her dress caught on the post, making a ripping sound and causing her to stumble until it tore free. At her entry the mother dog, who had been sleeping lightly in one corner, rose from her place and charged forward in defense of her brood. Her bark was higher and lighter than the growls of the mastiffs outside, but it testi-fied that she was not happy with the presence of strangers. Han-nah had to hope that the dog found her less of a threat than the mastiffs, and after a moment's hesitation, she did. Turning her stare to the two large beasts, the mother dog growled deep in her throat.

The pugnacious stance of another dog was enough to halt the mastiffs for a moment, but Hannah feared it would not stop them for long. She searched frantically for a weapon with which to defend herself. There was nothing. Calling again for help, she backed into the farthest corner, shamelessly allowing the puppies' mother to defend her. Each time one of the mastiffs tensed to spring she added to the little dog's threat with a repeated, "Stay!"

The dogs could not deal with their own confusion. On the one hand, they longed to attack Hannah; on the other, their training demanded they stay on command. In addition, another dog resented their proximity in noisy fashion. They hesitated, tiny brains trying to puzzle it out.

Suddenly a voice shouted, "Mars! Venus! Come!" and the dogs turned toward the sound in perfect synchronization. Two men stood a short distance away, one with a stout cudgel in hand. Both dogs whined in frustration, but their master repeated, "Come!" and their tense bodies slumped. This quarry would not be theirs. With a last look at Hannah, they wheeled and trotted obediently away. The spanielle, certain that she had accomplished the rescue, added a few more barks of disdain as the man guided the pair to their pen and fastened the gate.

Hannah fought back tears of relief as the second man approached. "Are you all right?"

"Yes." It was all she could manage.

"Hannah?" At the sound of her name, she looked up and actually saw who extended a hand to help her out of the puppy pen. His name did not immediately come to her still-scrambled mind. "It's me, Giles Fuller."

"Master Fuller." His strong hands felt reassuring, and she

was glad when he continued to hold hers as he led her away.

"I saw you crossing the yard and wanted a word. It is a good thing I followed, but I turned the wrong way at first. When I heard the commotion, I called for the dog boy."

"Yes." Dimly she knew her responses were tepid, but reaction to recent fears lingered.

The dog handler had secured his charges and now joined them. "I know I closed that gate. I can't say how they escaped, but I'm sorry."

"It was closed," Hannah managed. "I looked at it as I passed because the dogs were so anxious to attack me." She shivered violently in a delayed reaction.

Fuller watched her closely. "Do you mean that someone opened it after you passed?"

"I saw nothing until those beasts appeared behind me."

"You did well to delay them."

Hannah managed a smile. "I had help from Mother Spanielle, who informed my attackers that they would be unwelcome in her home."

Giles took over then, thanking the dog handler for his quick response and shepherding Hannah to the courtyard, where he set her on a sun-warmed wall. She recovered gradually, and he regarded her closely, judging when she was ready to consider what had happened.

"If someone set those dogs on you, it was a warning, or perhaps worse, an attempt on your life. You have been asking questions about certain matters at Whitehall, probably for the princess. I fear someone does not want you to do so."

She thought of the plant that had fallen so close to her. This was a second warning. Surprisingly, she reacted with anger, not fear. How dare this killer, whoever he was, try to silence her? She would be more careful, more watchful, but she would continue. The princess was threatened, and Simon was not here to help. She must do what she could.

The two travelers followed Beverley's course all day and found, in a small village called Leek, a church where he had spent the night. The gaunt, half-blind priest confirmed that the man they asked about had indeed traveled northwest. "He asked directions to Bury. In the morning he took a bowl of porridge and went on his way." He added, stabbing a finger skyward as if calling God's attention to his words, "Not even a coin in the alms bowl." Taking the hint, Simon contributed with a clink the old man could hear clearly, which brought a smile to his face.

The day was a study in frustration, for the road, such as it was, often branched in two, even three directions. They followed each until they found someone to ask about the passing nobleman, retreating when no one had seen him. Only too aware that a man might journey through the more desolate areas without being observed at all, they judged their chance for success slight. Still, Calkin's sense for tracking, the intuitive streak that took into account terrain and direction, brought a logical estimate of what Beverley would have done, given the choices he had.

Around noon, they heard hoof-beats on the trail ahead and looked up to see a rider coming at some speed. "Make way!" he called, and they reined their horses right, making room on the narrow track for him to pass. As he moved to his own right, however, the rider failed to see a low-hanging branch at the road's edge. It caught him directly across the chest and swept him from the horse's back like grain before a scythe. The horse ran on, but the rider landed on the road with a loud grunt of exhalation and lay gasping for air.

"Are you all right?" Simon asked, dismounting and hurrying to the prone figure. He was about fourteen, plainly dressed, clearly agitated, and out of wind. Seeing that he would recover,

Calkin turned and started after the horse, which disappeared around a curve.

"Why don't you watch where you're going?" the youth snarled as soon as he could speak.

"We tried to give way, but you came up fast."

"I must make all speed to London." Rising with painful slowness, he rubbed his landing area and groaned. His tone signaled he intended to blame them for his fall despite the evidence.

"My friend will catch your mount, and you will soon be on your way."

A second snarl conveyed that it was the least they could do. Calkin returned in moments. "The beast was grazing only a short way down the path and has decided to make no further trouble," he said cheerfully, possibly enjoying the surly young man's discomfort.

As the messenger rose and examined his clothes for tears, Simon asked, "May I ask what message is so vital for London?"

The youth wavered between a haughty refusal to divulge the information and an obvious desire to tell. "I suppose it is no secret. Baron Rochdale is dead."

Simon tried to recall what he knew of the man. He had a hunting lodge near here where he spent most of his time, spurning the company of his beautiful wife. "What happened?"

The messenger already seemed to regret telling the strangers his news. With a grumpy admonition that they watch for opposing traffic in the future, he mounted his horse once more and went on his way with no further explanation.

Simon stood looking after him for a while then said to Calkin, "I think a trip to Rochdale is worthwhile, do you agree?"

It was easy enough to follow the messenger's tracks, since it had rained the night before. In less than half an hour, they approached a house that seemed to Simon like something out of Mallory's tales of King Arthur. Built into a hillside, it had a projecting log roof and a façade of stone barely visible through the moss that grew up around it. In a cleared space at one side of the building's entry stood three people: a man, a pregnant woman, and a half-grown boy. On the ground before them, something was laid out on an oiled skin and covered with a coarse blanket. The man was digging a hole.

"Greetings, friends," Simon called out. "Can you say if we are on the path to Blackburn?"

They had not heard them coming and looked up in surprise. After a moment the woman said, "You are. It is a few miles on to the east."

Simon appeared to notice the corpse for the first time. "I'm sorry to see that you've had some misfortune."

"Aye, that we have," the man said, his tone revealing more than his words.

"Nothing good can come of it." The woman laid both hands on her belly as if protecting her unborn child.

The boy looked from his father to his mother nervously. "It's Sir Andrew," he volunteered. "Someone killed him."

Simon raised his brows. "In some quarrel?"

"It were brigands," the husband replied. "A miracle that we found him at all, but my boy here noticed the scavenger birds circling. He was wrapped in his own blanket and buried in a shallow grave, but eventually the beasts sniffed it out."

Simon was immediately suspicious. "Brigands. Are there many of those hereabout?"

The huntsman grimaced. "Not in some time. We patrol the roads and deal with them harshly. But it were brigands. We found a campsite where someone spent several days in wait."

"You're sure it is the baron's body?"

"Yes, although they stripped him. There was a scar from when we were boys together. I knew it well, for I was at fault, though he never said so." The man was genuinely grieved, but he tried to keep to facts. "They took his horse, too, or we would have known sooner. The beast would have found its way here if left to it."

"Did you not miss him and start a search?" Calkin asked.

"We did not know for certain he was coming. His other lands demand his time in the spring, though this place is—was his favorite."

"When do you suppose he died?"

"At least two weeks ago, judging his—the condition of the body." Simon bent and removed the covering from the corpse's head, holding his sleeve over his mouth to reduce the stench. The woman turned away with a whimper; her husband stared stoically at his former employer. Swallowing his distaste and using his kerchief as a glove, Simon felt the skull until he located a soft spot at the back. A crushing blow from some heavy object. A tree branch would have served.

"We've sent word to London, to the baroness," the man said. "Our eldest will find her. Then we shall know what to do."

"You know what will happen," the woman said, her voice rising. "They will turn us out."

He put an arm around her shoulders. "Hush, Cathy." Apparently unwilling to discuss the matter before strangers, he changed the subject. "If you can spare a moment, goodmen, I will be grateful for help in the burial." His face clouded. "It is best if we put him in the ground quickly."

"It's what he'd want, to be buried here," the woman said, "and you shall serve as witnesses." She seemed relieved to have objective observers as to the manner of their master's death. Blame might easily fall on them, and there was little they could do about it.

They dug a sizeable hole in the soft, dark earth. Simon's weak arm made it difficult for him to handle a shovel efficiently, but he insisted on taking his turn. The day had warmed, and they were all damp with sweat by the time they finished. Once the grave was deep enough, Calkin and the huntsman picked up the corners of the thick wool blanket that lay under the body. Andrew Rochdale had once been a large man with hands the size of dinner plates, but his corpse was both desiccated and incomplete. Two easily handled the weight of it, though the task was unpleasant.

When they had covered the grave, the huntsman, whose name was Peter, said a simple prayer. Afterward, he offered the only reward he could for their help. "It is cooler inside, and my wife has fresh bread and beer, if you will share it with us."

The house was dark but dry and comfortable, and the welcome smell of bread hung in the air, mitigating somewhat the horrors of smell, touch, and sight they had just experienced. As they moved into the hillside, the air indeed became cooler, which was also a relief. Taking places at a table with benches on either side, they blinked as their eyes adjusted to the dimness. The woman brought a bowl of water and they washed their hands, Calkin first, then Simon, and finally their host. "Blackburn is your destination, you say?" he asked, wiping his hands on his shirttail.

"Only briefly," Simon answered. "We are sent by a knight named Charles Beverley, who traveled north from London some days back. Perhaps you saw him?"

As he gave a brief description, the woman brought bread, sliced each man a thick slab, and smeared it with grease. Taking a bite, Peter said as he chewed, "I saw no such man. I hope he did not encounter the same fate as His Lordship."

"No, he returned safe to London but left some important papers somewhere along the way. He sent us to retrieve them, but it is difficult, since he does not recall his exact route."

"We think he was lost most of the time," Calkin put in with a wink.

"I see your difficulty." The wife set a pottle of beer on the table, and they drank by turns, the host again going last.

"We've been asking where he might have stayed here and there between Leicester and Blackburn," Simon said, passing the jar to Calkin.

"He would not have stopped here. His Lordship sought quiet and did not encourage others to visit. He would have stayed in this place permanently if he could, I trow."

"And his wife?"

"She came with him once, last fall, it were." He rubbed his sidewhiskers. "I think she wanted to see where he spent his time, but her presence made him uneasy. They were an odd pair."

Calkin asked, "Your master was angry with her?"

They both looked surprised. "No," the man said. "Not angry."

The woman tried to explain. "Shy, he was, and most comfortable here, with us he knew well. Having her here with her long silences made him twitchy-like." She summed it up in a tone of pride. "She was his wife, but we were his family."

"Not really family, o'course," Peter put in self-consciously. He finished his bread and wiped the crumbs from his beard and shirtfront. "But Cathy is right, here is where he wanted to be. The old baron never understood it." The huntsman stopped, probably reminding himself that he spoke to strangers.

"I hope you will be able to stay on here."

"It may be." The huntsman's wife forced a cheerful tone. "Her Ladyship spoke to me at some length just before they left. Her questions I think showed some liking for this place."

"What did she want to know?"

She clasped her hands under her swelling belly. "When my child will arrive and if I would have a woman to help me with the birth. I told her Peter has served well enough with the first two, and she should not worry." She leaned toward them, sharing the secret. "Then she said she hoped to have a child of her own soon. She said she would ask His Lordship to let her return here to have the child, to make me its nurse."

Peter said eagerly, "You see? We may yet have a place and not be turned out." It was clearly a topic much on their minds. Their home, their livelihood, and their place in society all depended on a hunting lodge that served no hunter now that Andrew Rochdale was dead.

Something Elizabeth had told him brought Simon's next question. "Why did the baron send his wife to London? Is there no physician nearby competent to birth a child?"

Peter looked confused. "I cannot say. It does not sound like something he would do, but I suppose he wanted reassurance, since he is the last of his line." Embarrassed, he continued, "To say sooth, I think he had no hope of an heir, but things change, and Man cannot understand the ways of Heaven." He glanced at his wife's rounded belly and grinned. "Nor the wiles of women."

Simon rose to go, and Calkin followed suit, pushing the bench under the table with a scrape. "I pray that things go well for you all." Thanking their host and hostess, they left the lodge. Peter walked with them for a while to be sociable, so they had to travel some distance out of their way to give the impression that they were truly bound for Blackburn.

CHAPTER EIGHTEEN

"Andrew Rochdale is dead," Kat reported to Elizabeth. "His body was found near his lodge."

"A hunting accident?"

"More likely brigands. He was struck with something and his possessions taken."

"How terrible!"

Kat shivered. "Death comes in threes, but now there have been four, two of them purposeful." Hannah, sitting quietly nearby, saw in Elizabeth's face the same thought she had. They believed three were "purposeful" deaths. And what of the fourth?

Elizabeth was silent for some time, and Hannah suspected she was building a theory. As soon as Kat went off to do some household task, she mouthed the word "Window," which after a moment Hannah realized meant she was to find something to look at outside. Obediently she wandered to the window and leaned on the casement, staring out over the rooftops.

Soon the princess said behind her, "Are you looking for your lover, Hannah?" She joined her, apparently idly, but side by side at the window, they could speak without being overheard.

"I think Beverley killed Rochdale."

"What?" Remembering discretion, Hannah quieted her voice.

"He wanted the man's wife, though it is clear she did not want him."

Hannah chewed gently on her lower lip. "She reacted to news of Beverley's death."

"Relief. He pursued her; she was glad to be rid of him, even by such a terrible method."

He pursued her. Hannah's mind grabbed at the phrase. What would Charles Beverley have done to get a chance at the beautiful Ellen? They knew he was ambitious for wealth and prestige. Hugh suspected he had married and killed two women. Such a man might well have planned two additional murders to advance his goals.

Elizabeth thought along the same lines. "He needed money. He wanted a chance at a seat on the council. Simon thinks he lied about where he went. What if he went to Rochdale and killed the baron while his confederate arranged Amberson's death here? He would have gained control of a fortune without becoming a suspect. And on his secret journey, he laid the way to another fortune."

"But why would the baroness marry Beverley?"

"He must have had some means of forcing her." Elizabeth watched the movement below them, which from here was picturesque, removed from the smells and press of bodies. Hannah shivered despite the sun that warmed the window. Beverley had indeed been a long-range planner, as Daniel said. Like a demonic chess master, he had moved players into certain positions until their next move was inevitable. How had he captured the baroness?

They needed to learn what had passed between Beverley and Lady Rochdale. No one they questioned had even seen them speak to each other, so any contact they had was secret. She had tried twice more to speak with Daniel, suspecting that as Beverley's loyal admirer he might have been the go-between, but he was adamantly unfriendly. Sorry that he was hurt but too busy to fret about it, Hannah kept her expression pleasant and let him glower past her.

With more hard riding, Simon and Calkin made the trek east to Beverley the next morning. The place proved depressing, obviously neglected while the owner spent every cent he could garner on making the proper impression in London. The workers in the fields looked put-upon and listless; the reeve was curt to the point of rudeness.

"He were here a fortnight back," he told them, hardly opening his mouth to speak. "Left me my orders and went off again." He spat noisily and added, "Like to kill that horse, he is."

"Why did he not change horses while he was here?"

The man eyed them, one scornful brow raised. "Because there's just the one, maybe?" He glanced at a nearby worker with a grim smile at the newcomers' ingenuousness.

"There is a second now," the man offered before the overseer gave him a glare of warning.

"Beverley had a second horse when he arrived here?"

The reeve chewed on a green stalk of hay for some seconds before replying. "It weren't a horse for use, you see. It belongs to a friend, and we're keeping the beast till he comes for it."

Simon glanced at Calkin. The reeve was as crooked as his master. Knowing they would learn nothing more in this place, they took their leave.

"Where did he get a horse?" Calkin wondered as they rode south, toward London.

"Rochdale's horse is missing."

"But we found no sign that Beverley went to Rochdale. It was miles out of his way."

"Peter said they found a campsite where a man spent several days."

"Waiting."

"Yes. He could not have known exactly when the baron would arrive. He had to wait."

"To kill Rochdale? Why?"

"To make his wife a widow. Beverley has set his mind on having Ellen Rochdale. Amberson's wealth will help him, but he wants more. He wants the baroness."

"But her husband's death doesn't guarantee he can have her. And marriage won't assure him the baron's title. It doesn't work that way."

"It works the way Northumberland wants it to, these days. If Beverley controls a fortune, marries a rich woman, and makes himself indispensable, there is no telling how high he may rise."

"I saw them, and it was plain she despises him. She might as well have slapped his face."

"I doubt a woman's reluctance would deter him." Ducking a low-hanging branch, he grabbed his cap as a twig caught it. "Beverley has a plan, and the baroness is part of it. It makes my skin crawl to speculate on how he plans to get what he wants from her."

Around noon, the travelers passed a crossroad with a large rock on which was painted, "Fuller" with an arrow pointing west. "Now there's a name you mentioned to me," Calkin said. "Giles Fuller comes from that place."

"So near Beverley's lands?"

"Their lands share a border, though the road goes its own way."

"How do you know this country?" Simon asked. "Are you not London born and bred?"

"I am, but as a youth I spent summers with an uncle. He had need of an extra hand around the property, and my parents had need of one less mouth to feed. I learned to be at home both in the city and the country." He surveyed the tree line. "It was not but twenty miles or so from here."

"Did you know the Fullers?"

"Only the name. I first met them when they descended upon London in search of a wife for young Giles."

Simon considered. He wanted to get back to London, to assure himself that Hannah was safe, but there might be something to be learned here. "Do you think a visit worth our time?"

"You're thinking Beverley pulled Giles into some partnership of murder?"

"Or Giles' mother, who is most anxious for a match between her son and Madeline."

"It is late." Calkin surveyed the darkening sky then nodded in the direction the sign pointed. "Maybe they have a spare pallet or two. Nice to sleep in a bed, don't you think?"

Fuller Town was not much of a town, though there was some evidence it had once been. There was a fairground, but the structures that lined its edges were rundown, many abandoned. The few shops left seemed resigned to minimal business and lack of upkeep. The manor house that served as home to the Fullers was modestly sized and unchanged in at least a century. There was, however, activity outside the house as several men herded the sheep in for the night. Simon approached a man of about forty who appeared to be in charge. "Is this the Fullers' holding?"

"Aye. I am Lionel Fuller."

"An honor, sir. We are travelers from London, Thomas and Clarence. If you have a spare crust of bread, we will in exchange give news of that city and its events."

Fuller gave a muted snort of objection. "Nothing in that place interests me, but you are welcome at our fire. We've heard each other's stories so oft we could recite them from memory."

The evening meal was plain; the company genial. In spite of his earlier protest, their host eventually asked about matters at

Court. "My wife fancies herself an addition to the king's companions," he confessed. "I tried to dissuade her, since we have no extra money for frippery and frolic, but she would go, and take my only son, too."

"London is a place where a young man may make his future bright."

Fuller scowled. "That is what she says. She took Giles there to seek a match when he should be here, learning how this place works. It's hard enough to make a living with prices so high, and he has to run off and play the courtier!" It was hard to say who angered the man more, his scheming wife or his idle son.

"Have you some hope that they will succeed?" Calkin asked, his face innocently curious.

"None!" He slammed a fist on the table, rattling the serving dishes. "We have nothing to offer a rich man like Amberson, who has title, lands, and position. She says our Giles will win the girl with his looks. That may be so, but it is the father who will have say."

"Have you not heard? Lord Amberson is dead."

Fuller turned wide eyes on Simon. "Dead? How so?"

"Poisoned, they say, though no one has been arrested."

He took a moment to absorb it, finally muttering, almost to himself, "Then perhaps they will come home and forget this foolish errand." Simon guessed that Fuller's wife had sent no word of Amberson's death lest her husband demand just that. "I told her from the start we should stay where we belong, here on this land that gives us all that we need."

All that we need. Simon thought that Lady Fuller might disagree with her husband. Need was a matter of definition. Did she "need" a brilliant marriage for her son so much that she had collaborated with Beverley, providing a helpful, murdering hand? Had he promised the girl to Giles, then gone north to accomplish his own end, Ellen Rochdale's widowhood? As things now stood, both Beverley and Lady Fuller had a clearer path to the marriage each one sought.

Her Grace the Princess Mary arrived at Whitehall with a small crowd of servants, friends, and hangers-on. Elizabeth went down to meet her, kissing her sister's cool cheeks dutifully and expressing joy at her robust health. Unspoken between them was the fact that their brother's health was just the opposite. Which of them would succeed him, or would they both be denied the throne? For either, the other's ascension meant danger, for who could be trusted to accept second place meekly? For now, they carefully kept the appearance of amity, two loyal subjects of His Majesty, Edward VI.

Hannah watched from a distance, judging the much older Mary vapid and spinsterish. Listening to the stilted speech in which she accepted, with veiled reluctance, the squirming puppy, she tried to decide what sort of queen the older princess would be. Catholic, of course, but how much religious freedom would she allow her people? Could she manage finances? The military? Foreign princes? The strong-minded men of her own government? Observing the prim face, Hannah doubted it. Could they not see that only Elizabeth was strong enough to lead, dedicated to the work her father had begun, a Tudor to her very core?

Once they returned to their rooms, Elizabeth suggested they take Minster for a walk in the gardens. Kat rolled her eyes and muttered about whispered secrets. "Tell me what happened at the dog kennels," the princess ordered, as soon as they were away, and Hannah grimaced. She might have known Elizabeth would find out; there was little about her household that she did not know. When Hannah finished the story she asked, "You are unharmed?"

"Yes, Your Highness, though I admit I was frightened. I agree with Giles Fuller, though. Someone released those dogs."

"Perhaps Giles himself."

"What?"

"Twice now he has appeared at your side out of nowhere. The first time he probably wondered if you had found green glass. This time he may have arranged the warning he so plainly pointed out to you."

She considered Giles' open smile, teasing manner, and apparently idle existence. Could sinister traits lurk beneath a pleasant demeanor? And how had he known her name?

Elizabeth had followed her own line of thought. "We must do something to protect you."

Hannah smiled. "I appreciate the thought, Your Grace, but what can be done? We have no real evidence. A fallen pot, a careless dog boy. That is how things appear. With two murders to investigate, who will guard your newest serving maid?"

"Then we must assure that you are not alone at any time. You will remain with me."

"How will I speak with the other servants and learn what we need to know?" She was aware that she was dangerously close to arguing with a royal princess.

"We must find a way, now that your questions have been noted."

"If I am in danger, you are, as well. Whoever sought to harm me must know I pass information on to you."

"Yes, we must both be vigilant, but I am used to cautious living."

Hannah knew exactly what she meant. Everything the princess did was scrutinized by her enemies, every word carried off and analyzed. After some notable mistakes, she had learned to give away nothing, to guard herself even with those she trusted. From the age of three, when her own mother died on the block, she had known that life was fleeting. Once Henry's darling, Anne Boleyn died at his command, an inconvenient wife. In a similar way, an inconvenient princess might be disposed of so that those who controlled the throne had one less worry.

CHAPTER NINETEEN

Simon and Calkin rode even harder than before on the last segment of their journey home. Both were anxious to see the gates of London, Calkin to return to his work and Simon to see Hannah again. Her image came to him in his dreams, patient, good-natured, but hopeful for the day when they could marry. It was hard on a man to wait, and he sensed it was hard for a woman as well.

He also looked forward to sharing what he had learned with Elizabeth. Although he had little to prove his suspicions, Charles Beverley had indeed gone to a place he had not admitted. During that time, someone had killed Andrew Rochdale. "It was murder," Simon muttered. "But what do we do about it?"

Calkin leaned forward, easing his muscles. "The princess must take it to Northumberland. He has both the power and the diplomatic skills to deal with Beverley." He paused. "She will be careful, will she not? She might be taking her life in her hands, accusing one like him of murder."

"She is most cautious, having learned some hard lessons, I think," Simon replied. "And I will tell what I learned on this trip, so they will know that Beverley lied."

"The horse is solid evidence," Calkin observed. "And Beverley's men will tell the truth when the Lord Protector asks the questions."

But their plan disappeared like smoke as they rode into London. Nailed to a post they found one of the dreadful publications rampant in London that purported to give news but more often slanted toward scandal. "Another poisoning at the king's palace!" it announced. "Beverley dead!"

"How can this be?" Simon asked. He took down the sheet and read it, but it was almost useless, recounting only one fact: that the knight died of poison three days earlier. The writer attached to that speculation of the wildest sort. Three people were suspects: Princess Mary, Northumberland, and Elizabeth. The writer hinted that the latter, a known wanton, had carried on an affair with the man and killed him in jealous spite when he turned his affections to another.

Simon wondered how they tolerated it. Lies regularly circulated about the nobility and royal family, printed in news sheets or whispered in alehouses. Some, all too willingly, believed without examination whatever they heard. The slandered had few ways to combat such stories, since it was hardly worth the effort to hunt down those who invented or inflated them. Every word, every action, was fodder for scandal, and there was always someone willing to report, usually with outrageous twists, what Elizabeth, or any of the Tudors, did. It was enough to drive a person mad, at least to one unused to living that way.

The collapse of his theory made Simon unsure what to do next. Accompanying Calkin to the palace, he waited outside while his friend learned what he could. "It is a cipher," he reported. "There were guards in the corridor. No one entered his chamber, so no one could have done it."

"Yet it was done."

"The poison was in his mead, and it was potent stuff. He had not been in his room for more than an hour when the guards heard a crash. When they entered, he was already dead."

"We knew there was someone else in all this, and now that person has killed Beverley. If we do not discover who it is, they will say that the princess herself conspired with him."

Calkin rubbed the beard that had sprouted over their time away. "You said Hugh suspected murder some years back. Might he know who Beverley would have conspired with?"

"I will find out," Simon answered. Hugh might be more willing to talk now that the man responsible for his misfortunes was no longer a threat.

After he had asked three people on Pembroke's estate and been misdirected twice, Simon found his friend seated on a low wall that ran perhaps twenty feet between two structures, the stable and a storage bin of some sort. The sunlight provided assistance as he squinted to see the holes he was punching into a leather harness with a sharp awl.

"Simon!" He rose briefly and took his hand. "What brings you here?"

"A man we spoke of earlier has been murdered." Simon did not offer the news sheet, knowing his friend did not read.

"I heard it. Beverley is dead, poisoned."

"Just as Lord Amberson was." Simon sat on the wall, shifted to ease his saddle-sore rump, and briefly explained his recent trip. "Calkin and I thought him guilty in Amberson's death."

"So this may be revenge?"

"Amberson had only two children. The daughter is no candidate for murderess, as far as I can tell." He recounted his visit to the earl's rooms as a tailor's apprentice, and Hugh chuckled.

"You still enjoy the art of disguise, I see."

"It is often useful to take on a different role. We thought Beverley might have killed His Lordship to advance his own cause."

"That sounds like something he would do, but would he take the chance without some certainty of success?"

"Calkin says Amberson was losing his ability to reason. If his deterioration was noted, the authorities might have examined his affairs, even disregarded his will."

"Beverley would not want that. No doubt they would find he was stealing the old man blind."

"You said his first two wives died under suspicious circumstances."

Hugh sighed. "I know nothing that can be proven. The first wife was, by an account I heard from a man who knew her well, a harpy straight from Hell. Beverley's father arranged the marriage to regain some of their wealth, and the son was more than agreeable. After a month or so of her temper and screeching, however, he stayed away more and more. She took to following him from place to place, making his life miserable with her scenes. At first, he was furious. Then he seemed to settle down and try to be the husband she demanded. Shortly afterward she became ill, showing the symptoms I told you before, and over the course of a month, weakened and died."

"You think he reconciled with her so he could poison her."

"At the time, no one thought that. They were in the north, and we heard only that she was taken with illness and died."

"But at the death of a second wife, you became suspicious."

"I did, but no one listened to me." Hugh stood and stretched brawny arms above his head with a sigh of released shoulder tension and the crack of shifting vertebrae. "You see, I knew the second Lady Beverley, who deserved neither the marriage nor the death she got."

"How did you know her?"

"Millicent Trowton was ten when I first met her. Her father came to the attention of the old king and received some honor for improvements in farming techniques, of all things. He was given a permanent position, and almost through no fault of his own, became rich."

Simon knew of others whose fortunes came through such service to the crown. "That is how he met Beverley."

"Yes. He ran through his first wife's money within a short time and was on the lookout for a likely bride. Poor Peter Trowton was thrilled when Beverley offered for his daughter's hand. Even Millicent thought it a stroke of luck."

"You liked her."

Hugh waved a hand to banish thoughts of a relationship. "She was a simple girl, without airs or self-importance. She sometimes brought us cakes she'd made or fruit she'd picked, saying we deserved a reward for devotion to duty."

"As you did," Simon commented, recalling Hugh's dedication to the guard.

"A genuinely kind soul. When she married Beverley, however, all that stopped. She was discouraged from even greeting us. I watched her become sad and stiff-faced, fearful of her husband's displeasure or the rasping tongue of that hideous sister of his."

"And then she died."

"Quite suddenly. They said she miscarried a child and it killed her."

"But you didn't believe it."

Hugh wiped the sweat from his forehead with a sleeve. "A woman came forward, a healer the servants called in when Millicent took sick. Shortly after she arrived, Beverley returned home and ordered her out, insisting his wife had no need of witchcraft. Millicent died later that day, and her husband was once again rich and free to do as he liked."

Simon was appalled. "He didn't want her saved."

"That's what the medicine woman thought. She went to a local constable with her story, and he sent her to me. I did what I could, which amounted to nothing."

"And soon after, you were dismissed from the guard."

"Yes."

"And the healer?"

"I never saw her again. She said she would return, but if she did, it was after I was gone."

"You never searched her out?"

"I knew no more than that her name was Martha." Hugh cleared his throat and added gruffly, "What could she have offered to counter the power of a man like Beverley? He was a master at manipulation." Simon discerned that Hugh had been through this rationalization before, to soothe a sense that he had failed to achieve justice. "I had objected, man-to-man, that his penny-pinching weakened the guard and put the king in danger. When I questioned his wife's death he took my objections and twisted them, making me seem a disloyal troublemaker."

"They lost the best petty captain the guard ever had."

"I thank you for your confidence," Hugh said with a rueful grin, "but I don't think they want the best these days. Just the quietest and the most obedient."

Simon stopped at Whitehall to report what Hugh had told him. Calkin whistled softly. "Hugh had a witness who would attest that Beverley killed his second wife?"

"He believes it is what turned Beverley against him."

"He never told me."

"He could gain nothing by telling you and could have caused your dismissal as well."

Calkin scratched his head vigorously. "Who killed Beverley, then?"

"Might the baroness have done it in revenge for her husband's murder?"

"No one here knew Rochdale was dead until after Beverley was poisoned."

Simon dropped his head in disappointment. "True."

"Besides, Beverley, perhaps more aware of how easily poison is administered than most, had posted guards. They attest to the fact that no one went into his rooms, with or without him, that whole day. Nor was anything delivered to him. The room contained only what he himself brought there. The mead was in a jack like those he kept for gifts and his own use. Somehow, poison was added, though the stuff was untainted the day before."

Simon paced a few steps. "What are the other possibilities?"

"The sister often disagreed with him," Calkin suggested. "Heaven knows she came and went in the palace as much as she was allowed, claiming to be helping her brother. The guards might not have thought a visit from her worth mentioning."

"But with him dead, she loses everything here in London. According to the princess and Hannah, Beverley is not a place one such as she would voluntarily retreat to."

Recalling their stop at the dreary estate, Calkin nodded. "What about the Fullers? If they were in league with Beverley, they might have killed him."

"But if they were plotting with him, it was to gain Madeline for Giles, and that has not been accomplished. Again, they would have killed the golden goose."

Calkin clicked a thumbnail against his teeth, a habit he had when deep in thought. "Lukas Seawell might have killed Beverley, whether he was his confederate in Amberson's death or not."

"That's a possibility, I'm afraid." Simon liked Seawell, or at least he admired him. He did not want to believe the man a hypocrite, preaching Christianity while he plotted murder. "I will speak with him again."

As Simon took his leave, Calkin said, "I hope Hannah is recovered from her fright."

His questioning look brought an explanation of the incident with the mastiffs. "The dog boy insists the gate was secure," he finished. "Hannah herself said it was fastened when she passed.

Someone let the dogs out, hoping they would attack her."

Simon groaned. "When the princess asked us to look into Lord Amberson's death, I wanted to help. I never thought that it would lead Hannah into danger."

"Well, the good of it is she is warned now. We must see that she is never alone."

"I would like to see her back at Hampstead," Simon muttered, "safe from all but damp."

CHAPTER TWENTY

Simon found Lukas Seawell at the church where it seemed he spent a good deal of his time. With him were four men Simon had not seen earlier, their behavior and dress just different enough to suggest that they were not part of the usual group. As Simon approached, he heard one of them speak in a heavy accent. German, he thought.

"Goodman Seawell, I am here about Charles Beverley."

Nodding to his companions to continue without him, Seawell led Simon to a far corner of the room. "What does that hound of Hell want of me now?"

Simon's brows rose. "You have not heard that he is dead?"

For a moment, he stared as if Simon had spoken in another language. "Beverley is dead?"

"Yes."

"May God have mercy on his soul." Simon sensed that Seawell's plea was all the more heartfelt because the subject did not deserve it. "I must go to my sister."

"May I walk with you for a way?"

Seawell retrieved his hat from a peg on the wall by the door and they went outside, joining the crowds on the busy street. As they threaded their way, often stepping sideways to get through the press of people, Seawell said to Simon, "You seem much entangled in this affair. I suspect you have spoken to those associated with me under one pretense or another."

Holding his hat on as they passed a trio of brash youths who seemed to feel they owned the pathway, Simon answered, "I seek justice, as I'm sure you would in my place. As I told you, my master was called in to attest to the manner of your father's death."

"I remember."

"And now Beverley has been poisoned as well."

He stopped and turned toward Simon. "And you think me capable of murder?"

Simon took the wall, stepping close to the building to let traffic pass. Doing so kept him from being pushed around by passersby, although his shoes would almost certainly be soiled from the slops thrown from balconies above. "A man might be tempted if he thought another murdered his father and planned to steal his sister's inheritance."

Seawell sighed. "My faith teaches that this wicked world offers no justice. God will deal with Beverley. In fact, He already has. Remember Christ's words to the thief: 'This day you shall be with me in Paradise.' While I doubt he is in Paradise, I believe his judgment was immediate."

"Will you petition now for guardianship of your sister?"

Seawell smiled thinly. "Madeline hardly knows me. She would be unhappy with the sort of life I lead. Besides, I would not be considered a suitable guide for her." Seeing an opening in the crowd, he started on his way again, and Simon hurried to keep up with his long and determined stride. "Because of my beliefs, I expect someday to be jailed, perhaps killed. Like Peter and Paul, I glory in the prospect, for if I were silent the very stones would cry out against me. But I would not expose my sister to that."

Again, Simon felt respect for Lukas Seawell. Fanatic or not, he was a man of principle, one who had considered his faith and arrived at his own conclusions. Whatever others said or did, he knew what he stood for. At least that was how he appeared.

Outward appearances were often deceiving, and he had to remember that.

As a result of his admonitions to himself, he parted from Seawell and returned to the house where he rented rooms. Since the man was on his way to see Madeline, this would be a good time to interview people about his activities over the last few days.

The landlady was no more talkative than before, and Simon soon gave up trying to get more than a word or two from her. In the sunlight at the front of the house, however, he found one of the other lodgers, a garrulous sort who was peeling the bark from a green branch. "Lukas is an odd one, he is," he said when asked if he knew Seawell. "We make some sport of him, you know, for the days he spends at church and all the reading he does of tracts and letters and the like. He is never quarrelsome, though, and one must admire him for that."

"He seems to me a good man," Simon said truthfully.

The stick's under-layer appeared, stroke by stroke, as the knife made soft sounds of friction against the back. "He is that. Has no need for money or fine clothes, neither—gives what's left once rent and board is paid to the poor. Odd, as I say, but a man respects them that practice what they preach." He chuckled to himself. "But he do preach, young man. He do preach!"

"Have you seen anything in the last few days that is different from his usual behavior?"

"Of course I have, young sir. Why, he has no less than four foreigners staying with him, has for a seven-night or so. They don't speak a word of our language." He sniffed slightingly. "And they don't know what decent food is, either. The place smells something awful. He says it's a cheese of some kind, but you never smelt anything like it."

"These men have been here for some days?"

"Missionaries, he says they are. Come to teach his group

their foreign ways."

Simon left the man to his fast-fading sunny spot and made his way toward Whitehall. He had a lot to tell Hannah, and a lot to mull over as well. Could he convince her to leave the palace? He had miscalculated the danger, but now he knew better.

Hannah waited at the outer gate. "Her Highness will join us. We have much to discuss."

His heart sank. He could not argue that Hannah should invent an excuse and leave Whitehall with Elizabeth present. "We must talk first."

"Well, be quick. She said she would be in the garden as soon as she could politely take her leave from some entertainment. She hates to be kept waiting."

"I know about the dogs."

Hannah stopped for a moment, thought about denying it, he guessed, then touched his cheek lightly. "It was nothing, Simon."

"You might have been seriously hurt, and it was no accident."

A careless gesture dismissed his fears. "We are more vigilant now, and the princess has forbidden me to venture out alone." She chuckled. "One advantage to royalty is that odd requests must be obeyed. She simply told the palace guard I must have an escort whenever I request it."

"You must listen to reason." His voice was heavier than intended, and her tone changed.

"I can reason on my own, Simon Maldon. I don't need someone to do it for me."

After that, persuasion was hopeless. Hannah refuted or dismissed all his arguments. She would stay in Elizabeth's household. When he finally gave up, he had gone too far. Her pretty face was set in an expression he had never seen before: anger. At him. With heavy heart, he followed her to the meeting place, noting her stiff spine and taut shoulders.

Elizabeth stood in a charming archway of flowers, the pale

petals like tiny lights in the growing darkness. She tried to appear idle but peered at them impatiently, obviously interested in hearing Simon's news. Hannah moved past her, taking Minster from her and settling him in her arms in an ungentle manner, causing the dog to squirm and Elizabeth to look to Simon questioningly. He tried to remain expressionless but was doubly miserable: Hannah was in danger and resentful of his concern. What was a man to do when a woman behaved irrationally? He would ask his father, since his mother was prone to such behavior.

"Walk with me," Elizabeth ordered, and they set off through gardens redolent with lily-of-the-valley. Simon told the story of his journey, ending with, "I returned to find the principal suspect murdered. We are no farther along than when we first began."

"We know more about those involved," Elizabeth corrected. "Knowledge is always worthwhile." They walked in silence for a while, cataloging and assimilating information separately before fitting it together. Hannah hung back, saying nothing and clutching the dog tightly as he whined to get down and run through the grass.

"Beverley probably murdered two wives," Simon said after some moments. "That may have led someone related to one of them to kill him."

"But that has nothing to do with Amberson," Elizabeth replied. "Are we to believe someone waited years to take revenge?" She sat down on a bench, and Hannah moved to stand beside her, avoiding Simon's eye. As the princess ruminated on murder, he felt Hannah's displeasure. What did she want from him?

Trust. It was almost as if she whispered it in his ear. What he and Elizabeth shared, what made them friends though their stations were widely separate, was trust. Elizabeth believed she could trust him with her life, and he believed the same of her. But Hannah! It was not a question of trust, he argued. He wanted her protected, removed from harm's way because he loved her so much.

Now it was the princess' spirit that whispered into his ear. *You treat her as a possession, not an equal.* He had had at times heard Elizabeth rail against being female and therefore assumed to have no intelligence. He understood her objection. Could Hannah feel the same way?

Like Elizabeth, Hannah had a good mind, could see the consequences of her actions, and deserved his trust. He had to let her do as she felt she must, had to view her as his equal, as he did the princess. Odd that it was easier with a friend than with the woman he loved.

"Tell me again what we know," Elizabeth was saying. "I must hear it spoken."

He dragged his mind back to the topic of murder. "Four dead, possibly murdered. I believe money was the motive in Amberson's case. Marie's knowledge of some part of it probably led to her death." He paused before adding the newest conclusion. "Baron Rochdale may have been killed to clear Beverley's path to his widow."

"Then who killed Beverley?" Hannah asked.

"If the motive was revenge," Elizabeth said, "then Seawell is the most likely suspect."

Simon raised a dismissive hand. "I do not believe him a murderer."

Elizabeth raised an eyebrow. "Are you such a great judge of men that you can tell a killer from the rest of us?"

He grinned, glad to react to teasing instead of Hannah's cool stare. "I am no judge of men at all, Highness." He turned his eyes to his future bride. "And I am a poor judge of women as well. I do realize of late that I should trust a person to make his—or her—own choices in life. That is the wisest I suppose I will ever be."

Elizabeth's brows met as she puzzled that out, but behind her, the line between Hannah's brows relaxed. She had received the message. Simon relaxed a little, too, as he went on. "Aside from my judgment, the fact is that Lukas Seawell is currently part of some exchange between churches and has as his guests four German reformers."

"So it would be difficult to creep off to do murder, especially in a guarded hall of the palace." Elizabeth took Minster from Hannah, set him down, and watched him scurry into some bushes with obvious intent. "Besides, his presence in the dog pens would have been noted. He could not have set—" She stopped, fearing she had betrayed Hannah's secret.

"I know about the dogs." He tried to keep his tone even.

She did not ask how. "Giles Fuller was there when it happened." She reached out a hand to Minster, who returned to see if it held anything edible. "Conveniently nearby to save Hannah once she'd been frightened enough. Then he spoke of warnings, said she must stop asking questions."

"I cannot believe Giles is involved." Hannah's comment brought a pang of jealousy as Simon recalled the handsome young man's interest in learning her name. Did she like this Giles?

"What about the mother?" he asked, recalling his visit with Lionel Fuller and the knight's disgust at his wife's ambitions.

"She certainly is forbidding," Elizabeth replied, "and she does press their suit. Robin spent some tedious hours listening to her argue that Madeline is in love with Giles." When no one spoke, she admitted, "Murder is something else, of course."

"I agree. Ambition is one thing, murder another. It takes a cold-blooded sort to kill an old man who never harmed anyone."

They were distracted for a time as Minster, scenting some

small creature, bounded off, sending Hannah running after him. The dog circled, enjoying being chased as much as he had enjoyed chasing. He would pause, allowing her to get close, and then take off again, staying just out of her reach. Soon they were all laughing at his enthusiasm for the game. Finally, he paused a few feet from Hannah, rear raised and head low, ready to take off again as she approached. Playing Judas, Simon sneaked up behind, picked up the squirming puppy, and handed him over. When she touched his hand in the darkness, Simon knew for sure that Hannah understood his message and accepted his apology. Things between them were back to normal.

Elizabeth returned to the purpose of their meeting. "Henrietta Beverley had been to the kennels with Madeline. She knew about the mastiffs and might have seen a chance to frighten Hannah, perhaps so much she would leave Whitehall and go home to Hampstead."

Henrietta was a poor judge of character if she believed that, Simon thought, but he held his peace on the subject of Hannah's resolve.

"There are so many possibilities!" Hannah exclaimed, revealing frustration. "When we think a person is eliminated, another reason to suspect him or her arises."

Elizabeth sighed. "It will be said that I murdered Beverley. He was trying to prove I'd killed Amberson, so who more likely than I to remove him?"

Simon suppressed a stab of fear at her matter-of-fact assessment. No need to tell her that the rumor was already circulating. "Let us go back to the beginning. We agree that Beverley must have planned Amberson's murder, to gain wealth and to take one step closer to his dream of a seat on the council."

"Yes. He meant it to appear a natural death, but when your master named it murder, he blamed me, probably with you as supplier of the means."

"Later he saw the advantage of circulating the story that Marie saw you in the corridor."

"Yes. A dead witness is convenient, since she cannot be questioned." Elizabeth stopped suddenly on the pathway, and the others continued a step or two before they returned to her. "He might have used Marie's death in another way as well: to send a message to the baroness."

Hannah grasped her meaning first. "A threat of what could happen if she questioned the tale of wandering brigands."

"But why did he imagine she would marry a knight once she was widowed?"

"And a knight as disgusting as Beverley." Hannah realized a moment later that she had criticized a nobleman and hastened to add, "That's how she would see it, I suppose."

Elizabeth was unfazed by her honesty. "Though ill-matched in Rochdale, I doubt Ellen would have exchanged him for Charles."

Simon thought he understood the whole if not the details. "Beverley always had a plan to reach his goals. For reasons we do not yet know, he believed he would wed the baroness once she was free. If your assessment is correct, Highness, she feared he would get his way."

"Poor woman," Hannah said. "First wed to a man apparently cold and demanding, then pursued by one even worse who sought to force her into marriage."

"Pregnant, far from home, and unused to such manipulation. She must have been terrified."

Elizabeth voiced a more sardonic view. "Convenient for her, then, that Beverley is dead."

Simon looked up in surprise. "You think she killed him?"

She wanted to say yes. He saw it in her face; but she could not. "No. Honestly, I cannot imagine that woman garnering the backbone to kill. Ellen is like a porcelain figurine, lovely to look at but somehow lacking, like an empty shell."

Simon recalled the baroness' words to him. "Yet she has some sense of others' feelings and fears, I think."

"Yes. But she is like an oracle, her pronouncements emotionless."

That was true, he had to admit. Her message to him, perhaps kindly meant, was oddly cold. He wondered what she had told the princess, what doubts of hers she had quelled.

"Charlotte, the duchess' maid, says she has the Sight." Hannah said it shyly, knowing Simon did not put much stock in such things.

He sniffed dismissively, ignoring the topic. "What we know for certain is that she did not go into Beverley's room that day, nor did anyone else, according to the guards."

"Might someone have climbed in the window or crossed from a neighboring balcony?"

"I considered that possibility when Amberson was killed. With the distances involved, it would take a ladder, ropes, or something similar to accomplish it. The materials would have been impossible to conceal."

"Even if someone used ropes and entered through the window, it could not have been the baroness," Hannah reminded them. "Such a feat would be impossible in her condition."

"And the apartments on the other side are occupied by old Grinley," Elizabeth said. "He can hardly climb the steps, much less swing from one balcony to the next."

"So we return to the idea that Beverley himself must have poisoned his drink."

"Suicide?" Elizabeth was incredulous.

"He is not the type for that. Someone tricked him."

They were silent for some moments, unable to determine how that might have happened. Why would Beverley have added something to his own bottle of mead, something that killed him?

"What do we do now?" Hannah finally asked.

"We have to take what we know to Northumberland," Elizabeth said.

"Beverley is dead, Highness. If it was he who sought to blame you, the danger might be over."

"Beverley didn't set the dogs on Hannah."

"Or try to hit us with a potted plant."

"What potted plant?" Simon demanded.

Hannah's expression showed dismay at her mistake, but the princess stepped in. "Another warning. They have known our intent from the beginning. None of us is safe until the truth is out."

Suddenly Simon recalled almost being run down by a man on a black horse. "Beverley's horse is black as ink," he muttered. When Elizabeth asked for clarification, he said, "Beverley tried to frighten me, or at least distract me. When we continued asking questions, he and his partner turned on all of us, arranging accidents and turning us into suspects."

"I thought he was the clever one, but it seems his partner is every bit at apt as he."

"And we have no idea who this clever killer is."

"There must be someone we have not considered." They fell silent, reviewing the prospects, looking for new perspectives.

Hannah spoke tentatively. "There is a guardsman who told me Beverley would someday rise to the highest levels of government." Elizabeth and Simon turned to her. "His name is Daniel. When I first came here he was quite friendly. He asked question after question about Her Highness, and I thought him a gossip."

"There are enough of those hereabout," Elizabeth said, her tone both irritated and resigned.

"Daniel turned against me when he discovered that Simon and I are affianced. I thought he was disappointed that . . ."

"That a pretty girl was spoken for," Elizabeth supplied, seeing her embarrassment.

"But maybe it was not that at all."

"You mean he realized you were part of my investigation."

Hannah would not have put it that way, but it did have a nice sound. Part of an investigation. Part of a princess' investigation. She went on. "Daniel is certainly not the type to be a clever killer, but he might know something that will help us."

"Find the fellow in the morning," Elizabeth ordered, and Simon bit his lip to avoid contradicting her. If he had his way, Hannah would do nothing more to catch a killer, but she had made it clear he was not giving the orders. "Simon, ask Calkin for the names of guardsmen Beverley favored. If this Daniel cannot help us, maybe others can." At a nod from Elizabeth, Hannah gathered up her silk bag and shawl, tucking them under the arm not holding Minster. "I will continue to ask questions where I can, and we will compare reports tomorrow."

"Will people be suspicious if you accompany us two nights running?"

Elizabeth looked up at several heads silhouetted by rushlights in the windows above. "They already are. Your name may be linked to mine in the tomorrow's news sheets." She turned away, but not before he glimpsed a smile at his discomfort. She had little enough to smile about, so he did not begrudge her humor, even if that sort of renown shocked him more than a little.

Simon met Calkin as he exited the palace, and one look at his face revealed bad news.

"They're looking for you, Simon. To arrest you."

"Arrest me! What have I done?"

Calkin's freckled face was solemn. "Killed two men with your poisons. Possibly pushed a certain maidservant down the palace stairs. Your presence in the palace at the time was noted."

"I don't understand."

Calkin looked around anxiously. "Let's go inside, where all eyes cannot gaze on us." He led the way to a small alcove out of direct line of sight.

Simon grasped his friend's arm. "Tell me what you know."

"The new head of the King's Guard was approached by a certain guardsman."

"Daniel."

"Yes. You know him?"

"Hannah does. We believe he was in the employ of Charles Beverley." Simon briefly explained their conclusions. "I was coming to tell you and enlist your help."

Calkin frowned. "I will do what I can, but the order is already given for your arrest."

"Elizabeth is the target. Hannah and I will be tools to bring her down."

"Yes. They will try to force you to implicate her." Calkin did not elaborate, but Simon felt a chill. Commoners could be held indefinitely, even tortured, for the general belief among the nobility was that torture was the best way to make them tell the truth. The only person willing to speak for them would be the princess, who was in no position to help.

"I will find Hannah and Elizabeth, and together we will decide what to do."

"I will delay things as much as I can, but hurry."

The two parted with a brief handshake, much unsaid but understood between them. Calkin would risk his job to turn pursuit away. Simon could only hope it was enough.

His first problem was gaining entrance to Elizabeth's apartments. Searching his mind for an idea, he remembered Minster.

Hannah had told how she used the inquisitive creature to explore the palace. He turned toward the kennels, keeping an eye out for those in search of him.

He needed to change his appearance. Nearby were the kitchen, the bake-house, and several pantry sheds. As he passed, he peered into each, finally finding one that was empty. Inside, several aprons and two jackets hung on pegs by the door. He put on one of the jackets then turned his cap inside out so the unbleached lining showed. Hunching low and changing his usual gait, he left the building looking quite different from Simon, apothecary's apprentice.

The kennels were fairly quiet at this time of day, but of course there arose a great din at the approach of a stranger. A boy rose to meet him amiably, probably glad for some human company. "I am sent by the Princess Elizabeth," Simon told him. "She would like a second dog, as like the one she now has as possible."

The idea appealed to the lad. "Two would make a pretty picture, running along behind her. Let's see if there's one that looks the same."

There were two others from the same litter, and one of them looked enough like Minster to pass. "I will take him to her tonight, and she will decide if he suits."

"Tell her they will be company for each other and cause less mischief," the boy said, nodding at his own wisdom.

Thanking him, Simon tucked the puppy under his arm and went back the way he had come. Navigating his way to the private quarters, he approached the guards on duty. "I believe this dog belongs to Her Highness 'Lizbeth. I found him on the grounds, wandering free."

"I will take it to her," one of them offered.

"Your Worship, might I take the dog myself? She may reward the one that found him, and if she does"—he smiled meaningfully—"we all will benefit."

The guard thought about it then said to his partner, "I will take him up."

When they knocked at the door of Elizabeth's apartment, Kat Ashley answered, looking at Simon in surprise. "What's this?"

He met her eye in a silent message that belied his words. "Ma'am, I found the princess' dog wanderin' on the bowling green and brought him back to her." He hoped the real Minster did not appear and that Kat realized it was essential to let him in.

She paused, considered, and said, to his immense relief, "Wait here, boy. The princess will want to thank you." She nodded to the guardsman. "You may go. I'll see that he leaves once Her Grace has spoken with him."

As soon as the man was gone, Kat let him in and shut the door. "I assume you are Hannah's Simon. What's wrong?"

"We are in danger."

Kat seemed to wilt like a parched flower. She had been through this before. After a moment, however, she sighed deeply and straightened her spine. "Come with me." She went to a side room, knocked gently, and gave terse orders that sent several women scurrying elsewhere. Alone with Kat, Elizabeth, and Hannah, he told what he had learned.

"Arrested! For killing Lord Amberson?" Kat was aghast. "Elizabeth, what have you done to bring this on?"

"There isn't time to explain it," the princess answered. "We must get Hannah and Simon away from here. If they cannot be found then I am safe, for they will not arrest me on the word of a dead maidservant. They'll need to make one of you implicate me."

She spoke in a matter-of-fact manner, but Hannah's eyes met Simon's. Not only were they in great danger, but they might be tortured into implicating Elizabeth. He tried to summon a re-assuring smile, but his lips did not seem willing to bend upward.

Kat paced a few steps then returned to them. "What will happen now?"

He considered. "They will try to find me first, since they know where Hannah is. They will search the shop, my home, and perhaps Hampstead. When they do not find me, they will come here, to make Hannah tell what she knows." They were all silent for a few moments. Laughter sounded in the next room, a world away. Where could they go? "Is Pembroke in London?"

"No, he's gone to his estate," Elizabeth replied. "Why?"

"Hugh is his man now. He will hide us."

"Then we must get you there."

"How can that be done?" Kat asked, her practical mind tackling the biggest question.

Elizabeth looked at Hannah appraisingly. "I believe that by morning Hannah must become a lady," she said slowly. "And Simon may serve as her maid."

CHAPTER TWENTY-ONE

Early the next morning, while the palace was still gray with the dregs of night, the doors to Elizabeth's apartments opened a slit, then a bit wider as Kat Ashley peered out. Seeing no one, she motioned to three figures behind her, and they moved forward.

"Walk slowly and keep your nose tilted upward," Elizabeth told Hannah. "And Simon, keep your face lowered."

"Have no fear of that," he grumbled. Attired in one of Kat's old dresses, with a powdered wig and a large shawl to shadow his face and hide the fact that the dress did not close over his broad back, he appeared to be a taller than average, rather homely, serving woman.

Hannah, however, was stunning in one of Elizabeth's dresses, a flamboyant red wig, and the accoutrements of a grand lady. She tried to obey Elizabeth's command, but her face showed apprehension. "They will surely catch us," she whispered.

"Only if you fail to play your part," the princess said firmly. A woman rounded the corner just then and came toward them, a young manservant close behind. She was dressed for an outing, a long, protective cape over her clothing.

"Catherine," Elizabeth greeted her. "Do you go out this morning?"

"Yes, Your Grace."

"Then you are come on a wish. Will you show this lady the way to the Holbein Gate? She is of my sister's household and has never been to Whitehall before."

"Of course, Your Grace." The woman's eyes swept Hannah and turned cold. Another beautiful woman at Court was obviously unwelcome.

"Anne, this is Catherine Carey, my cousin. She will show you to the gate, and from there you will easily find your way."

"A p-pleasure, madam." At Hannah's reply, Simon released the breath he'd been holding

"Please commend me to my sister and tell her I will visit tomorrow."

"Thank you, Your Grace." Hannah settled into her role, dropping a curtsey before turning to her guide. "Come, Gwenyth," she called over her shoulder. "Don't keep the lady waiting."

As they navigated the passages, Catherine made general comments of the sort that new acquaintance generates, and Hannah answered without stammering. Yes, she was enjoying London. No, she did not mind the noise and confusion.

They had been lucky that Catherine Carey appeared when she did. Guardsmen in the passages and rooms hardly gave them a second glance. Warned to watch for two commoners, a man and Princess Elizabeth's pretty maidservant, they largely ignored two ladies, one of them the familiar Mistress Carey, with their servants, a homely woman and a boy.

Once at the gate, Hannah thanked Catherine prettily as they parted ways. After a short distance at a dignified speed, she and Simon picked up their pace, headed for Pembroke's house on the strand and what they hoped was safety.

As they hurried along, Simon wondered how women managed all the clothing they wore. His skirts kept bunching between his legs, making forward motion a lot like wading through deep water. When he grumbled, Hannah said primly, "If you walk as a lady should, that won't happen." He wondered how a lady was supposed to walk but in the end decided it wasn't worth the effort to learn the trick of it. He would be out of this disguise as soon as was humanly possible.

The man at the gateway of Pembroke's house seemed surprised at the well-dressed woman who asked to see Hugh Bellows. With just the right tone of haughtiness Hannah explained, "This Bellows is the last surviving relative of Gwenyth here." She leaned toward him and whispered, "The plague took them all." Simon hid a grin. Hannah was enjoying her role-playing just a bit.

As the man went to find Hugh, Simon shifted from one foot to the other, worrying and resisting the urge to twist his wig just a little in order to relieve the itch it had generated all over his head. Would Hugh dismiss the message, knowing that he had no Welsh relatives named Gwenyth?

He need not have worried. Hugh appeared within minutes, eyes widening at Hannah's borrowed finery. With a twitch of humor on his face, he addressed his "cousin."

"Little Gwen, is it you? I would never have known, for you've grown so!" Thanking the man who had fetched him, he led Hannah and Simon away. "What sort of trouble has this lad led you into, Hannah?"

"It isn't Simon's fault, but we are in trouble."

"It's Her Grace, then." He turned to Simon. "I warned you."

Simon gave a brief version of events since they last met. Hugh seemed pleased that Calkin had assisted them. "He's a good man," he observed when Simon finished.

"Her Highness got us out of Whitehall, but she is in as much danger as we."

"Yes," Hugh agreed. "You two are a means to someone's goal."

"How do we stop him?" Hannah asked. "Beverley is dead—who left alive knows his name?"

None of them could say, and the question hung in the air, unanswered.

Elizabeth watched Simon and Hannah disappear through the palace gate, feeling some release of tension as they parted from Catherine Carey and started for Pembroke's house. Hugh would keep them safe. She turned back to the room where her people had begun their day's activities, only Kat aware that anything was wrong. She would betray nothing, although Elizabeth heard her sniff from time to time, an unconscious catching of her breath as she fought to control her fear. They had had their share of such moments, but they never got any easier.

Elizabeth dressed for a turn through the palace. Hannah had planned to interview the guardsman—Daniel—but that was impossible now. Hannah was running for her life. It was up to Elizabeth to find someone with knowledge of Charles Beverley's plans. He had been a schemer, had fawned on Lord Amberson shamelessly, had used his power over the King's Guard to further his own career. That was not so unusual. She needed more, something of substance. Having already canvassed everyone she knew, she resolved to go farther afield today in her search for Beverley's character. It turned out to be something else entirely that she found.

It was more difficult than she had anticipated, walking the rooms and corridors of Whitehall as if she were perfectly at ease when in reality she was almost stiff with dread. Few knew the peril she faced, but that did not make it any less. Real or imagined sounds often caused her to turn to assure that no one spied on her, that the footsteps she heard were her own.

Forcing herself to appear aimless, she wandered from acquaintance to acquaintance, striking up conversations and leading to the subject of the dead man. Nothing new arose, and she continued on, determined but ever more discouraged.

Finally, she came upon a group of women, none of whom she recognized, working on a large tapestry in a sunlit room. Approaching, she learned that they had accompanied her sister to the palace. Mary was with the king, and the ladies used the time as ladies should, by being useful.

Elizabeth seized on the chance to make herself part of their conversation. One woman hurriedly gave up her chair for the princess' comfort. Dragging it close, she began with questions about their work: what scene would be pictured, where would it be displayed, and so on. Invited, rather hesitantly, to join in, she declined, claiming her skill would never equal theirs. "I would be embarrassed to have someone point out a corner poorly done and ask whose fault it might be!"

That settled them somewhat, and she turned to her practiced litany of innocuous remarks, letting them get past the shock of having Mary's rival in all things join their little group. As the conversation became slightly less stilted, she steered the topic to the recent tragedies.

"Terrible," one woman—Winifred, she thought—said with a doleful sigh. "Two dead by a murderer's hand, in the king's own palace." Unspoken was the thought that such things would never have happened if God, in the form of the Catholic Church, had not been banished from Court.

"There was an accident," said another whose name she could not recall. "On the stairs."

"And Baron Rochdale," Elizabeth put in. "That was not in the palace, but his wife is here, and it is a terrible loss for her." She added, "I wonder if he knew Lord Amberson or Sir Charles."

"I think not," said a small woman who had been silent thus far. "The baron was not a man for the company of others."

"I had heard it was so." Elizabeth turned to the woman with interest. Older than the others, her face had the kind of loveliness age cannot destroy. Introduced as a cousin to one of the other ladies, she was on her way to live with her daughter in Calais. Elizabeth searched her mind for the woman's name. Florence, she thought, possibly Florence Bolton, but she was not sure. "Did you know the baron well, madam?"

"I knew his father. My late husband's lands were north of Rochdale." Her face tightened, perhaps with recent grief. "The last time I saw Andrew was at his wedding."

"So you know the baroness as well?"

"Yes, Your Grace. I have known her all her life."

"Such a beauty!" one of the others said.

"And as sweet as she is lovely."

Florence was quiet, but Elizabeth sensed she held back a comment.

"You knew Ellen's father too, then?"

"Oh, yes. We knew him well."

"I have heard it said that he was difficult."

Blue eyes disappeared under lowered lids. "That may be so, Your Grace."

"He was a knight with a very small holding, if I remember," Winifred volunteered. "They say he was determined that his daughter would marry the heir to a title, that he traded on her beauty and forced her to accept Andrew Rochdale even though he is—was—peculiar."

"Not that she complains," another said. "The baroness told my sister Anne that her father's choice of her husband was his right, and she would make the best of it."

"A wise attitude," Margaret opined, twisting a thread in two with a sharp snap. "If every woman abided by her father's wishes and her husband's desires, the world would run smoothly."

All the more reason never to take a husband. Elizabeth nodded as if the woman had said something very wise.

"The baroness says not a word against him," the unnamed

woman commented. "But everyone knows she was mistreated. Her father did not choose wisely."

"Her father did as he was forced to do," Florence blurted, and there was a shocked silence around the little circle. Embarrassed, she lowered her head. "I meant to say that we may not know all there is to know about a situation, so we should not judge." She did not elaborate, and the conversation moved on. Elizabeth kept up her part, watching Florence at the same time. Two spots of red gradually faded from her cheeks as she regained control of her emotions.

When the group finally broke up in preparation for the midday meal, Elizabeth followed Florence from the room. "May I ask a question, madam?"

She turned in surprise. "Of course, Your Grace."

"You know something of the negotiations that brought about the marriage of Ellen Doan and Andrew Rochdale. I would like to hear what you know."

"I am not one who likes telling tales, Your Highness."

Elizabeth put a reassuring hand on her shoulder, feeling bone as light as a twig. "This is important, Florence, and you are not telling tales, but helping us understand why the baron died."

"But he was killed by—" Understanding dawned. "His death is related to the others."

"It's possible. I would appreciate it if you would keep it to yourself, though."

"Of course." She glanced around. "Here is what I know. Thomas Doan was a good man, not one to force anyone to do anything, especially his daughter, whom he loved to distraction."

"So how did the mismatched couple come about?"

"Baron Rochdale, the elder, wanted grandchildren, heirs to his land. He feared his son would never marry on his own." She blinked several times. "I think he was blind to what the rest of us saw in Andrew, or at least was determined to ignore it."

"The younger Andrew was a lover of men?"

Florence's chin set. "I cannot say that, Your Highness. He was a good man, decent and kind. But in truth, he had no interest in women." Having said it, her voice grew stronger. "Such men may prefer to remain strangers to the physical act of love rather than sink to perversion, and I believe this was Andrew's choice. Still, Baron Rochdale was convinced that his son would become a husband in fact if they provided him a wife of great beauty."

"So he chose Ellen."

Something sparked in the woman's bright eyes, something that might have been anger. "Ellen herself did most of the choosing, but the old baron was no fool. He had a contract drawn that demanded a child within three years, or the wife could be set aside and another chosen."

A canny move, designed to see that Ellen exerted all her energies in pursuit of her own husband. There would be an heir, whether the son desired his wife or no. "She must have felt great pressure, given a timeline."

"She was more than willing." Florence looked as if she wanted to spit.

"I take it she wanted more from life than her father could provide."

A hard little smile showed agreement and more. "Thomas was a simple man with little wealth. His willful, greedy daughter wanted both, and he almost beggared himself to achieve it."

The picture she painted of Ellen was very different from what the Court had seen. "How does she now seem so sweet?"

A shrug. "Perhaps now that she has what she wants, she is content. Or perhaps the babe she carries has changed her. They often do."

"But you said the baron was disinterested in his wife."

229

Grace's smile was knowing. "Men do what they must. Perhaps the elder Andrew was right after all. He will have his heir, though he never lived to see it."

Elizabeth thanked Florence and went on her way, thinking about Ellen Rochdale, who needed to produce a child to fulfill her marriage contract. If her husband had not done his part in the two years since their marriage, she might have taken matters into her own hands. Would she have allowed Charles Beverley to father her child? Or was the father someone else, and Beverley had merely learned her secret? Either way, she now understood why he had felt certain that his next wife would be a baroness.

CHAPTER TWENTY-TWO

Hugh had work to do, but he led Simon and Hannah to an unused storeroom that, although it smelled of horse sweat and linseed oil, provided safety and privacy. At first, they relished the quiet, but after an hour, they began to chafe at their inability to help Elizabeth.

"What if they arrest her even if they can't find us?" Hannah questioned, although Simon was as unlikely to have an answer as he'd been the first two times she asked. "Do you think Robin Dudley will come to her aid?"

He did not reply, since that, too, was a repeated question. "Let us go over it again," he said softly, lest someone passing hear voices inside. "Perhaps together we can think of a way to help."

They both jumped at a sound at the door, but it was only Hugh, carrying a cloth bag that Simon hoped contained different clothing for him. "I have received a rather strange message."

"From Elizabeth?"

"It seems so. A boy appeared at the gate, asking for me. He said he was sent because the princess has written a play called 'Orion's Wife.' She seeks to know if Pembroke's wife will play the faithless Side, who was so beautiful that Hera cast her into Hades in jealousy. I am also directed to send greetings to Carthburt's child."

They were silent as they considered Hugh's words. Elizabeth well knew that the apothecary's child was dead, and while plays were a constant source of diversion at Court, it was unlikely that she planned one, given her current situation.

"Pembroke's wife," Hugh said, "besides being away from London, is no rival to Hera in beauty. It is for us to figure out what message she intends, which means you, Simon."

"To begin with, Orion is the Hunter."

Hannah caught on quickly. "Baron Rochdale."

"The clue mentions the *wife*," Hugh reminded them. "Rochdale's wife, Ellen; I remember you asked me about her."

"Orion's wife was indeed beautiful," Simon said, "but she was not faithless."

"So she put that in as a clue, something you would note but the messenger would not."

"A faithless wife whose husband is a hunter." There was a long silence while they each worked on the message. Simon let his mind float, allowing pieces of information to meld as they would. Finally, Hugh asked, "Could the baroness have been Beverley's confederate?"

"We think not. Besides being physically hampered by her pregnancy, she is unlikely to commit murder due to her timid nature."

"Timid?" Hugh's tone was skeptical. "I have not met the woman, but what I hear makes me doubt that."

"What did you hear?"

Hugh ran his hand over his brow as if there were still hair there to arrange. "It was some time back now, perhaps a fortnight. One of my men was waiting for Pembroke at Whitehall when he heard a commotion in a room nearby. He peered in and saw the baroness berating that girl of hers. Such scenes are common in the palace, where privacy is nonexistent, but he noted the woman's ferocity. First she slapped the girl then began striking heavier blows, all because of some forgotten item. He was not surprised, he said, that a woman in her condition might be overly emotional, but he almost intervened, fearful that she might harm her child with the exertion."

"And did he?"

Hugh shook his head. "It is the baroness' affair if she beats her maid, and she stopped when the girl fell to the floor in tears. She composed herself, quite comically, he said, pulling at her clothes as if angry with the child within. My man crept away, not wanting to be noticed." Hugh looked from Hannah to Simon. "The maid could probably tell you what the baroness is truly like."

"If she were still alive." Feeling slightly sick, Simon forced himself to reexamine all that he knew about the baroness. Layer by layer, he moved past what they had heard from gossips, past his pity, past his admiration, past his desire to believe in her goodness. Elizabeth had called her a shell with no warmth. What if the shell was deliberately constructed to hide the person beneath? What if under the shell there was only greed?

Baroness Rochdale was a beautiful wife who did not love her husband. Once he accepted that she might not be an innocent pawn, it became all too clear that she had as much to gain from the death of her husband as Beverley had from the murder of Lord Amberson. "Beverley traveled north to do the baroness a favor."

"Kill the baron," Hannah said.

Hugh glared at the two of them, completely at sea. "Take me with you, you two."

"The baroness and Beverley made a pact. He killed her husband, leaving her a rich widow. She killed Amberson, opening doors for his future."

"And both were far from the scene, so they could hardly be suspects."

"But Beverley and the baroness make an ill-matched pair of lovers if ever I saw one."

"Love had nothing to do with it. It was purely a business arrangement."

"But the lady did not trust Beverley."

"Nor would I," Hugh said with a grunt.

"She poisoned him, just as she poisoned His Lordship."

"And Marie?"

"Must have seen her go into Amberson's room."

Hugh paced the dirt floor, trying to wrap his mind around the information. "So somehow, Beverley and the baroness meet, assess each other's character, and formulate a plan. She tells him that her husband will soon visit his hunting lodge near Rochdale, alone. Beverley leaves London, supposedly to do his spring planting, but takes a side trip, overtakes the earl and kills him, making it appear that he was waylaid by bandits."

"Then he went on to Beverley," Simon continued, "complaining about the terrible condition of the roads. His presence there proved he could not have poisoned Lord Amberson."

"Once he was safely away, she waited for the right time to poison the old man. Claiming to be ill, she stayed behind that day when the others went to dinner. Marie remained with her like the good servant she was, but the baroness did not want that."

Hannah gave a sudden gasp as she recalled, "Charlotte said Marie had a mark on her cheek when they returned from dinner that day. She would not say how she got it."

"Lady Rochdale berated the girl on some pretext, struck her, and sent her away. Once Marie was gone, she slipped into Amberson's room and poured poison into the cup Beverley had told her would be there."

"Marie was hiding nearby. She saw it and could not hide her disquiet."

"So she, too, had to die. Poor thing."

"It is a chilling story," Hugh said. "If the baroness is as you say, it only makes things more dangerous for you. Oh!" Remembering, he pulled several cloth bundles from his pockets and unwrapped them, revealing food purloined from the kitchens. "I guessed you would be hungry."

"What about the part where the princess sends greetings to the apothecary's daughter?" Hannah took the food and divided it between them.

"She must want me to consult Carthburt, perhaps as to methods of poisoning."

"But she said his daughter, did she not, Hugh?"

At his nod of assent, Simon threw up his hands in frustration. "I do not know what it means! And how did she become suspicious of the baroness? Would I could speak to her directly!"

Understanding his need to digest what they had learned, Hannah and Hugh went silent. Simon tried to stop berating himself for stupidity and instead figure out what Elizabeth wanted him to comprehend. It was hard to let go of his embarrassment, though. He had been a fool.

Despite the wisdom of adages concerning outward appearances, he had been taken in by Ellen Rochdale. Beauty in her case was indeed only skin-deep, if what they now suspected was true. What kind of woman could murder an old man she hardly knew? What kind of wife sent a killer after her unsuspecting husband? And what kind of person could let an innocent suffer for her crimes, as Elizabeth might suffer? He would not let that happen. Taking up the food Hannah pressed into his hand, he began to eat. He would need his strength.

When they had finished their makeshift meal, Hannah asked, "How will we prove any of it, Simon? With Beverley dead, there is only our belief that the baroness is involved in the murders."

He stared unseeing at the wall, remembering. "Somehow, Beverley learned early on that I was helping the princess. That has to be why he tried to run me down as I left Seawell's house."

"Who could have told him?"

"Both of us felt that someone was listening when we first discussed the matter."

Hugh leaned in eagerly. "Who was nearby?"

"A maid and a guardsman were the only two I saw."

"What did they look like?"

"The maid was very young. Pretty, I suppose." He glanced nervously at Hannah to judge her reaction. "The guardsman had a lot of very dark hair, the type that defies combing."

"Daniel!" Hannah stood up in surprise, and her wig slipped comically to one side. "He knew your purpose at Whitehall. He said so."

"And when he discovered you were part of my plans, he feared you'd figure things out." Simon tapped his lip in thought. "He tried to frighten you with the dogs. Probably the planter as well. We need to talk to him."

Hugh brought them back to reality. "You cannot go looking for a guardsman. Orders are out for your arrest, and you either have to answer the charges or run."

"We can't run," Simon said firmly. "Elizabeth is in danger."

"So how will you prove your innocence?"

Righting her wig, Hannah stood. "I will return and tell the princess what we know."

"Impossible. We were lucky to escape arrest once. Luck cannot be counted on forever."

"Why don't I go?" Hugh offered. "She will know I come on your behalf."

"And what will you tell her?"

Hugh shrugged. "What you think best, but keep in mind, she does not take orders easily."

Simon considered their best course of action. "She must call on her friend Robin Dudley, ask to see the Lord President in private, and explain the situation before it comes to the formality of a hearing before the council."

"And what will she offer as proof?"

Simon shook his head. "We must depend on her persuasive skills and whatever she found out about the baroness."

Hannah made a gesture of contradiction. "Accuse a dead man and a pregnant saint of murder? She has no proof, and since she herself is accused, little chance of success."

"Then what do we do?" Unable to stand still, Simon prowled the room like one of the mastiffs, Hannah thought, disquieted but unfocused on a clear target.

"Might we convince her to escape?" she asked. "She has friends who will take her to safety, somewhere outside of England."

"She will never go. Elizabeth will face whatever trials she must rather than retreat to some place where it can be said she surrendered her right to the throne." Knowing he was right, Hannah's enthusiasm faded.

"I will talk with her," Hugh said. "You find proof of what happened. Something."

"Or someone," Hannah said thoughtfully. "There is still Daniel. If we convince him of our innocence, he might tell what he knows, perhaps of communication between Beverley and the baroness."

"Yes! Someone had to be their messenger, since they were careful to remain apart."

Hugh had been listening carefully. "This Daniel knew the maid who died?" he asked.

"Marie. Yes."

"And do you think he could have killed her?"

"No," Hannah said. "He claimed her death was no accident, and was very upset by it. Why would he say that if he pushed her?"

"Then consider this. This guardsman was probably paid to

spy for Beverley. That is not unusual, since many at Whitehall augment their income with favors for those above them. But what turned him from mere spy to one who threatened your life? You say his behavior changed when he learned you were connected to Simon here."

Hannah saw his direction. "Someone convinced him Simon killed Marie."

Simon finished the piece of cheese he had hardly tasted. "Once he thought of us as killers, he was willing to act against us, even felt justified in hurting you, Hannah, because of me."

"What can we do to convince him to tell us what he knows?"

"Make him understand that we are innocent of murder, no matter what Beverley said."

"Beverley was to him a hero. Why should he believe us?"

"I don't know, but I must try." Simon took up the clothing Hugh had provided and began creating his disguise. "Daniel must know some of the truth. If I assure him he need not blacken his own name, he may yet be honest."

Hugh left then to do his part, giving Hannah a brief hug and Simon a nod of affection. When he had gone, Hannah urged, "I should speak with Daniel. He knows me."

"But I am less known in the palace, and well able to disguise myself. I stand a better chance of getting to him." Simon held up a hand as she drew breath to answer. "You know it is true."

Her eyes filled with tears that he would have kissed away, had there been time. "I must know what happens."

"I will try to send word." He touched her face lightly. "Hannah, you know I love you."

"And I you."

"Then if the message is that you must escape, please do it. I will come to you if I can, no matter what, but my mind will be easier if I know you are safe."

Tears burned, but she would not let them fall again. "We will all escape this, Simon. You and I and Her Grace as well. We have done nothing wrong, and God will not let us suffer."

He gripped her hand briefly and left. She stared at the closed door for a moment then turned away, unable to bear its opaque blankness.

Elizabeth paced her room, incapable of tolerating even her closest companions. When would they come for her? Had Simon and Hannah managed to get away, and if so, what would they do? Anyone with a shred of good sense would leave London as quickly as possible, lose himself in the country, and forget he ever met anyone named Elizabeth. But Simon would not do that. He would risk his own life to help her escape this plot. Hannah, too; she was sure of it.

She could not help but wonder what made them devoted to her. What in her makeup inspired those two to take up her causes? How did she engender such loyalty? Thus far in her lifetime, few had found her an irresistible force. Those who approached her with promises of loyalty and service always had ulterior motives, always retreated when she would not stoop to treason or respond to flattery. Still, if someone as forthright and earnest as Simon Maldon was dedicated to her, she could not see herself as undeserving. Simon was no fool, and he respected her. In fact, she thought with a smile, he liked her.

The smile faded quickly. They were all in danger, and she had to find a way out. While Simon would try to save her, she must try to save them all. But how?

Blanche knocked lightly on the door. "Madam, there is a man below. He said to tell you Hugh craves a word."

Hugh! Then Simon had made it to safety. That was something, at least. Hugh could spirit the two lovers away, and she would have only herself to worry about. It was something. Used to being on her own, she would defend herself to the death once her friends were safe. "Tell him to wait in the west garden, by the sundial."

When she arrived at the appointed spot, she took a moment to watch Hugh Bellows before he turned and saw her. He was older, but there was still a reassuring sense of solidity about him. Another man whose honesty she did not question, although she did not know how he felt about her. Duty was Hugh's master, and she had no idea how an extraneous princess fit in.

"Master Bellows."

"Your Grace." Hugh's face was unreadable. Did he disapprove of her? He liked Simon, and she had once again pulled him into danger. He probably resented that.

"Simon is safe for the moment," Hugh began without any social pleasantries. "He has a plan." He paused before adding, "For your consideration."

Elizabeth nodded and tried to keep a telltale brow from rising at his discomfort. "I am glad of it, for I desire his safety and trust his judgment."

Hugh seemed pleased. "He has grown into a wise man, I think. He suggests you ask your friend Robert Dudley to arrange a private audience with the Lord President tomorrow before you break your fast. Simon thinks he will do that much for you, though he will risk no more."

"Simon is probably correct."

"Ask that the audience be held in the same chamber where Hannah, um, overheard Charles Beverley speak to the duke."

"The one with the small anteroom at the back."

"Yes."

"Simon thinks it wise to lay what we suspect before the Lord President?"

"Better with Northumberland alone than before the council, he says."

She considered, tapping her knuckles against her lips in

unconscious tension. "If I can convince the duke that lies have been spread about me, the matter will be solved. If I cannot, I will in all likelihood be arrested on the spot."

Hugh looked unhappy. "Yes, Your Grace."

"But what trick has Simon got up his sleeve?"

The smile he managed was grim. "He will try to get a certain guardsman to come with him to that meeting. He hopes to convince him to tell what he knows of the matter."

"I see. And I must be at my most eloquent until then."

"Yes, Your Grace." Hugh turned to go, adding a benediction, "May you all fare well in this."

Robert Dudley was skeptical about relaying Elizabeth's request to his father. "You know what is afoot," he told her. "Is it not best that you stay out of sight? He has not found the two he seeks, but once they are arrested, they will surely implicate you, if only to save themselves pain."

Elizabeth shuddered. It was dangerous for Simon and Hannah to reenter the palace. But Simon was good at disguise, and the assumption was that they would escape the city, not creep back to where guardsmen stood at every corner.

"I will prove to your father that I had nothing to do with these murders," she told Robin.

He sighed heavily. "All right. I will ask." He looked as if he wanted to add something, perhaps that he was sorry her life had been so uncertain, but in the end, he merely bowed and left to do as his childhood friend asked.

Watching him go, Elizabeth gave way briefly to nervous spasms that shook her whole body. She groped for a chair and fell into it just before her knees gave out with fear. What had she done? It was one thing to be bold, another to invite trouble. Northumberland wanted her out of the way, and she had probably just given him the impetus to begin the process.

On the other hand, and here she actually watched her hand as the shaking subsided and she regained control of it, it felt right somehow to depend on her wits and her powers of persuasion to get her out of trouble. She had a sense for such situations, knew instinctively what to say to her accusers, whether it was conciliatory, angry, or counteraccusation. It was vital that she trust herself—and Simon, Hugh, and Hannah as well—to put an end to this nightmare.

There. Her hands were still. She rose with knees that had regained their sinew and returned to her room, at peace with her decision.

Simon left Pembroke's estate dressed as a lowly sort, with tattered clothes and dirty, bare feet. He had even chopped his hair off with his knife, making it go every which way. Gobs of tar over several teeth gave him a gap-toothed smile, and when he passed another person, he evinced a blank stare that made him appear a lack-wit.

The plan they had concocted was not much, and even that turned out badly. "Daniel is nowhere to be found," Calkin reported when Simon found him outside the palace gateway. "He was on duty yesterday, so he's free until early tomorrow morning."

Simon forced himself to remain calm. Elizabeth had by now done as he suggested. She would face Northumberland without proof of her assertions, and that was dangerous. How much easier it would be for the duke if she was guilty of a crime! Northumberland dreamed of being grandfather to England's future king, so who would he *want* to believe in all this?

"I could find Her Grace and tell her we have lost Daniel," Calkin offered.

"Not yet. If we have not located him by morning, I will try to get her out of the palace so they cannot arrest her. That will at least give us more time to prove her innocence." He hobbled away in a feigned limp, unwilling to compromise Calkin's position in the guard. As he went, he wondered where he would take Elizabeth if escape became necessary, and how he would keep both her and Hannah safe. It was not difficult to appear bowed down, for he felt as if the cares of the world rested squarely on his back.

Chapter Twenty-Three

By late afternoon, Hannah knew she could not sit in the pungent little storeroom while Simon risked his life. There had to be something she could do, she told herself, and she already had a disguise. She had promised to stay away from Whitehall, but it occurred to her that Joan, the Beverleys' serving maid, might be of help. Sharp-eyed and insightful, she had known Beverley well. Busy with preparations for leaving London, it was likely that Henrietta would not know of the order for Hannah's arrest. It was worth a chance.

After peeping carefully out the door, Hannah left the building and headed for the street, head up and eyes forbidding approach. A few on the grounds seemed interested, but not overly so, and she made her way through the arched gate. It would have been quicker to take one of the boats lining the shore, but she had neither the money nor the nerve to try it. She would walk.

It took some time, mostly because she had to keep stopping to ask the way. London was a maze, and even the river was lost to her for a while as she followed one twisted street after another. She was so tired when she finally approached Beverley's town house that she was not looking where she was going and almost bumped into Tiny Joan, whose view was obstructed by a pile of blankets she carried to a waiting cart. "Hannah?" Joan asked, dumping her load and peering at her friend's costume in disbelief. "What is this?"

"Oh, Joan, I am in trouble."

"Come inside." Taking her arm, Joan escorted her to a quiet room under the stairs where the sounds of climbing and descending formed a background for their conversation. "Tell me."

"We are suspected of murder, Simon and I and the princess."

"I see."

"But we did not kill anyone. We were trying to discover who did."

"And have you?"

"We believe one of the king's guardsmen knows something of the matter."

Joan looked at her askance. "My guess is that you know more than that."

"I hope you will not think me untrusting. I would not put you, too, in danger."

Joan's expression turned knowing. "Is Baroness Rochdale involved?"

Hannah gasped. "How did you know?"

Smiling, Joan counted off her reasons on her fingers. "First, the very fact that you asked about her piqued my interest. Second, I have long suspected that she is not as she appears to be. Since we spoke, I have investigated her character."

"Why did you do that?"

Joan stopped, her hands still before her in counting mode. "Her eyes, I think. She keeps them cast downward, meek as a lamb, but once I observed her in an unguarded moment. If ever a woman's gaze belied her exterior, it was then."

Hannah felt some comfort in Joan's assessment. As soon as Simon left, she had begun to doubt their conclusions. Were they, was the princess, jumping to the wrong conclusions about the baroness? Everyone said she was a saint, an angel, mistrusted and mistreated by her husband. But Joan had seen something else. It would not be the first time the public perception of a person did not match her true nature.

Joan continued with the account of her search for knowledge. "The Carlson sisters claim she is lazy and selfish. No one believes them, because they themselves are lazy and selfish. Still, they lived with her."

Something clicked in Hannah's memory. Elizabeth had mentioned the Carlsons' disgust that Ellen came with them to the ambassador's ball. Charlotte, who stayed behind to do the packing, claimed the baroness had wanted to help but was cajoled into attending by the sisters.

"Apparently," Joan went on, "she is quite intuitive. She makes it a practice to find some aspect of a person that he or she is fearful of or embarrassed by, then she gives a bit of positive advice, always with a sense of mystery. With her looks, she needs do little else to make most people decide she is both wise and wonderful. It is especially useful with servants like us, who are seldom treated with any civility at all. She gains a horde of admirers in the palace with little effort."

Hannah remembered her one meeting with the baroness. She had indeed been impressed, simply by a smile from one not required to notice her presence. "But the duchess' maid, Charlotte, claims the baroness is an angel, too good for the rest of us."

"Then Charlotte must be one the baroness thought it worthwhile to cultivate."

"She is only a maid."

"The duchess' maid. And she does exactly what the baroness wants: spreads tales of her goodness to all who will listen."

"I see." Hannah began to comprehend the scope of Ellen Rochdale's planning. "She is unable to hide her true personality completely."

"No one can play a role forever. Her mask slips from time to time, but only with those who can do her no harm." Marie, the maid who spoke little English and had no friends, was a likely victim. How cold, how calculating, how clever!

"It seems she really does have the Sight," Hannah murmured. "Not to see the future, but to see into people's personalities and know how to deceive them." Reminded, she told Joan the story Charlotte had related. "She was convinced the baroness has the Sight."

Joan's practical mind framed another explanation. "I'd say a messenger probably brought the letter early in the day. The baroness read it, used the information to appear all-knowing, and handed over the letter later, proving her supposed gift."

It was difficult for Hannah to take in the complexity of Ellen's thinking. "She must have planned all this some time ago, and in some detail."

"But it would not be difficult to take on a role temporarily, especially for an accomplished actress. But listen to this!" Joan had saved her best bit of information for last. "My mistress mentioned something strange about the baroness that I put little importance to until recently."

"What is that?"

"The day after Lord Amberson was killed, Henrietta remarked that she saw Ellen Rochdale outside the palace in the early morning. She carried a spade, and Henrietta, a curious sort, followed, to see what she was up to." The image of Mistress Beverley creeping along behind the baroness was comical, and Hannah's mind dwelt on it for a second before catching up with Joan's account. "—buried something in the midden. She was intrigued, since she dug a hole rather than just throwing the trash on the heap."

Hannah took a second to digest this. "Did she see what it was?"

Joan expression turned ironic. "Henrietta is curious, but her interest did not extend that far. She would not go near the midden to save her life."

Hannah rose and righted the wig once more. "We must ask her to show us the spot."

"Are you mad?"

"No," Hannah replied, "merely determined."

They met Henrietta Beverley coming down the stairs as they went up to find her. At first confused, her expression quickly turned to outrage. "What do you think you are about, girl? If you stole those clothes, I'll see you horsewhipped!"

"Madame, you can help to capture the person who murdered your brother."

She sputtered, tried to maintain her outrage, then deflated like a pierced sheep's bladder. "You know who killed Charles?"

"I believe you saw a certain woman dispose of something in the palace midden."

She thought for a moment, trying to recall the incident. "I did, but what of it?"

"Is it normal, do you think, for a pregnant noblewoman to dispose of her own trash?"

"Of course not," Henrietta said coldly. "That's what those of your station are for."

"I believe she killed Lord Amberson, and you caught her hiding the evidence."

Her eyes widened, first with surprise then with pride at her own cleverness. "And Charles?"

Hannah said a brief prayer before telling the lie. "He must have suspected her, so she poisoned him, too."

She teetered for a moment between belief and disbelief, but in the end seemed happier with the former. "My poor brother! Devoted always to the king's service, and in return? Murdered at the hands of an evil woman!"

"Could you show us the exact spot?" Hannah added what

she hoped was an irresistible suggestion. "And you must tell His Lordship what you saw, to avenge your brother."

The large bosom swelled even more. "Of course," she boomed. "He will be grateful, I am sure, to put the matter to rest." Then she was off, sweeping along before Hannah and Joan, who exchanged triumphant glances as they followed. Henrietta was now on their side.

As they passed through the palace gates, Hannah again took on the persona of a lady, raising her head and pulling her face into a haughty expression, although inside she trembled so badly she could hardly put one foot before the other. Joan glanced at her with some interest, her plain face showing both amusement at her outer demeanor and understanding of her inner terror. As they passed a small shed, Hannah whispered, "Could you see if there is a shovel inside, Joan? I, um, it would look odd if I did so dressed like this."

Good-naturedly, Joan did as asked and emerged with a small spade. "I suppose I'll do the digging, as well." She smiled at Hannah's embarrassment. "Don't worry. I don't mind."

The midden was along the riverbank, a depression rapidly filling with bones, shards, and foul-smelling household waste. As they neared it, Henrietta wrinkled her nose in disgust and stopped far back from the edge. "Of course the baroness did not wade into the midden. She stopped just over there." She pointed to a spot a few feet farther on. "Go forward, and I will direct you."

Hannah and Joan did as ordered. Once they had found the general area, Henrietta directed them somewhat off the path, a few feet to the left. The search took some time. "I was standing farther away, of course, and it has been many days, so my memory is not clear. Still, I think you are close, Joan. Try digging there." Obediently, Joan dug a shallow hole, Hannah almost in her way as she tried to see. Nothing. "Perhaps a few more steps that way."

Joan moved farther to her left and began a second hole. "Try scraping the blade across the earth," Hannah suggested. "She wouldn't have worked very hard at it."

Seeing the wisdom of that, Joan dragged the shovel over the damp ground, turning up a half-inch of soil. On the third stroke, a glint showed, and another pass revealed several pieces of glass. "It's green," Hannah said triumphantly. Picking up the visible bits, Joan handed them to Hannah then scraped up more. Soon they had what looked like most of a goblet. Green, with a stem, a carved bowl, and a wide lip. Hannah knew that the piece she had found below Amberson's window was part of the whole. Now it was a matter of timing, of getting things in place. With Henrietta's backing, she could prove that Ellen Rochdale took the pieces of the goblet away and buried them so they would not be found. If Simon located Daniel, and if Daniel knew of a relationship between the baroness and Charles Beverley, they could prove their theory. She hoped.

Simon entered the guardhouse, changing his walk, the way he held his shoulders, and even his face by pulling his chin back and lowering his brows. He had to find Daniel, and the only starting place was here, where the most danger lay at the moment.

He found Daniel's belongings, but there was nothing to indicate where he spent his free time: a few articles of clothing, a broken belt, and a pair of boots in need of polish. As he picked up the boots and upended them, something fell out onto the floor, a scrap of fabric too fine for a guardsman, in fact, too fine for a man. It was a woman's scarf, and in it were tied several coins.

He pocketed the bundle and quickly looked through the rest. Nothing. Simon left the room, avoiding a couple of guardsmen in the passageway by ducking into a dark corner. He was almost out of the building when he was grabbed roughly from behind. Ducking quickly, he spun out of his attacker's grasp and turned to face the man who must be Daniel. He blocked Simon's escape route. The only retreat was the guardroom, where he would be easily be cornered and arrested.

"I heard you was looking for me."

"To give you a chance to tell the truth. If you reveal what you know about Charles Beverley, the princess will help you escape the hangman's noose."

"Why would the hangman think he could have me? I ain't done nothing." Before Simon could react, Daniel was on him, raining blows on his body and face so hard that for few moments he could do nothing but crouch defensively. The man was bigger, stronger, and fully trained to fight. Simon was smaller, strong perhaps but untrained and hindered by his crippled arm. His panicked brain fought for clarity, his body soon rang with pain. He fell to the floor, trying to protect himself until he could launch a counterattack. Daniel kicked him in the ribs, and he heard his own grunt of agony. Rolling away, he found the wall and tried to stand, but Daniel brought an elbow down on his cheekbone that almost sent him into unconsciousness. He let his body go limp, hoping it would appear he had succeeded.

Daniel took advantage of his apparent defeat to catch a few breaths. Simon lay quiet, gathering his strength and planning his strategy. He was already badly beaten. There would be only one chance, and he had to make it good.

He heard Daniel mutter, "Let's finish this." Opening one eye just enough to see his enemy pull a foot back for another kick to the ribs, Simon waited. At the last possible moment, he reached out with his good arm, grabbed the planted foot, and pulled it toward him as hard as he could. Daniel's arms flailed helplessly against the air, but there was nothing to keep him upright. Simon rose to one knee, desperately holding on, and Daniel went over backward, landing hard on the packed earth. An exclamation of pain burst from him as his head slammed against the opposite wall of the passageway.

Rising quickly, Simon kicked Daniel in the ribs, hoping to wind him and achieve submission. However, his boots, unlike the heavy ones worn by guardsmen, were too soft to inflict any real damage. He had to render the man unconscious, and quickly, since someone might come by at any moment. Cutting off his air supply would subdue but hopefully not kill him. Putting one knee onto his opponent's throat, he pressed firmly. Daniel thrashed violently, but Simon grabbed the front of his tunic, keeping the knee firmly in place as he watched his face. He struggled, pulling in tiny gasps of air whenever he could. His hands flailed at Simon's head, buffeting him in random but still painful blows. Simon took hold of his tunic with his good hand in order to keep the knee in place. It seemed to take forever, and his whole body screamed in objection. In all likelihood, that last kick had broken a rib, maybe two. But he had to persevere, had to keep the pressure on just until Daniel passed out. He was their only possible witness. Simon could not afford to let him die.

Finally, Daniel slumped back, inert. Simon waited a moment more to assure that he was not playing dead, then looked around. A door down the passageway looked promising: a storage room for weapons. Dragging Daniel inside, he spent a few minutes tying his hands and legs tightly to a support post, sacrificing strips of his tunic for bonds and a gag. The guardsman would be where Calkin could find him, if Simon could prevent his own arrest long enough to get word to him.

CHAPTER TWENTY-FOUR

Hannah spent a restless night at the Beverley town house. The place was a mess, since Henrietta was in the process of packing for the return to her holding, where she would not have rent to pay. She had adamantly refused to go to Whitehall until morning, and Hannah supposed that was just as well. If Simon located Daniel and brought him to the morning meeting with Northumberland, they could present all their evidence at once and prove beyond doubt that Elizabeth was guiltless.

Still, she did not sleep. Assigned a four-by-six space built into a wall, she crawled into the curtained enclosure and lay back on the slightly lumpy straw mattress. The light of the fire across the room made dancing shadows on the curtain, and she watched them rise and then fade to a dull glow, wondering if Simon had escaped capture, if Hugh had succeeded in his part, if Elizabeth was facing her last night of freedom. Life was unfair; she knew that. Orphaned children had to make their own way in the world. Economics, politics, and social status separated couples who might make each other happy. And those who should lead, who had both the intelligence and the will, were passed over for reasons that had nothing to do with the good of all. At this point, all they could hope for was that Elizabeth would survive the machinations that threatened not only her right to rule but also her very life.

Simon crept into the guards' sleeping quarters and touched

Calkin's arm. His friend was instantly awake, and, hearing the whispered, "It is Simon," relaxed. In one motion, he threw off his blanket and sat up, rubbing his face.

"What?"

"Come with me." Simon led the way to a corridor where they could speak in whispers. "I've got Daniel, who we think knows something of the crimes."

"Lead the way." Calkin followed Simon to the storeroom where he had left his captive. When they reached the door, he took a torch down from its holder and disappeared for a moment. When he returned, it was lit, and he led the way into the room.

Daniel was awake and had managed to sit up. He glared at them in the torchlight, and Calkin turned to Simon. "Daniel spied for Beverley," Simon explained. "He shifted his allegiance to Baroness Rochdale after Beverley died. When I tried to get him to go to Northumberland with his information, he attacked me."

Calkin's lip twitched. "And you subdued him." He bent over Daniel and removed the gag. "Yeoman Mann," he said formally. "You will answer my questions concerning these murders with no further trouble, or things will not go well for you."

There was no answer, but Daniel lowered his eyes, used to obeying authority. "I know nothing of any murders." He was surly and looked much the worse for the struggle with Simon. Not that Simon looked good.

"The Baroness Rochdale killed Lord Amberson," Simon began, hoping to shock Daniel into cooperation. "She poisoned his wine and threw the cup out the window in the confusion of the corpse's discovery the next morning. You must have seen her there."

Daniel looked surprised, thoughtful, and finally scornful. "There were a dozen people in the room before Dudley ordered them all out." His expression turned sly. "It's more likely you got rid of it, when your ancient master was called in to investigate."

"I know you listened to my conversation with the princess at Richmond. You told Beverley I was investigating for her, and he tried to kill me."

"Did he now? A shame that he failed. The man knew a murderer when he saw one."

"He was the murderer. He killed Marie after you told him she had a secret." Simon saw a slight narrowing of his eyes. "You didn't know your tattling resulted in her death, did you?"

Daniel's face turned hard "You killed her. I saw you there afterward, in the crowd."

"Why would I have done that?"

"She saw your precious princess sneak in to poison the old man. He was trying to disinherit her, and she killed him for it."

Calkin took a turn at trying to make him see reason. "Daniel, Beverley lied to you to hide his own crimes. He killed your friend Marie because she saw too much."

Simon wondered if that was true. If Daniel spied for his master, reporting everything he heard and saw, Beverley might have used the information to protect himself and his partner. The death of a servant would mean little to him. But he was beginning to understand that the girl's death would have meant little to the baroness, either.

"What you didn't realize," Simon told Daniel, "neither you nor Beverley, is that Ellen Rochdale is not comfortable with others knowing her sins. She has done away with Beverley. How long before she decides that you, too, have outlived your usefulness?"

Daniel looked at him as if he were a bug he would like to step on. "Who do you think I will believe? A creature like you or a woman like the baroness? She is pure and honest—generous, even, though I would serve her cause for nothing. And you? You serve a bastard: half-witch, half God-knows-what, who seeks to take the throne away from the rightful children of Henry Eight."

Ignoring the jibe, Calkin tried again. "Did you report their meeting to Beverley?"

"As a loyal guardsman, I reported to my superior what I saw in the course of my day. There's no crime in that."

"Did you know your superior was involved in Amberson's death?"

He looked surprised. "I swear it is not so. He asked me to discover what the princess was up to. When I told him, he ordered me to hinder her in any way I could." He spread his hands in justification. "I did as I was ordered."

"You tried to hurt Hannah."

Daniel looked to Calkin as if for some man-to-man understanding. "I thought she was a pretty thing, but then someone told me she was promised to this . . . apprentice." He said the word as if it were a curse.

"So you turned on her," Simon accused. "You pushed a planter off the balcony and almost hit her. You set two dogs loose that might have killed her."

"She is a false woman and deserved a scare or two. But I did not hurt anyone."

"What about Marie?"

Daniel' face took on a surprised expression. "I would never hurt Marie." He was telling the truth, at least as he saw it. He pointed at Simon. "Marie was sweet, not like your girl, who lied about being engaged and plots with Nan Bullen's daughter that everybody knows is a witch."

Simon felt a stab of pity for the absent Elizabeth. Would she never hear the end of accusations that her mother was unnatural, immoral, and wicked? He pressed on, determined to clear her name to the best of his ability. "When did you begin working for the baroness?"

Daniel wet his lips nervously. Up to this point, he could claim he had done his job as a guardsman in response to orders from his superior. Now, however, he was on shakier ground.

"The lady asked me to do for her as I had for Beverley, keep watch on these plotters and see what they were up to."

"Did she tell you to try to beat me to death?"

Daniel looked at him squarely. "No one had to ask. I only wish I had succeeded."

"But she did pay you to spy for her."

He hesitated, and Simon pulled from his pocket the scrap of cloth with the coins tied inside it. "I could ask the lady's companions to identify this scarf. Then you can explain how it came to be in your spare pair of boots."

The man slumped in defeat. "She paid me, yes. But it was for good, because she wants to prevent more murders."

Calkin spoke, his voice harsh with condemnation. "Your greed has made you blind, Yeoman. Did you never wonder why those two slunk behind the scenes rather than making their accusations plainly? They sought their own ends, and you assisted them, bringing about more murder." He handed the torch to Simon. "I will have some men take him into custody."

He was back in a moment with two guardsmen who avoided Daniel's eyes as they untrussed him and took him away. Calkin watched them go then turned to Simon. "What next?"

"The princess requested an audience with Northumberland first thing tomorrow."

"That tomorrow is today, I'm thinking. The watch has changed already."

"Then we must take Daniel there and make him tell what he knows."

"It will be done."

At that moment, one of the guardsmen hurtled into the room, his nose gushing blood. "He got away, Captain! He seemed docile enough, but when we came to a turning in the corridor, he pushed us sideways, into the wall. He was gone before we knew what happened."

Calkin uttered a phrase Simon had not heard him use before. "Find him! Get the rest of them up and hunt him down!" The man left, grateful, Simon guessed, to be out of his superior officer's presence. "They will find him," Calkin assured. "There's no place for him to hide."

He was wrong, and Simon knew it. There were a hundred places to hide in Whitehall if a man was desperate enough. And having worked here for months, Daniel would know them all.

Calkin suggested that Simon stay where he was, out of sight, until Daniel was recaptured and the order to arrest him could be rescinded. After his friend went off to oversee those matters, however, he found it hard to remain stationary. Pacing the tiny room, he looked out the sole window each time he passed in hopes of seeing guardsmen with Daniel in custody. Daniel would get out of Whitehall if he was wise, but where would he go? He might have family in the city. He might know friends who would hide him, no matter what he had done. Suddenly Simon stopped.

Where would Daniel go? To Ellen Rochdale, of course. She was close. She was his friend, at least he thought so. And she had the cleverness he lacked. He would almost certainly turn to her.

Simon doused the failing torch, left the tiny storeroom, and made his way along the dark corridor. It was not yet daylight, but the deep black of night was starting to dissipate to grays, so he kept to the walls and the still-dark edges of night. The palace was as quiet as it ever was, the revels over, the inhabitants gone to their beds. He had to stop a few times and back into a corner to let sleepy servants pass, one with a blanket and one with a cup of something, probably a sleeping draught. They never saw him, which was for the best, since in his present costume no one would mistake him for someone who should be inside the king's palace.

Whitehall, a maze at the best of times and even worse in the gray-black of predawn, threatened to defeat him. Unable to ask directions, Simon wandered in and out of different areas, looking for something familiar. Finally, he recognized a doorway. From there he retraced the route he and Carthburt had made that first day, knowing that Ellen Rochdale's rooms were next door to what had been Amberson and then Beverley's sleeping quarters.

Once he found the right place, he stood outside the door uncertainly, wondering who might be inside the apartments. He listened, ear to the door. There was a muffled conversation going on, a man and a woman. He understood little of it. The man spoke quickly in low tones. The woman's voice was slower, the tones reassuring. Simon caught a phrase now and then: "Don't worry," and then "He cannot—" He could not make out the end of it, but he was almost certain the speakers were Daniel and the baroness.

"What are you doing here?" A voice behind him almost sent Simon's heart to his throat. "Guard!" He turned to see a round, red-cheeked woman who first brought to mind his own mother. Even her expression mirrored his mother's when she was outraged.

The door opened, and Ellen Rochdale stood in the opening, taking in the scene before her. Now past his infatuation, Simon felt as if he could read her mind, see her turning the situation to her advantage. It only took a second. "Simon," she said, her tone chiding, "you are almost come too late. I depart soon."

"You know this young man?" The woman looked scandalized.

Ellen laughed, a silvery, tinkling sound. "I do, but not as you see him, Charlotte. Simon is a friend who asked me to help him with his costume for a pageant they are preparing. I feared he would come too late, and I would already be on my way, but you have found him." She pulled Simon into the room, gesturing for the woman to follow. There was no one else in sight, but a door to his right stood slightly ajar. He guessed Daniel waited there to see what developed.

Charlotte eyed Simon distrustfully, digesting the lie. "I came to say good-bye."

"How kind you are." To continue the ruse she had begun, Ellen made a critical examination of Simon's attire. Turning her back to the woman, she held Simon's eye as she spoke to her. "I will pray that no harm befalls you until we meet again, no accident or tragedy." He got the message. The woman—Charlotte—was in danger if he did not play along. An appeal for help would result in her death as well as his. He had to wait until she was safely away.

There followed a tender scene in which the earnest but slightly dull-witted Charlotte took leave of the woman she believed to be an angel on earth. From their conversation, Simon realized she was the maid who had praised the baroness to Hannah, innocently building one of several walls that had kept them from the truth. Ellen Rochdale was an excellent judge of whom she could manipulate, and this ability had served her especially well to ingratiate herself with servants, the worst gossips in the Court. Probably Marie had known of the hag that hid behind the beautiful mask, but Marie had had no power, no one to turn to.

Charlotte finally backed away, "Please be careful on your journey home," she cautioned. "The bandits who killed your dear husband may still be a threat."

"I'm sure Andrew's men have hunted them down and punished them by now," Ellen replied, her eyes sorrowful at the subject of her husband's death. "I must see to his affairs, as he would want me to do."

As she closed the door behind Charlotte, the baroness' expression changed. Simon saw in it pleasure at the control she wielded over others. When Daniel emerged from the side room her face changed again, innocence dropping behind her eyes like a curtain closed to hide a garbage heap. Stepping between Simon and the door, Daniel folded his arms across his chest. The guardsman would not underestimate his crippled opponent again.

"Daniel tells me your princess has an appointment with the duke this morning. What lies will she tell him about me?"

Simon hoped his voice would remain steady. "Elizabeth does not lie." It was not quite true. The princess' truth-telling could be capricious, but she was as honest as one in her position could be. "She will say that you, not she, killed Lord Amberson and Charles Beverley."

"Liar!" The blow that accompanied Daniel's roar of objection sent Simon staggering to one side, and he knew nothing for some time.

Chapter Twenty-Five

When he came to himself, Simon felt cool air on his face and a terrible pain in his middle. Opening his eyes added a sickening lurch to the mix, and he feared for a moment he might vomit. He was slung over a man's shoulder, Daniel's, of course, and they were ascending an outdoor staircase. Turning his face to one side, he saw a crenellated wall and starlight above it. Though groggy with pain and nauseated from hanging upside down like a slaughtered hog, he forced himself to think. One of the castle towers, unused except in wartime. A high place. A lonely place. A place he would probably not depart alive.

His first response was to struggle, but it was a feeble attempt. A gag of silken fabric forced his jaws painfully apart and at the same time made it difficult to breathe. His hands were tied behind his back. Daniel's shoulder jabbed into his damaged ribs with every step, making it hard to think, much less concoct a plan of escape.

Reaching the parapet wall, Daniel stopped and dumped his burden unceremoniously onto the tower floor. With some difficulty, Simon managed to avoid letting his head bounce off the wall. He closed his eyes briefly, trying to pull his wits together. If he lost focus now, he was dead. Elizabeth's cause was lost. And Hannah would suffer, too.

Ellen stood facing him, and her image wavered softly for a few moments, as if she were moving to some unheard music. It was not true, of course; it was his vision blurring and then clearing. In fact, now that he knew Ellen better, Simon could not picture her dancing or singing or joining other innocent pastimes. For someone as wicked as she, only plotting was worth doing.

As she regarded Simon dispassionately, he wondered how he would die. She was planning how to get rid of him, hardly bothering to maintain the innocent façade. "Daniel, you must find out where this meeting with Northumberland is to take place, and when."

He nodded. "I will."

"Be careful. The guards will be looking for you."

"I will." He seemed hesitant to leave.

"I am safe with him now. He is securely tied." Her tone was perfect, half-assuring, half-fearful. Simon could almost believe she depended on Daniel's strength, being herself so fragile. Almost, except he saw her now for what she really was.

Daniel did not. He hovered nearby. "What will you do if the Whore's Bastard convinces Northumberland that you are guilty of some crime?"

Ellen smiled bravely. "God will not allow that to happen. The innocent are under His protection. I will go to this meeting and tell His Lordship the truth. Elizabeth will be punished."

"They should all be punished," he insisted. "This one, his trollop, and Anne's bastard."

The baroness gave a sigh of feminine passivity. "God sees to such things, not man."

Daniel left then, shutting the trap door quietly behind him. As soon as he was gone, Ellen's demeanor changed, and Simon saw what he had only glimpsed earlier: smug satisfaction, eager anticipation, and enjoyment of the extent to which she fooled the world when she chose.

"He will kill you when he returns," she said matter-of-factly. "I have not yet had him kill, but we have been working toward it, and I think he is ready. He believes you are evil, and that you want to destroy me. He believes I am good, and therefore, acting to defend me is justified. Soldiers are taught how to kill. They merely need to be convinced the killing is righteous."

Stepping forward, she removed Simon's gag. He ran his tongue around his mouth and coughed, sending a stabbing pain through his body. She seemed interested in his pain, but not in a sympathetic way. "I leave for Rochdale this morning," she told him. "Of course I want to return to my husband's lands to have his child."

The part of Elizabeth's message they had not understood suddenly became clear to him, and his own knowledge filled in the gaps. "What child would that be?"

One eyebrow rose in the first sign of real humor he had seen from her. "So you know?"

"You plan to make the huntsman's child heir to Rochdale, so you control everything."

She patted her stomach and then, with a mischievous grin, pulled at the mound, moving it off to one side so that her shape altered comically. At Simon's look of disgust, she chuckled. "I hope she has a son, but I will take a daughter if I must." She restored her "belly" to its previous position. "You understand why I must be away from London. There is much to do." Her tone implied dire events, and he shuddered. Would the huntsman and his family suffer death by poison, too, so that no one knew of the substitution?

Ellen read his thought, as it seemed she was uncannily able to do. "The huntsman may yet fare well. They want a home, and I think a child is a fair exchange for that privilege."

He marveled at her planning while at the same time deploring her depravity. "You have gone to a lot of trouble to arrange this charade."

"Yes," she agreed. "It was a lot of trouble. My father-in-law, in his wisdom, decreed that I must have a child within three years. I thought it would be no trouble at all, but I underestimated my husband's unwillingness to participate."

"So you were about to be set aside."

"But I am unwilling to give up my title and access to my husband's wealth."

"When you realized there would soon be a child you could pass off as yours, you faked your pregnancy."

"Unfortunately, Andrew could attest that the child, if there had been one, could not be his, so he could not hear of my so-called pregnancy. I came to London, supposedly with reluctance."

"But the baron had to die before you could produce the theoretical heir to Rochdale."

"Fortune was on my side, for I met Charles Beverley on my first day here. You have noted, I am sure, my talent for reading people's secret desires. His lust for advancement was plain to all, but I looked deeper and saw what he might do to accomplish it. After that, we struck a bargain."

"You wanted the baron dead, and you had to be far enough away that your innocence was beyond question."

"Yes. My part was to clear Beverley's path to riches, which was easy enough."

"Except your maid saw you slip into his room."

She frowned at the remembered inconvenience. "She already suspected there was no child, I think. She would have been lost overboard on the way north, so her spying merely hastened her end by a few weeks."

"And Beverley had outlived his usefulness, so he had to die as well.

"I had not planned for him to die so soon, but it turned out well in the end, since there is one less who knows the whole tale." She untied the cords at his wrists. "Daniel will escort me home. When he does not return, few will notice or care."

"He'll die of poison, too?"

"Probably. It is hard to detect, both for the victim and for those left behind." Her expression turned briefly resentful. "Your Master Carthburt disturbed my plans when he called the old man's death murder, but only slightly."

"You turned the blame on the princess."

"Mere convenience," she said almost apologetically. "I have nothing against her." Simon wondered if he could struggle to his feet and overcome her before Daniel returned. The trap door was closed, his arms were trussed to his body, and the wall was low. If he stood, Ellen would simply push him over the parapet. He had to wait for a better opportunity.

"Once Daniel is gone, you will return to Rochdale alone, spinning some tale that he abandoned you, and make your bargain with the huntsman's wife."

"It will bring things to a nice conclusion. The crimes here in London are already laid at Elizabeth's feet, and Daniel will simply be another wandering soldier who had had enough of city life. Your pretty girl will fall with the princess, and with you dead, there will be no one left to accuse me. Even the method of your death will help to prove your evil intent."

She pulled off the beaded coif she wore and tousled her hair with her fingers. Watching to note the point where he understood, she tore the sleeve of her dress, ripping it from the shoulder seam with a ferocious tug. Last, she kicked off one slipper and let it fly across the circular space, hitting the wall with a soft thud and spinning to a stop some distance away.

He slumped against the wall. "When Daniel returns, he will find me attacking you."

"He already thinks the worst. When he sees the struggle, he will have no trouble acting as his training demands. Your interference changed my plan but did not ruin it."

"Do you always get what you want? Is there always a man willing to do anything for you?"

She shrugged delicately. "Can I help it if men are as they are?"

"Did Charles Beverley think to replace the baron in your bed?"

Her face turned hard for a moment. "The baron never found his way to my bed. He was a man I could not reach, no matter how I tried."

"Perhaps he saw beneath your façade, to the real woman."

She shook her head, unwilling to believe it. "They never do unless I choose to show them. Even Charles, I think, convinced himself that he was doing a service to me by killing a husband who did not appreciate me." She gave a huff of disdain. "I suppose he planned to take Andrew's place in my life, but I would never trade one problem for another."

"How did you manage to poison him? The door was guarded."

"Apparent pregnancy is convenient." Her tone was smug. "One cannot imagine a woman in my condition spanning the distance between the duchess' window and Amberson's, but it was easy enough. When workers made repairs due to a recent fire, I asked for a plank to put under my bed, claiming that it would relieve my overburdened back. They were glad to help a mother-to-be."

"You used the plank as a walkway between balconies."

"Exactly." Her forehead furrowed briefly. "If I'd thought of it earlier, I would not have been seen the first time. If one does not look down, the feat is quite simple."

"You poisoned his mead."

"He sent a bottle of it to Northumberland as a gift, but the duke drinks only wine. I poisoned the bottle he had sent and switched it with the one on his worktable. I was only a few minutes delayed for the midday meal." She smiled and touched

Simon's arm with a conspiratorial air. "In truth, Beverley's mead is better than most. I intend to take the bottle with me and drink a toast to dead friends when I am close to Rochdale and success."

The sound of footsteps rose from below, and she moved quickly. Pulling the cord that held Simon's arms, she released him and then screamed piercingly. "Help!" He had only a second to consider his course of action. He could stay where he was, evincing no aggression, but he doubted Daniel would believe she was acting. He had to meet him head on; it was his only chance.

The trap door burst open, its lid striking the stone floor with a clatter. Daniel appeared, bellowing, "Leave her alone, villain!" He rushed forward, and Simon barely had time to dodge to one side. Daniel hit the parapet wall, stumbling back from its edge, but recovered quickly and came at Simon again, this time with more control. Behind them, Ellen closed the trap door and stood on it, preventing Simon's escape. Her intention was clear: one of them would not leave the tower alive.

Daniel was no student of human behavior, but he had learned from his previous encounter with Simon. He approached watchfully, crouched low and intense. "You are brave enough when it is women you face, cripple, but your deeds have caught up with you now."

Simon glanced over the wall, unable to keep from thinking what was sure to happen. Four stories, his mind screamed. A fall that far would kill him. He would be unable to help Elizabeth, unable to save Hannah. He would never see her again.

His attacker lunged at him, and again he spun away, but this time Daniel anticipated the move and followed, taking the back of his tunic in one strong hand. He jerked Simon backward, catching him against his chest and grabbing him under the arms. In an instant, Simon was lifted off his feet. He clawed frantically at Daniel's head, but his hands could not reach. His damaged ribs screamed with pain, and his shoulder joints strained from the weight of his own body. Despite that, he fought, sensing Daniel's intent. The guardsman moved to the parapet, a low wall that separated them from the long drop. Simon braced his feet against the outer wall, but Daniel simply lurched backward and then tried again. The struggle continued for some time, both men silent in concentration. Only their grunts of exertion sounded: Simon pushing back each time his feet connected with a hard surface, Daniel staggering a few steps, renewing his hold, and pressing forward again. In spite of his predicament, Simon sensed Ellen's interested gaze. She really did not care who won. Either way, she would find an advantage and use it.

He felt himself tiring. It took all of his strength to keep his legs extended in front of him, to keep pushing himself and Daniel away from the wall. Worse, the pendant position squeezed the air from his lungs. It became harder and harder to fight at all. His leg thrusts grew weaker, the distance Daniel had to retreat shorter. Ellen waited, calm as fallen snow, cold as death.

Then his foot slipped. His ankle banged hard against the crenellated edge, and suddenly his feet dangled over air. Now he reached back in desperation, grabbing the neck of Daniel's tunic. It was all that kept him from plummeting to the ground below, for Daniel released his grip, slamming Simon's back painfully against the wall. His efforts turned to making Simon release him. The weight dangling from his clothing pulled him forward so that he, too, leaned over the parapet wall. Simon used his right arm to hold on as he desperately tried to find a hold with his other hand, to get a purchase that might allow use of his good hand to pull himself back inside. It was no use. The arm obeyed only halfway, and he dared not trust his life to it.

Above him, Daniel made unusual sounds, and Simon realized he was having a hard time breathing, pressed against the stone wall by his opponent's weight. That was both good and bad; his enemy was weakening, but only he kept Simon from falling to the ground, far below.

Simon's options grew fewer by the second. With no good choices, he took the least dangerous. Pulling himself as far upward as he could, he jabbed the fingers of his weak hand into Daniel's eyes, then quickly transferred his grip from the man's shirtfront to the wall. He hoped to make his opponent retreat long enough for him to pull himself back inside the parapet wall. It was not to be.

With a scream of pain, Daniel clapped his hands over his eyes. That was as Simon had hoped, but Ellen saw her chance and took it. Rushing forward, she pushed with all her strength, sending the blinded guardsman over the wall. The impact of his body sent Simon hurtling downward with him, and after a brief sensation of floating, he felt an impact and then nothing.

Chapter Twenty-Six

Elizabeth could not help pacing the small audience room as she waited for her early morning meeting with the duke. She had little evidence to prove her case, although she believed she knew almost all of it. Beverley was dead. Marie was dead. Only Ellen and Daniel knew all of the truth, and they had good reason to keep it to themselves. How would Simon convince Daniel to tell the truth? she wondered.

She wanted to ask Robin if anyone had seen Simon but dared not. Although she felt so tense that her tendons might split her skin, she had to appear serene. And innocent.

Only a short while after the appointed time, the Lord President entered the room, his face a stern mask. "Your Grace," he said with no warmth. "My son tells me that you crave a word."

"Yes, my lord duke. I have come to put to rest certain rumors that have arisen concerning the deaths of Lord Amberson and Charles Beverley."

"Madam, these rumors, as you call them, are quite serious. I hope that you will be able to answer them before the council. It is not meet, however, that we discuss them here."

"My lord, I would save you embarrassment," she said quickly, for he turned as if to leave. "If I am accused of murder before the council, and the charges are proven false, as they will be, will it not weaken your position that you allowed lies to be aired against a princess of the blood?"

He paused, apparently unwilling to give anyone cause to call him incompetent. "I will listen, but be advised. You will appear before the council unless I am fully convinced. I do not conduct the nation's business in private."

Ignoring the irony of that statement, she said meekly, "I understand." He eyed her impatiently, his body almost humming with anxiety. Northumberland was not a dishonest man, she knew. Self-absorbed, crafty, and greedy, yes, but not dishonest. He did not want to falsely accuse her of murder. Her best chance was to convince him here and now that he should not accuse her at all, that it was to his detriment to do so. But how?

There was nothing to do but put before him what she knew. "I believe, Your Lordship, that your evidence against me comes from two sources. Charles Beverley first approached you, saying someone had seen me leaving Lord Amberson's rooms on the day he was poisoned. That person was a maid, one Marie, who later fell on the stairs and died."

"That is true."

She relaxed a little. Her first guess, that Beverley had carried the tale, not Ellen, had been correct. Ellen would try to remain as far as possible from accusation and counteraccusation. "The servant is dead. We cannot question her to learn exactly what she saw or why she might lie." The duke's mouth moved as if to say something, but he pressed his lips together and maintained silence. "I believe Marie did see something that day. She saw her own mistress entering the room carrying poison with which to kill His Lordship."

Even absent, Ellen Rochdale's influence remained, and Northumberland rose to her defense. "The baroness had no reason to kill the old man. It was she who reported what her maid saw to the captain of the guard."

Elizabeth ignored the hopeless feeling that Northumberland had already made up his mind. "Here is the truth of it: Ellen and Charles Beverley made a pact. He disposed of her husband, whom she found tiresome and repugnant, in a way that was attributed to robbers. In return, she poisoned Lord Amberson while Beverley was far away, leaving him in control of His Lordship's estate through Madeline, his heir."

The duke's face was almost comic as he struggled to digest this. Elizabeth wondered grimly if there was any chance at all he might believe her and if so, would he feel surprise or admiration for so clever a plan. Such removal of inconvenient persons might appeal to him, given the problems England faced at the time. Still, she was a princess. He had to listen.

"Beverley claimed he and the baroness were unacquainted, that he'd never spoken to her until she came to him with the story." He turned to his son. "Have you ever seen them together?"

With a reluctant glance at Elizabeth, Robert shook his head. "I have not."

"Find Ellen Rochdale and bring her here." With a bow of obedience, Robert left.

"We believe there was a go-between," Elizabeth said when the Lord President's questioning gaze moved back to her. "A certain guardsman who assisted them."

"And has this guardsman come forward to admit he served in that role?"

"I had hoped to see him here this morning, but—" She stopped. She had proved nothing, only made baseless allegations against a woman known for meekness and for the sort of beauty that made fools of men. Even the most powerful man in England, it seemed.

Northumberland's voice was devoid of sympathy as he returned to his own interpretation of recent events. "You were seen exiting His Lordship's room with a bottle in your hand, Your Grace. Your maid's lover sells poisons."

"Medicines, my lord."

"Substances that kill." Northumberland glared at her. "And there is this." He drew from his tunic a folded scrap of paper and handed it over. As she glanced at it, her heart seemed to stop in her chest. She put on a brave face, however, and scanned the note quickly. The words were not hers, though there was a wax seal formed in an "E," broken into two pieces where the letter had been opened. It was the note she had sent to Simon's house, but her words were gone and new ones written: *I was observed. Assure that the maid Marie does not tell. E.*

"A fair copy of my hand, but not perfect."

"It has your seal. It was found at the shop where the apprentice works."

"Someone took a note I wrote, scraped the ink off the parchment, and composed a new message." He did not look convinced, and she added, "If I had written that, Simon would have destroyed it. He is not such a fool as to keep something that incriminates us both."

"Perhaps he thought it would benefit him at some time in the future."

Elizabeth laughed, or at least gave the best imitation she could in her present position. "My lord duke, you do not know Simon Maldon. He thinks nothing of his own benefit, now or for the future. He is a man of integrity."

"We have only your word for that."

There was a scratch at the door, and a servant put his head in. "My lord, the princess' servant Hannah is outside. She begs to bring in a witness."

Northumberland frowned. "What? Is this woman not hunted throughout London, and she walks boldly through the very palace and asks to enter here?"

"Your Worship, if you will listen." Hannah stepped into the room. The red wig was gone, but she still wore Elizabeth's dress.

"I have with me one who may shed some light on this matter."

"Bring him in, then."

"It is a lady, Your Lordship." She turned to usher in Henrietta Beverley. Seeing her air of importance, Elizabeth felt a glint of hope for the first time in hours.

Henrietta was both nervous and proud to be in the presence of the Lord President. She tried for a coquettish smile but achieved instead a rather frightening grimace.

"My lord, Mistress Beverley is come to tell what she saw the morning after Lord Amberson's death."

Northumberland was less than patient. "Very well. Tell us what you've come to say."

After a few false starts, she succeeding in making sound. "I was coming to see my brother, Charles Beverley. He was—"

"I know who your brother was."

"Of course, Your Worship. I only meant to be clear." She stopped, made a few more soundless starts, and then found her voice again. "I came up from the river, having taken one of the boats that bring people to and fro so nicely. They are—" At a slight rise of Northumberland's nose, she forced herself away from the topic of boats. "At any rate, I came past the midden, and there was the baroness, digging with a little spade. I thought it odd, you know, her so far along with the child and having servants who should be taking care of such things for her."

"You're sure it was the baroness?"

"Oh, yes, Your Worship. I had seen her several times before. She was all they could talk of when she came to town." Her voice reflected slight resentment. In all likelihood few spoke of her presence in London, at least not approvingly.

"Did you see what the baroness buried?"

"Uh, no, Your Worship."

"But we went to the spot and found this, Your Lordship." Hannah pulled a cloth from her pocket and unwrapped the pieces of green glass.

The duke leaned in to look. "They are very like the cup he kept on his table," he admitted.

"Someone threw the cup out the window and later buried the pieces," Hannah said firmly.

"And that could have been anyone," the duke replied. "Being seen near the midden does not make a person a murderer."

A stir at the door distracted them, and they turned to see Robert Dudley escorting Ellen Rochdale through the doorway. Her clothing was in disarray, her hair hung loose, and her were eyes wild. "I did not have to look far," Robin told his father. "She was looking for you."

"Your Highness. My lord. I am sorry—. It is a terrible thing. I—" The baroness' throat stopped, and she turned away, weeping almost silently into her hair.

"There's been an incident." Robin Dudley took up the account in deference to Ellen's distress. "The baroness was abducted by one of the guardsmen, one Daniel Mann, who had apparently become diseased in his mind. He forced her to the west tower, intending—" Robin stopped as the baroness sobbed aloud. "Intending harm to her. She was rescued by a brave young man whom I think Her Highness knows, Simon Maldon."

"The one whose arrest had been ordered?"

"A mistake, sir. Apparently, young Maldon had suspicions that this Daniel was the murderer of both Lord Amberson and Charles Beverley. He was trying to prove that when he came to Whitehall and happened to see the baroness' abduction."

"So we have this guardsman under arrest? The matter is resolved?"

Ellen's tearful face was as lovely as an angel's when she raised it to answer the Lord President. "Not arrest, Your Worship. He is dead. He and that poor boy went over the wall in the struggle.

Simon Maldon died to save me!"

Simon thought there must be a fish rotting in his mother's kitchen, though she was not usually one to overlook such things. The smell was distinct and close. He opened his eyes and was surprised to see a few last stars above him. They were fading; day was imminent. Slowly his mind cleared. Slowly it came to him that the stench and the stars above him meant he was not in his own bed. Then where? He searched his memory: Ellen Rochdale's satisfied face appeared, then Daniel's angry one. Everything came together. He had somehow survived the fall from the tower.

Get up! he told himself, and his outraged body tried to obey. His shoulders ached from the struggle in the tower. A spot over his ear throbbed from a blow Daniel had administered, and his ribs felt as if they had been seared with a blacksmith's iron. He rolled slowly to his strong side and pushed himself up. He lay on something—no, someone. Daniel sprawled beneath him, inert, his skin cool. Simon's fall had been broken by the body of the man who would have killed him, had he been able. His head was turned to the side in a position impossible for muscles and sinew to take, and below it, a dark stain spread over the rocks and into the ground.

Turning from the gruesome sight, Simon took stock of where he was. Below the castle, between the Thames and the outer wall. Two stories above, Ellen Rochdale schemed and maneuvered. He should have died in the fall; she undoubtedly thought he had. He had to act quickly, while she believed she was safe.

Simon stood. One ankle objected, but he probed it carefully. No swelling, no obvious fractures. It held his weight, although it felt like he was stepping on glass. If it could work, then it had to. He had to find Calkin.

His friend was not in the guardroom; in fact, no one was.

Simon took the opportunity to change clothing and at the same time hide some of the marks the night's events had left on him. He sloshed his tunic in a fountain and used it to wash the worst of the blood and dirt from his face and hands. Taking a guardsman's uniform from its hook, he put it on. It was big for him, but he hoped to make up for that with swagger. With no idea how he would accomplish it, he knew he had to find the place where Elizabeth was meeting with Northumberland. He had to stop Ellen Rochdale.

Elizabeth took Hannah's hand in hers when the baroness announced Simon's death, but she could not have said whether it was to comfort Hannah or receive comfort herself. Simon dead! Such a thing was unthinkable.

Hannah seemed to shrink, her body closing on itself, making her less than she had been a moment ago. Tears streamed from her eyes, but with an effort she could not have explained, she did not sob aloud, did not make a sound. Had they been able to compare, they would have shared similar pain, similar memories, similar regrets. Never to see his thoughtful expression as he considered some matter important to him. Never to hear him say, "Hannah" or "Highness" in a teasing tone. Never to feel the surety that someone solid was there when needed, always, ever.

Another knock came at the door, and Elizabeth wondered irrelevantly if ever a meeting was so often interrupted. Yet another servant whispered to Robin Dudley, who approached his father and spoke in low tones. Northumberland looked at Elizabeth, then at Ellen. "Here is news," he said. "The guardsman was found below the east tower, as the baroness says. But there is no sign of Simon Maldon."

Hannah swayed, and Elizabeth squeezed her hand sharply. They had to finish this. The baroness could yet ruin them.

Ellen's face was a mask. The question in her eyes was the same one Elizabeth asked herself. Where was Simon?

Northumberland ignored the emotion in the room and kept to the practical. "Baroness, this woman claims she saw you burying something in the palace midden. They found green glass in the spot, and I ask you now, what were you burying in the midden?"

Ellen stood apart from the rest of them, her dress a ruin, her hair a mess, and her overall effect still stunning. When Northumberland turned his gaze on her, she shook her head, her manner perfectly representing a woman stressed beyond fairness but composed nevertheless.

"I am embarrassed to say it, Your Lordship, but it seems I must, or you will think worse of me. I am become quite clumsy as the child grows within, and I broke one of your wife's favorite figurines. Rather than admit to it, I hid the pieces, hoping she would believe it was lost in the move to Warwick." She paused, and her face turned pleading. "I am sorry, my lord."

She made it sound so believable, so simple. Elizabeth wondered irrelevantly if she could ever learn to lie so convincingly, so remorselessly. There was nothing more to say. Daniel, the only person who might have been able to convince the duke, was dead. He would decide now whether to accept her version of recent events or the baroness' plausible pack of lies.

Northumberland was silent for some time, considering all facets of the situation. "I suppose this ends the matter," he said finally. "This Daniel was guilty of the crimes, and he is dead."

Elizabeth could not believe it. How could he ignore the fact that Ellen had accused her of poisoning Amberson? Or that she had buried the pieces of the goblet in secret? The answer came quickly: with Daniel dead, there was no way to prove either her or Ellen guilty. Further investigation would create more problems, possibly a split between those who supported her and those who chose to believe Ellen. He probably suspected that Beverley had incited Amberson's murder, but the rest was speculative. The death of Marie was already seen as an accident; the baron was deemed the victim of bandits. If Daniel took the blame for Beverley's murder, it would end the matter. She was relieved of suspicion, but so was Ellen Rochdale.

The baroness recovered quickly and turned to the duke, laying a light hand on his arm. "My lord, if you are finished with me, I must go. I return home today, to Rochdale." Her voice almost broke as she said it, and Elizabeth marveled. *She would have been a worthy addition to our entertainments, playing the grieving wife.*

Northumberland's face softened. "I wish you a safe journey and such comfort as home might provide in your circumstances, madam."

Ellen approached Elizabeth, her expression sincere enough to convince almost anyone. "Your Grace, I must apologize for having caused you trouble. It is obvious to me now that my maid lied to implicate you in the crime she must have known her lover was responsible for. It grieves me that I was used in such a way. I would like to believe that it was her foolish emotions that led her astray rather than any animosity toward you."

With a proper curtsey to each of them, the Baroness Rochdale left the room. Elizabeth detected in her final glance a trace of smugness. Ellen had won. She closed the door quietly, as if not wanting to break the spell she had woven.

CHAPTER TWENTY-SEVEN

Simon made his way through the palace, following the directions Hannah had given. Daniel was dead. He had failed. He had to think of something before they were all arrested. Beverley had planted the seed against Elizabeth. Ellen had nurtured it, sensing the Lord President's desire to have something against the princess. What accusations had she made?

He reached the room and hesitated. Should he knock? Rush in? Listen? He decided it was best to approach from the opposite side, try to get a sense of the situation, and act from there. If he had to fight his way out of the palace with her beside him, he supposed he would try it.

Northumberland departed, but not before giving dire warnings about princesses who meddle where they should not. There were four of them: Hannah, Elizabeth, Henrietta, and Robert Dudley, who could not stop shaking his head.

"What a wild sleigh-ride," he said, wonderingly. "And all before breakfast."

"I am to leave London today." Henrietta seemed slightly dazed by the events she had witnessed, unsure of what the truth of it all might be.

"I understand young Madeline goes with you," Robin said.

"Yes. It will be some comfort to have her with me, though I know it will not be for long. In truth I have become quite fond of her, and she of me, I might say."

"But she will wed Giles." Robin's glance at Elizabeth signaled that he had spent even more time with Dorcas Fuller and reached some settlement.

"Not until she is fifteen."

So both parties had won something in the battle over Madeline. It was an odd end to the matter, but Henrietta seemed genuinely pleased. Maybe she did indeed like the child.

"I must see to this business, so I will leave you now," Dudley said.

Elizabeth took his hands in hers. "Robin, I am again in your debt."

He bowed. "Life with you is never dull, Your Grace." He kissed her hands, made a pretty speech about how much Henrietta would be missed, bowed to Hannah as gallantly as if she were a lady, and then left, trailing a cloud of scent and an air of relief. To him it was over. Elizabeth was out of danger, the killer was dead, and breakfast was imminent.

Once he was gone, Elizabeth and Hannah exchanged worried glances. Where was Simon?

He kept turning left, hoping to end up on the opposite side of the audience room. There were few astir due to the early hour, and those who saw him ignored his presence. One more guardsman carrying a message was no surprise, although this guardsman's appearance was hardly up to the usual standards. His lip was split, he walked as if every movement was agony, and his uniform was so ill-fitting as to be ludicrous. Added to that, he smelled of sweat, fear, and the midden where he had spent an unconscious hour.

When he at last reached the anteroom where the meeting was supposed to be, he listened at the door. He heard only the murmurs of women. Impatient, Simon peered into the room. Hannah and Elizabeth stood on either side of Henrietta Beverley like two reeds beside a stump.

"Hannah!" At the sound of his voice, she rushed to him, wrapping him in her arms, which caused his ribs exquisite pain and his heart exquisite joy.

"Simon! We were worried about you! They say that Daniel is dead. What happened?"

Elizabeth stopped him from answering, putting her arm around Henrietta. "First let us see that this lady is returned to the comfort of her own folk." Her eyes warned that Henrietta need not hear details of her brother's wickedness.

Before she left, Henrietta reminded the princess that the state should pay for Beverley's funeral. "My brother was a loyal servant to the Crown who deserves every honor."

"You are no doubt correct," Elizabeth said, allowing the mistress of Beverley her illusions for a while longer.

Hannah guided Henrietta down the corridor to where Joan waited. "The princess says you must take your lady home," she instructed, indicating with her eyes that she would explain the details later." Joan nodded and led her mistress away. Once Charles' crimes were fully revealed, she would be lucky to keep Beverley, poor as the holding was. Her wisest move would be to return there as soon as possible and hope that Northumberland forgot she existed.

As Hannah returned, she heard Calkin call to her, and she led him to the room where Elizabeth and Simon had begun puzzling out the details of what had happened.

"I was worried, lad, but I should have known you'd be all right. You have a way of landing on your feet, like a cat."

Grimacing at the reference to landing, Simon told the story of the previous night as briefly as possible, leaving out the pain that hampered him even now. When he finished, Hannah took her turn, relating how she had gone to Joan for help and found it instead with Henrietta. "Not that it did any good," she finished.

"Hannah, it was brave but very foolish of you to return here. It might have meant your arrest." Simon had been thinking the same thing, but he let the princess chastise Hannah for taking chances. He took her hand in his, both to reassure her and to steady himself. The last few hours' exertions had almost used up his resources, and he wanted nothing more than a quiet place to lie down and rest. They stood, drawing strength from each other. Elizabeth stood alone, as usual.

"And you, Simon. Taking on that brute on your own? You should have called for Calkin."

"I managed, Highness," he answered through tight lips.

"Oh, don't be touchy. I meant nothing about your arm. It's just that . . . We thought you were dead!" The calm tone she intended did not quite come off.

Simon sighed. "I kept thinking of you facing Northumberland alone." He rubbed the lump on his head gingerly. "I wanted Daniel to tell what he knew, but he is beyond that now."

"I'm glad to know he was misguided but not evil," Hannah said. "He spied on me, but at least he did not murder anyone."

That reminded Simon. "The message you sent us was cleverly done, Highness. It pointed our suspicions toward the baroness."

Elizabeth explained what she had learned from Florence Bolton. "Once I looked beyond the meek matron, I began to see she had much to gain from her husband's death."

"A child will allow her to remain a baroness and control Rochdale for many years."

"But there is no child." Simon told them about the fake pregnancy.

"We can unmask her, then!" Hannah proposed. "She can be examined, and her lies will catch up with her."

"But she is gone," Calkin put in. "Her boat sailed with the

tide, some while ago." Knowing the woman who had threatened them was out of the reach of justice silenced them for a moment. By the time anyone caught up with Ellen, she would have her story in place and an heir to display.

"I told you she did not walk as Kat did when she was pregnant," Elizabeth said after a moment. "Much too graceful for a woman in that condition."

"Things like that began to add up in my head," Simon said. "Although she would not dance because of her pregnancy, it did not keep her from beating her poor maidservant."

"I told you the Carlsons commented on her shyness before other women, even her servant."

"And I mentioned that Charlotte was missing a pillow, though I never thought about why it might have been taken."

"It took a long time to put all those things together." Simon shook his head ruefully. "I cannot believe how blind I was."

"She is quite beautiful." Elizabeth's tone was droll. "Beauty has an effect on most men. And she is as clever as anyone I have ever met."

"She is a murderer, Highness!"

She slapped his arm lightly. "I only admire her planning, Simon, not her deeds."

He looked at her with some concern. "Is it certain that you are safe?"

"For now," she said, sounding much older and very tired. "We know the truth, and that is some comfort. There was no plot against Edward, and the man responsible for Lord Amberson's murder is dead, even if the murderer herself has escaped."

Calkin coughed deferentially and spoke, earnest concern evident in his plain face. "I think you—all of you—would be well advised to stay out of things from this point onward." His tone hinted what he could not say. Elizabeth had escaped a dangerous situation, and Northumberland had decided to pursue his ambitions in a different way. She would not be branded a killer, but she was still an obstacle in his path to controlling the throne. Best to return to the image she had spent recent years building: meek, unassuming, and unexciting. Crime-solving was not part of that image, and the princess could not afford to be part of Ellen Rochdale's downfall, murderess or not.

She folded her hands as if consciously taking on once again her unassuming demeanor. "We have all escaped a great deal today. We are lucky His Lordship is an honest man."

Calkin raised an eyebrow. "I think we are lucky that his son is fond of you, Your Grace. I hear it was he who shamed his father into listening to your case."

Elizabeth's face showed a flash of genuine happiness. "I have a friend. Someone who will stand for me in hard times."

Simon glanced at Hannah, who nodded slightly. "You have many friends, Highness, if you were ever to need them."

"Thank you, Simon, but even from you I will hear no more. Let us keep our conversation short of treason."

Calkin and Simon started for the door, but Elizabeth held Hannah back for a moment. "If you will, I would like you to stay with me one more day."

Hannah realized with a jolt that her stay with the princess was over. She had come to Whitehall for a reason, and that reason was now gone. It was back to Hampstead for her. Although it was home, she found that it was not the pleasant prospect she had envisioned just a few days ago.

Elizabeth watched her face, reading her emotions. "I would be pleased if you could stay permanently," she said. "But such a life is not for you, a girl with opportunities before her. I am an unwanted appendage to the royal house with no future. Better, I think, if neither you nor Simon is associated with me."

Hannah could think of nothing to say. What Elizabeth said

was true, and despite her admiration for the princess, she knew that her heart was not at Whitehall. It was in an apothecary shop that did not yet exist, helping Simon in his work, raising his children, being happy. "I will be glad to stay with you one more day, Highness," she said. "We will discuss recent events until we understand everything, absolutely everything."

Simon and Calkin left Whitehall together. They, too, wanted to talk the matter over. Unresolved situations lead to repetition and more repetition, and Calkin took an hour's leave to make time for it, letting his young friend go over and over things and assuring him that he could have done no differently, and certainly no better, than he had done.

When Calkin returned to his duties, Simon started for home, knowing his parents would be frantic. The apothecary shop was on his way, and he realized that he should also speak with Carthburt, whom he had not seen since he left London. Due to recent events, he had neglected his master, and he felt ashamed.

"Master? It is Simon." He opened the door and called inside gently, not wanting to disturb the old man if he was resting. There was no answer, and he stepped into the gloom of the enclosed place. After his time away the shop looked different, smaller somehow, and very still. He thought of it as a busy place, but now the implements lay useless on the workbench, the jars sat with mouths shut. An odd odor told him that some of their ingredients had gone bad and needed clearing out. Again, guilt struck. He had left the old man to do everything. Moving to the back of the place, he paused at the curtained doorway, "Master?" He looked inside, and his heart sank.

Hannah left Whitehall the next morning with a small bag and a promise to visit the princess from time to time. Simon waited for her outside the Holbein Gate, his face serious. "I have news."

Her face tightened in anticipation at his somber tone. "I went to the shop yesterday. When I called for Master Carthburt, he did not answer. I thought he was napping, but he was dead."

"Oh, Simon!" Hannah gasped. "What happened?"

He paused a moment before answering. "I suppose his heart could not take the strain of Rachel's death. He was, my father tells me, a walking shadow these past days, and now his body has given up the fight. I spent most of the day arranging for his funeral."

"I am sorry, Simon. He was a good man."

Hannah's eyes sought his, and he knew she was thinking of their future. Their marriage depended on Carthburt's certification of his abilities as an apothecary, and she feared this would delay it even more. She would not say it, though, from respect for the dead.

"A good man, indeed. He signed my papers and arranged my certification. And more than that, he left me the shop. I have a profession and a business."

"Oh, Simon!" Hannah threw her arms around his neck and buried her face in his chest to hide her tears. "We can marry!"

"As soon as possible and proper."

"Can we invite Her Grace to the celebration?"

"I flatter myself that she will not refuse."

"It would not be a true celebration without her. I have come to admire her greatly." Hannah moved closer to Simon. "I am wicked to be happy with your master so recently dead, my love. I am truly sorry. But he was so kind to think of us at the last."

"Yes. He was the best of men," Simon answered. He did not tell her of the note that had been among the papers Carthburt left. First, there had been his will, leaving everything he owned to Simon. Next had been the papers that certified his apprentice had completed his training. Under it all was a note sealed with wax and addressed to Simon alone. He had read it once the evening before, then he read it again, taking in the implications.

My dear boy,

Do not grieve for me. I am even now with my wife and daughter, despite what the priests say. My only sin, in my own view, is that I lied to you. You asked who the man was who frightened Rachel that last day, and I said he was a foreigner. That is not so. The man was Charles Beverley, come to buy physic for sleeplessness. I told him to return the next day and I would have the preparation ready.

When he was gone, I found Rachel as you saw her, hiding in the rafters, fearful that the dark man had come back to hurt her. That night, with patient questioning, I persuaded her to recall the night her mother died. The story came quite clearly; the sight of him brought it all back, and for once, she was able to tell it.

I had left the city for a journey of several days. As Rachel and Martha went about their usual business, a woman asked Martha's help, saying her mistress was very ill. The two of them went to the house to see what could be done. Rachel stayed outside the sick room, so she never saw the patient, but she heard the commotion that came later. A dark man shouted at Martha, saying he had not asked for her interference and did not want her there. Rachel became frightened at his menacing aspect, but Martha stood her ground, insisting there was something amiss with the patient. The man grew even angrier and ordered them from the house.

Rachel said her mother was upset by the incident and later that day told the local constable about it. He sent her to White-hall, where she spoke with a man in what Rachel called "a wondrous suit of red and gold." She did not hear all that was said, but she recalls that her mother promised to return the next day.

That night she woke to Martha's pleading voice and looked

down from the loft to see the dark man holding her mother by the hair. She climbed down the ladder, determined to help, and Martha begged the man not to hurt her child. Rachel had trouble with the name, called him Master Betty, but she remembered clearly the scar that crossed his eyebrow, dividing it in two.

Rachel saw her mother die. As she stood frozen in fear, the dark man struck her, too, and then left, believing he had accomplished his purpose.

That is the story Rachel told me that last night. The next day she was dead, fearful that, old and useless as I am, I could not protect her from her tormenter. You left to arrange her funeral, like the helpful soul you are. I had forgotten that Beverley would return, but when he did, I could not believe it. In his arrogance he must have thought three years had bought his safety, since he had never been connected to the death of my wife and child.

My heart was so full of hatred, Simon, that I had no trouble giving him poison—the strongest I could supply—in place of physic. I told him the medicine had an unpleasant taste, that he should mix it with some strong drink. He asked if mead would do. "Yes," I replied, my voice steadied by knowledge of what he was. He said he would try it when next he had trouble sleeping. If the stuff worked, he said, he would return for more. I assured him that he would experience a long and restful sleep. He thanked me, and I thanked God for delivering him to me.

I have no regret for what I did, but once news of my success came, the thought of living in this world any longer sickened me. I spent the last few days making the arrangements you find here, the only worthwhile task left to me in this life. Now that your future is settled, I will settle mine with a concoction of my

*own making. Bless you, my boy. Love your Hannah and be
well.*

Carthburt

It had taken some time for the elements to meld in Simon's
mind. First came a question. Ellen Rochdale thought she had
poisoned Beverley; Carthburt claimed he had. Who was correct?

He let the scene play out in his mind, watching as Ellen stole
into Beverley's room, using the plank she had obtained with a
lie and bypassing the guards at the door. He imagined her carefully laying the board from one balcony rail to the other, then
sidling across, not daring to look at the ground below. Once
inside the room, she took the jack of mead on Beverley's desk
and left the one she had laced with poison. Returning, she
stowed the plank under her bed once again, along with the
mead, and went to join the others at dinner.

That evening, Beverley had poured what he thought was
physic into his mead. Had he been doubly poisoned?

Suddenly he jolted upright. What if Beverley had already put
what he thought was medicine into the bottle in his room?
Everyone who knew the man spoke of his planning, his desire
to have things under control. If he had planned ahead, then Ellen had replaced poison with poison.

He pictured her, traveling the last few miles to the hunting
lodge alone, as she had to be. Her plan, as careful as any of
Beverley's, dictated that no one but the huntsman and his wife
would know that the child she would take onward to Rochdale
was not hers. He guessed she would claim the birthing pains
took her on the road, imagined her tearfully relating how she
traveled as far as she could, wanting to reach home for the
child's sake, but in the end got only as far as the lodge.

Her words came back to him: "I will drink a toast to dead
friends on the road north." He pictured her settled into some
protected spot, resting and nibbling on cheese and bread. She

would drink from the bottle she had stolen from Beverley, savoring the sweetness of the mead and the victory she had won over all of them. The agony she would suffer would be no less than what she had served others, and her body might never be found once the wild animals discovered it.

Could the stars play such ironic games? Did Destiny bring justice when man could not? The answer would come with time. Simon burned Carthburt's letter in a candle's flame, watching the paper turn to brown, to black, then to ash. When it was done, he had closed the shop and returned to his parents' home for the last time, for he realized, with both joy and sadness, he had a home of his own now, for him and for Hannah.

ABOUT THE AUTHOR

Peg Herring is a mystery writer from northern Lower Michigan who once taught high school language arts and history. In her spare time, she travels with her husband of many decades, gardens, directs choral groups, and works to keep her hundred-year-old home from crumbling away.

WITHDRAWN
FROM THE RODMAN PUBLIC LIBRARY